KEKLA MAGOON

— THE —

SECRET LIBRARY

KEKLA MAGOON
THE —
SECRET
LIBRARY

CANDLEWICK PRESS

Copyright © 2024 by Kekla Magoon
Illustrations copyright © 2024 by Brittany Jackson

First edition 2024

Library of Congress Catalog Card Number 2023945937
ISBN 978-1-5362-3088-8

24 25 26 27 28 29 APS 10 9 8 7 6 5 4 3 2 1

Printed in Humen, Dongguan, China

This book was typeset in Arno Pro.

Candlewick Press
99 Dover Street
Somerville, Massachusetts 02144

www.candlewick.com

For the adventurers, the dreamers,
and the secret keepers

1

Dally paused with her hand on the doorknob and took a deep breath. In all her eleven and a half years, nothing had ever felt so important. Clutching the large folder that could make or break her fate, she turned the knob and pushed her way through the door, into the outer office. A bright blue-and-gold block-printed rug led like a runway toward the receptionist's desk, but a few steps in, Dally forced her gaze up from the carpet. She pulled her shoulders back, held her head high. Confident. Assertive. Determined to get what she wanted.

"Hi," she said to the curly-haired woman behind the L-shaped desk. "I have a three-thirty appointment."

"Hello, Miss Peteharrington," the receptionist said. "You can go right in, of course."

Dally glanced at the digital clock on the desk. It read 3:28. "I'm a bit early," she said, hugging her folder. "Should I wait?"

The receptionist smiled gently, a mix of kindness and sadness in her expression. "I suppose so. Let me just ring her." She picked up the desk phone and pressed a single button. "Your three-thirty is here."

Dally nodded. She rather liked the formal sound of that.

"Will do," the receptionist said into the phone. To Dally, she said, "She's ready for you. Go ahead."

"Thank you," Dally said. She opened her folder and glanced inside one last time.

"Good luck," whispered the receptionist.

Dally hoped she wouldn't need luck. She had prepared a very convincing presentation, if she did say so herself. But out loud, she said a polite "Thank you."

Dally followed another blue-and-gold carpet toward the main office door, head high, folder in hand. The folder contained a tablet with her slideshow already cued up, plus a full backup printout of her presentation, complete with seventeen graphs, two pie charts, three research articles, and a flip chart of bulleted notes printed in her neatest handwriting.

If all that didn't convince her mother, nothing would.

Dally was prepared. She had made the appointment on Friday for this Monday afternoon. She didn't *always* have to make an appointment to see her mother, of course, but during business hours it was generally a good idea. Dally badly needed a yes today, and interrupting her mother's work without warning was sure to put her in a bad mood.

For the last three school days, Dally had spent her free time—the unscheduled hour after school ended and before her business lessons began—doing research and organizing her thoughts. Then, over the weekend, she'd practiced her presentation several times in front of the mirror. Her mother needed a good reason to do anything different, so Dally had a whole folder full of reasons.

"Hello, Delilah," said Dally's mother. She rounded the desk and held out her hand to her daughter. "It's nice to see you."

"It's nice to see you, too," Dally responded. She gripped her mother's hand and shook firmly, the way she had been taught.

"Please," her mother said, gesturing toward the chairs on the visitor side of the desk. It was a boss's way of saying, *Have a seat, but remember who's in charge here.*

The chairs were wingbacks and quite large. Dally perched on the very edge of one so that her feet still touched the floor. She usually enjoyed climbing into them and watching her feet stick straight out, but it wouldn't do to be kicking and flailing while she was trying to seem responsible and businesslike.

Dally's mother was always perfectly businesslike. Her wavy brown hair was tucked into a neat chignon at the base of her neck, resting on a crisply ironed blouse collar. The delicate features on her smooth, pale face appeared calm. Dally had not inherited the always-put-together gene. Her school uniform top was hopelessly wrinkled. She had restrained her generous black curls somewhat before this meeting, but her full, brown cheeks felt blotchy with heat that certainly was visible. Appearance was only one of the many, many ways that she and her mother were different.

Her mother settled back into her own chair behind the desk. "Interesting that you've made an appointment. I assume you have some business to discuss with me?"

Dally sat quietly for a moment. She had rehearsed this part

many times. She knew exactly where to begin, and yet it was all different now that she was in the stately office, with the huge brown desk and the glare of afternoon light through the windows and the pressure of her mother's gaze on her performance.

"This is your meeting," her mother prompted. "What's on your mind?"

Dally swallowed hard. "Yes, I have a presentation," she said, placing her tablet on the desk facing her mother and starting the slideshow. *Lead with the information, land on the ask,* she reminded herself. She opened her folder and pulled out page one.

"Did you know that ninety percent of students who get accepted to Ivy League colleges have a significant track record of participating in extracurricular activities?" She laid the research study on the desk and clicked to her next slide.

"And did you know that the life skills kids can learn from outdoor programs, like scouting and camping, enhance socialization, increase creativity, and actually improve their brains?" She laid the second research study on the desk.

"And did you know"—this was the tough one—"that children who are grieving benefit from finding a way to honor the memory of their loved one?"

Dally's mother glanced toward the framed photo beside her monitor: one quick, there-and-back tug of the eyeballs. If you blinked, you'd miss it. But Dally didn't blink, so her gaze followed automatically.

Dally did a double take. The photo was turned away from her mother. So instead of glancing at the back of the frame, as she had the last time she'd been in her mother's office, Dally found herself looking directly at the best photo ever taken of her and Grandpa. They were sitting at the kitchen table, contemplating a chocolate cake. Forks in hand, he was smiling down at her and she was smiling up at him. Dally had this photo herself, in her room. She liked to look at it every day. Why did her mother have it turned away?

"Um . . ." Dally laid the third research study, the one about children and grief, on the desk. Then she started in on the ask. "There is a new after-school program beginning at my school this week," she said. "It's called Adventure Club, and I'd like your permission to join. Here is why it is a good idea."

Dally clicked through her carefully prepared slideshow of charts and facts, with the photo of Grandpa smiling over her. She hoped that he would bring good luck to her presentation. (Suddenly she feared she needed a splash of luck after all.)

For her whole life, Grandpa had been Dally's favorite person in the entire world. He had always been there, with his soft belly laugh and crinkly-eyed smile and big strong arms that were excellent for things like hugging and swing-pushing and tree-climbing assistance. He had lived in the estate with her and her mother and their live-in cook and housekeeper. The whole estate used to belong to him, but it had been handed down to Dally's mother when she took over the corporation after Grandpa retired.

The Peteharrington family was, in fact, quite wealthy, and Dally's mother's main concern was keeping them that way.

She worked all day and half the night, and she always worried about money, even though Dally was certain they had plenty. Grandpa called it a terrible preoccupation, and once upon a time, he'd threatened to "snatch the business out from under you and leave you without a dime so you can begin to appreciate what is important in life." But Dally's mother was a shrewd and careful businesswoman, and when Grandpa had said this, she'd produced a pile of papers that made his cheeks redden and his hands ball into tight white fists. Dally had seen it all from behind the suit of armor in the hall outside the study, where she'd hidden to see what the commotion was about. "You are not the daughter I raised," Grandpa said, voice shaking. To which Dally's mother coolly replied, "You no longer have any voting power in the corporation." And when Grandpa began poring over the documents, she added, "The paperwork is perfect. I may not be the daughter you wanted, but I'm *exactly* the daughter you raised."

Grandpa had inherited the business from Great-Grandpa, and Dally's mother had inherited it after that. Dally, too, was being groomed to take over someday. From a very early age, she had been placed in classes and given tutors to help her learn important business-ish things, like economics and bookkeeping and the essentiality of profit margins. These lessons bored Dally down to her bones. She hated charts and numbers. She loved words and stories, mysteries and adventures, but there weren't many of those to be had within the gates of Peteharrington Place—unless you used your imagination.

Dally had imagination to spare, and many wonderful toys, but she longed for someone to play with. She had no siblings, neighbors were few and far away, and her classmates thought she was *strange*. She was too energetic, perhaps, or too quick to invent elaborate, unusual games.

Grandpa had seen Dally's sorrow and loneliness and tried to fix it. He'd negotiated an hour a day of free play, outside of school and homework. After that, the afternoon business lessons began. For two long hours, Dally sat at a small desk in front of a whiteboard while her economics tutor droned on about some chart or another that was meant to illuminate for her the world of high finance. While he talked, Dally's mind would drift backward, reliving whatever fun she'd had earlier that afternoon. Those single hours after school spent with Grandpa in the backyard, climbing trees or working jigsaw puzzles or leaping off the pier into the lake (it was a very large estate indeed), or poring through the delightful old books in the family library—those single hours were the best of any given day, and the best of her entire life, when she added them all up.

They'd had summers together, too, of course, when Dally was free of her daily lessons. Her mother enrolled her in a series of enrichment camps—math and science camp, communications camp, occasionally a regular old sleepaway camp, all of which were more fun than the lessons—but when she was home, she and Grandpa would steal away for an occasional weekend on Grandpa's sailboat. They loved to explore the South Carolina coast on land and sea alike—there was plenty to do right in their midsize hometown city of Welleston, from the downtown shopping district and historic harbor to the cultural centers and parks and dozens of diverse neighborhoods. They sometimes even ventured up the coast to Charleston or went camping in the Blue Ridge Mountains. There had been no shortage of adventure when Grandpa was around.

"In conclusion," Dally said, wrapping up her presentation, "I feel that joining Adventure Club would be an excellent way for me to honor Grandpa and keep his memory alive, while learning new skills and making friends. As you can see in the scientific studies, all of these things are important for people my age."

Dally let out a big breath. She had done a pretty good job making all her points and explaining each of the charts. She paused on the slide that said *Any questions?* and laid the print-out of the presentation on the desk, where her mother could see it. She would be proud of Dally for making a professional slide-show while also having a backup plan. "So, what do you think?"

"I think there's enough of your grandfather in you as it is," Dally's mother said. "This is not bound to help." She touched one of the research studies. "But I know that enrichment is important. That's why you have your evening tutor."

"Tutor in *business*," Dally emphasized. "But like Grandpa always said, there's more to life than work." It was the wrong thing to say, and Dally felt it the moment the words left her mouth. *Oh, no.* To her mother, there was nothing more important in life than work.

"My father was not a responsible man," Dally's mother said.

"I know he seemed like a lot of fun to you, but—" She shook her head. She leaned back in her chair and gazed at the ceiling for a long moment.

Dally allowed the silence to grow. "Please," she said, after quite a while. "It's important to me."

"Your grandfather is gone," her mother said. "It's time to move on from his ways."

Move on from his ways . . . and turn away his photo?

"Don't you miss him?" Dally's voice rose and, distressingly, cracked. This was a business meeting. She had to stay cool and confident, her mother's only language. Her feelings would have to wait.

"He was my father," Dally's mother said, which wasn't really an answer to the question.

Dally sniffed hard, pulling herself together. "Of course," she said. "Well, I think he would have wanted me to continue certain things in his absence. Adventure Club meets only twice a week."

Her mother pursed her lips. "During your free hour?"

"Yes. Well, it's two and a half hours after school, on Tuesdays and Thursdays. But—" Dally had anticipated this question, and she clicked to the final slide. "That is still only five total hours per week." She had done the math and had a nice calendar graph to show for it. "If I study extra on Monday, Wednesday, and—"

"Your tutor's schedule is already fixed," her mother said. "We've signed an agreement, the three of us."

"Yes, but that was before."

"So, you want to go back on your word? How do you expect to succeed if the people you do business with can't count on you to be reliable?"

"No, I . . . I want to adjust for . . . um . . ." Dally tried to find a professional thing to say. "I want to adjust the original plan . . . because of a change in information. The announcement about the new Adventure Club was only made last week."

"I'm sorry, Delilah. My answer is no."

"But . . ." Dally had expected the meeting to be hard, but she hadn't expected it to fail. She had done research and made charts!

Her mother folded her hands. "So, if that's all, you can see yourself out."

"No. It's not all." Dally leaped to her feet. "You're being unreasonable."

"I am your mother. I don't have to be reasonable."

"But—"

"Your lessons are the priority. That is the end of the discussion. Show yourself out."

"NO," Dally said louder, stamping her foot. It made no sound against the plush carpet, making her feel all the more foolish for losing her cool.

Her mother pushed back from the desk and stood up. "Well, it is my office. You've come to make a presentation. It was very well thought out, and I'm proud of you for doing it. But sometimes in business, we don't get what we want."

"In family, too, I guess." Dally sniffed again. The tears had not yet arrived in her eyes, but down in her heart she could feel them packing their bags and boarding the train.

"In family more than anywhere," Dally's mother said, her voice quiet but firm. The horrible truth of what she was saying echoed throughout the fancy office. *I'm not the daughter my father wanted. You're not the daughter I wanted.*

Dally abandoned her presentation papers and turned away, keeping her head high. She would be out the door before she cried. She would. *She must.*

2

Dally ran through the halls of Peteharrington Place, toward Grandpa's study. Fingers outstretched, she flung herself toward the door and—*oof!* Instead of passing smoothly through, as she expected, Dally slammed hard into the thick, carved wood. The familiar large brass handle would not budge.

The door had been locked since he died, but in her sadness and frustration, Dally had forgotten. She crumpled to the floor, pressed her back against the locked door, and let the train of her tears chug along.

"She's horrid," Dally whispered, wishing Grandpa were there to hear her. "How could you leave me?"

At the reading of Grandpa's will, she had learned that he had left her a bank account all her own, not to be touched until she was twenty-one. The lawyer had held out a big beige envelope with her name on it, and Dally had stepped forward to claim it, but her mother had gotten there first. "It'll go in the safe," she said. "Until you're of age."

Dally didn't understand. The envelope was for her. Even if she couldn't use the money until she turned twenty-one, it would have been nice to hold in her hand the only thing Grandpa had left for her. She had sat very still in her school uniform, staring at the package on her mother's knee, while the lawyer droned on about real estate and investments and distributions and all manner of other things Dally barely understood.

However, she did know enough about banking (thanks to her lessons) to know that you didn't need an envelope that big to pass a bank account to someone. If all Grandpa had left her was money, he wouldn't have needed an envelope at all.

There was something more in that envelope—Dally was sure of it. But it was locked away.

At least for now.

Through the door, she heard the grandfather clock strike four. Dally had only fifteen minutes until her lessons started.

"Miss Dally?" Hannah, the housekeeper, came bustling around the corner and opened her arms wide. "Oh, there you are, baby. You all right, lovebug?"

Dally scrubbed her cheeks on her sweater sleeves. "Yes, I'm fine." She pushed herself to her feet and scooted out of Hannah's path. She wasn't in the mood to be comforted by anyone who wasn't Grandpa, no matter how warm and soft Hannah's hug was likely to be.

Hannah put one fist on her hip. "Umm-hmm. Now, you know I hear everything that goes on in this house, and I figure it's about time for a cheer-up . . ." She held out her hand, revealing one of Dally's favorite orange hard candies, drawn from a hidden stash that Dally had spent days trying to locate when she was smaller. Hannah always had a "cheer-up" ready whenever Dally skinned a knee or took a hit to her pride.

Dally accepted the wrapped candy. "Thanks, Hannah. I'll take this with me to my lessons." There was a bit of time before she had to report to her tutor, but she wanted to be alone to think. As she rounded the corner, she tore off the plastic and popped in the tasty sweet. It didn't make her feel a whole lot better, but it certainly didn't make her feel worse.

It was tempting, of course, to blow off her lessons and go riding or something. Sometimes she imagined galloping off into the distance, never to be heard from again. No one would miss her. What would it be like, she wondered, to simply run away, make her own way in the world? But she was only eleven and a half.

The one thing that might change her fate: getting her hands on the envelope Grandpa left her.

That night, after the usual boring lessons and the usual dinner alone in the large dining room, Dally lay in her bed, thinking. Waiting.

She knew how to pick a lock. She and Grandpa had read about it in a book. They'd spent almost a whole week practicing on padlocks, and then they'd tried their skills on several different doors around Peteharrington Place, including Grandpa's study.

Dally rolled toward her bedside table and opened the drawer.

She rummaged through the hair ties and scarves and nail clippers and whatnot until she felt the soft lump of a leather pouch wrapped in its own strings. Yes, there it was. She still had her lock-picking tools.

She pulled them out of their pouch. Three slim, flat pieces of metal, cool in her fingers but heat-searing her brain.

Dally slipped out from under the covers. The air was chilly, so she slid on her lavender dressing gown and stepped into the dim corridor, clutching the tools.

Dally tiptoed through the halls of Peteharrington Place. She could hear Grandpa's voice in her head, as clear as if he were standing right behind her. *Dally-bird, I said twenty-one, not almost twelve.*

"Extenuating circumstances, Grandpa," Dally whispered back. "If you were really here, you'd understand."

Picking the lock on Grandpa's study felt like shaking hands with a long-lost friend: familiar yet new, and warm with the promise of reconnection. The shadows in the hallway made it hard to see her own fingers, but Dally didn't dare light up the whole place at this hour. It didn't matter, anyway, because lock-picking was done mostly by feel.

The last time she'd been in the halls this late was with Grandpa, the final night they'd snuck out to the lake to swim: Grandpa in his hilarious crescent moon of a Speedo that her mother (and everyone) always made fun of, and Dally in her most comfortable black-and-purple racing suit, the one her mother said was not very feminine. *Alone in the dark, we can be who we want to be, Dally-bird,* Grandpa had said. He was good at making her feel better about all the ways she didn't quite fit in the world. They had slapped five in solidarity, then run along the dock and dived in, splashing and giggling and racing out to the basking rocks. Grandpa always won, of course, because he was taller and stronger than Dally, but she was getting close. A small twinge struck her heart. Now she'd never have the chance to beat him, a milestone she had been looking forward to with every inch she grew.

Dally hadn't known that that swim would be their last dance under the moonlight, but if she had, she wouldn't have done a single thing differently, and there was a kind of joy in that, swirling next to the sadness. She smiled at the memory as the lock twisted open beneath her fingers.

Dally pushed the door inward, and Grandpa smells rushed at her. She closed her eyes and let them enfold her like a hug. Old books. Fresh wood polish. Echoes of pipe smoke. That ancient, woodsy cologne he loved that they didn't even make anymore. He had rationed his last few bottles carefully, but not too carefully. Dally moved toward the sideboard, where Grandpa kept a few spirits, his spare reading glasses, and the cologne in its leafy-green glass bottle. Dally remembered the day he'd cracked the seal on this final bottle. There was less than a quarter inch remaining in it now. "I don't want to outlive this bottle," Grandpa had said, "but I don't want it to outlive me, either."

"That's a conundrum," Dally had answered.

"More like a game," Grandpa had said. When Dally looked

confused, Grandpa had chuckled. "You'll understand someday, Dally-bird."

Dally touched the bottle. She supposed she remembered this conversation because it was one of the only times Grandpa had chosen not to explain something that confused her. He was usually the one person she could rely on to tell her the truth, no matter how long and complex and adult it might have been. Maybe that's what was in the envelope. Something long and complex and adult.

With the door closed and the heavy curtains letting in only a sliver of moonlight, the study was like a cocoon, so Dally dared to reach over and pull the chain on the desk lamp. Then she moved toward the safe, which was hidden behind a simple gold frame containing Grandpa's favorite map. Dally had never understood his affection for the ugly old scrap of canvas, but he'd once told her it had been a source of great adventure in his life. She barely gave it a glance now as she swung out the frame and reached for the lock.

She knew the combination, of course. Grandpa had been less than stealthy about dialing the eight numbers in front of her, and it was a sequence Dally was not likely to forget, given that those eight numbers spelled out her birthday in reverse.

She cranked the big dial, and the safe door popped open.

3

I t wasn't an extremely large safe, but it was quite full. Stacks of important-looking papers. Boxes containing the most valuable gemstones in Grandpa's beloved collection. Prints of a handful of precious family photographs. Dally riffled through a leaning stack of beige envelopes with labels like DEED, WILLS, CORPORATION until she found the one labeled DALLY.

She carefully closed the safe, leaving everything else as she'd found it. She laid her envelope on the carved mahogany desk and climbed into Grandpa's large leather chair. As an afterthought, she slid out again, grabbed the bottle of ancient cologne from the sideboard, and directed a spritz at the big chair. She settled herself into the fragrant cloud and breathed deeply. For some reason it felt right to read Grandpa's message to her here, in the closest thing to his arms that she'd ever know again.

The envelope was sealed with both regular flap glue *and* a flourish of Grandpa's fancy sealing wax, but Dally tore into it without caution—there was no chance of covering her tracks with all that going on.

Inside were three items. The first was a floppy old checkbook cover, with a single check-sized piece of paper inside. It had the name of a bank Dally had never heard of and an account number written on it.

The second item appeared to be a map. It was hand-drawn in blue ink on a regular sheet of white printer paper, probably hastily plucked from one of the stacks and stacks of reams on the bookshelf behind her. Dally smiled fondly. That was Grandpa's go-to way of scribbling things down. He never had a proper notebook within reach, nor an ever-present tablet like her mother.

At a glance, the map didn't make much sense. It was sketchy, and everything was labeled with either letters—DS, PP, PL, AM, TSL, X—or tiny numbers—26, 85, 41. To anyone else it might look like an abstract drawing or a scratch page for someone's math homework, but Dally had looked at many, many maps with Grandpa, and she knew one when she saw one.

The third item was a letter on similar paper, in Grandpa's familiar stocky handwriting.

At the top of the page, typed, was a small notation that read "The Last Will and Testament of John Peteharrington Jr.: Addendum 17." That must have been added by the lawyer later, Dally figured. But all she cared about was what Grandpa had written to her.

My dearest Dally-bird,

It pains me to know you are reading this letter at the ripe old age of eleven and a half. (We both know you will not wait until you come of age, don't we?) My fondest wish would be to have the privilege to watch you grow into the beautiful woman I know you will become, but the world has seen fit to separate us now.

I would prefer that you wait until adulthood to read further, but as they say, the past is prologue, and I know too well your eager heart. So, here we are.

The map is for you and you alone, and you know everything you need to follow it. If you choose to follow the map, you must tell no one. It will be our final shared secret.

I love you, sweet granddaughter. You know I've never been one to speculate about what happens once we are gone, but I trust in this, my precious Dally: we shall meet again.

All my love,
Grandpa

Dally read the letter three times, then hugged it to her chest. She slid it gently back into the envelope for safekeeping. The map she kept out. She needed more time with it. She didn't waste time resealing the envelope with tape—if anyone bothered to look, it would still be immediately clear that the envelope had been opened. Anyway, Dally wasn't convinced that what she had done was wrong at all. She returned the envelope to the safe, turned out the light, and tiptoed back to her bedroom wing.

Peteharrington Place was the sort of mansion in which a family's only daughter could have a whole suite of rooms all to herself. Dally had a bedroom, a playroom, a sitting room, a bathroom, and a dressing room, not to mention a walk-in closet big enough that she could make snow angels in the carpet without disturbing a single shoe. Her wing was practically a house unto itself.

Dally headed for the brightest light in her suite: the bamboo reading lamp in the sitting room. She flicked it on, and its beam arced over her favorite purple beanbag chair, in front of the built-in bookcase, beneath her wall of special family photos. The familiar images usually blurred into the background, but tonight Dally took a moment to look. The largest frame, in the center, contained a full family portrait, professionally done: Dally, age one, sitting on her mother's lap. Wild black curls framed her smiling, chubby-cheeked, light-brown face. Her hands were frozen in front of her as if she'd been caught in the middle of a delighted clap. Her grandmother sat alongside her mother, and Grandpa and Dally's father stood behind them. Smiling, all together.

Most of the surrounding photos were of her and Grandpa, including their favorite cake photo. There was one with her grandmother, holding her as an infant. Grandma had died before

Dally turned two, and she barely remembered her. Two photos with her father when she was a toddler: one of her standing on skis between his knees, and one of her riding his shoulders in a hiking backpack. They were clearly related—Dally favored her late father's dark skin and wide features. The final photo in the gallery was of her and her mother, smiling after kindergarten graduation.

And then there were two. Dally tore her eyes away from the photos, struck too hard by the sadness of that truth.

She pivoted the bamboo lamp toward the small tea party table nearby and plopped down alongside Raymond, her stuffed koala. She gave his paw a squeeze.

"It's been quite a day, Raymond."

Raymond's glassy black eyes gazed back at her with sympathy. Though Dally was certainly too old for tea parties, she had to admit it was nice to have a familiar friend with her now.

"You pour the tea, and I'll start on the map," Dally said.

Don't mind if I do, she imagined Raymond saying. She laid out the map and studied it closely now that she had proper light.

The first number that jumped out at her was 17.5. That was a significant number to Dally, and Grandpa had known it. It took Dally exactly seventeen and a half minutes to walk from her school to the front door of Peteharrington Place, though a good portion of the last minute was spent on the estate property, climbing the long drive. School let out at three o'clock, and Dally's business lessons started at four fifteen. This timing had been a bone of contention between Dally and her mother. (That

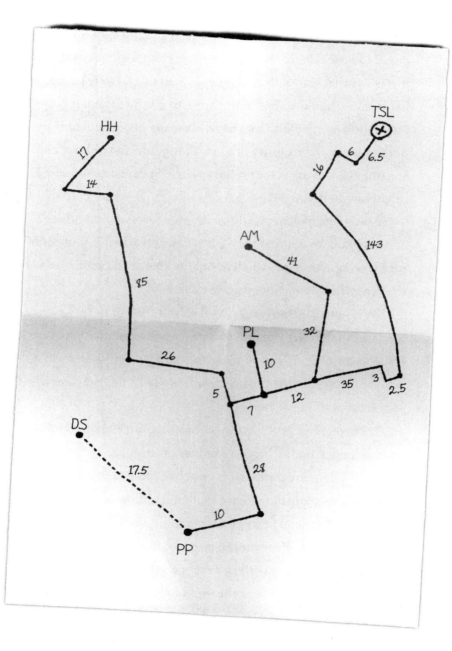

was a very Grandpa phrase: "bone of contention." It simply meant that Dally and her mother had argued.) Dally was supposed to have one free hour after school, and she did not think it was fair that she really had only 57.5 minutes. Dally thought her lessons should start at four thirty, to give her the full hour, but Dally's mother felt that she was already being generous by not including the majority of the walking time in the hour and starting the lessons at four o'clock sharp. Stalemate. (Or, some might say, compromise.)

So Grandpa had met Dally on the steps every day at 3:17:30, and they'd have approximately fifty-six and a half minutes of fun, leaving her approximately one minute to scramble from wherever they were to her private classroom.

The important thing was, she'd solved the puzzle! If seventeen and a half Dally-walking minutes was the distance between Dally's school (DS) and Peteharrington Place (PP), then that was the map key! All the other numbers on the map must represent Dally-walking distances, too.

There were two problems with this solution. First, naturally, her eye landed on the biggest number of them all: 143. A hundred and forty-three minutes would be almost two and a half hours. Dally simply didn't have that kind of time on her hands. A round trip would take five hours or more, depending on what there was to do at wherever the map led. Even on the weekend, she could not get away with an excursion that long by herself.

The second problem was the unit of measurement. Distance equals 17.5 minutes at Dally speed. That was true all through last school year. But she'd grown over the summer, and with her longer stride, she was now under seventeen minutes. It was another milestone Dally wished she'd been able to share with Grandpa. Especially now, because it would cause his math to be just slightly off. Dally knew it didn't really matter for the purposes of the map—17.5 was simply the key, and she could calculate the other distances accordingly—but that didn't stop her heart from twinging.

Where did the map lead? In the light, it was obvious that the X on the map was not just another letter, but the X that marks the spot, like on any good treasure map. It was right under the letters TSL. *Hmm.* TSL? The initials rang no bells, which of course made her all the more eager to get there and find out what they stood for.

Dally yawned.

D, are you planning to get any sleep at all tonight? she imagined Raymond saying, his beady gaze now one of concern.

"I'll figure it out," Dally told him. "But I guess I don't have to do it all tonight." She kissed his stitched gray nose and flicked off the bamboo light.

Patience wasn't really Dally's specialty, though. She crawled into bed and drifted off to sleep, her mind still a swirl of thoughts about things like map keys, how to convert walk time to drive time, and city bus schedules.

4

At school the next morning, Dally went to the transportation section of the library and examined the local bus schedule. Welleston had plentiful buses and shuttles operating throughout the city, but few routes served her wealthy neighborhood. Unfortunately, none of the options suited Dally's needs. Fortunately, she had a backup plan.

Dally's mother refused to give her a cell phone until she was twelve, which was still a matter of months away. So Dally borrowed a phone from a classmate (it was not difficult to find one whose parents were not so restrictive) and dialed a number she knew by heart.

"Limos and Co.," said a pleasant man's voice.

"Hi, Mr. Jerry, this is Delilah Peteharrington."

"Ooooh, Miss Delilah." Mr. Jerry's tone spiked from neutral to friendly. "How can I help you today?"

"I'm going to need a ride after school," she said. "May I reserve a car for one hour?"

"What's mine is yours, sweet thing," Mr. Jerry said. A keyboard clicked on his end of the call. "Three p.m.?"

"Yes. And after my errand, I'll need to be dropped home by four fifteen. So it's a little bit more than an hour, I suppose."

"That's just fine, sugar." Mr. Jerry clicked.

Dally swallowed hard. "Charged to our usual account, of course." That part was a bit of a risk, but Dally's mother ordered a lot of cars, so Dally suspected that the extra expense would go unnoticed.

"Of course. You are all set," Mr. Jerry said. "Driver will be waiting in the pickup line at three."

"Thanks, Mr. Jerry. You're the best."

"Don't you forget it, Miss Thing."

Dally clicked off and headed back toward Chip, the boy she'd borrowed the phone from. He was standing with two of his friends, talking excitedly about Adventure Club. It felt awkward to interrupt their conversation, so she lingered a few feet away. She endured the sting of witnessing their banter and their closeness and their plans for a fun afternoon. Then one of them, Amir, declared, "It's gonna be next level!" and spun away to speak to someone else.

"Hey, Dally," said the other kid, noticing her.

"Hi, Evan." She was careful to use his correct name. Evan had recently come out as trans and changed his pronouns.

"So, what did your mom say?" Chip asked, coming over to Dally as Evan went after Amir.

"Say?" she echoed.

"About Adventure Club." He slid a piece of paper out of his folder: the signed permission slip.

Dally sighed with envy. "Oh. She said no." How did Chip know she was interested in Adventure Club in the first place?

"So what?" he told her, waving his permission slip. "There's still a way . . ."

Dally wasn't sure what he meant, and she didn't know how to ask him. Sixth grade was proving difficult like that. She handed the phone back to Chip. "Anyway, thanks," she said.

"Sure." The redheaded boy plucked his phone from Dally's fingers and smiled. "It's kinda nice to know I have something you don't have."

Dally smiled, too, but his words made her feel a little funny. Chip had several things she didn't have, in her estimation. The phone, for one, and friends like Amir and Evan, and also the permission slip to join Adventure Club that very afternoon. That was something Dally could not buy or borrow. But she refrained from saying anything about it. She had learned that she should never complain about the things she didn't have. People had trouble understanding how you could have a lot of money and still be wanting.

Chip came from a family that was quite well-off, as did most students at Dally's private school. But the Peteharringtons were "richer than God," according to a recent newspaper article. Quite a few of Dally's classmates' parents worked for the corporation, which made Dally the boss's daughter. When they were little, her friends from school had loved to come play and explore at Peteharrington Place. But as they got older, the other children began to regard her as different. Dally gradually found herself with fewer playmates. Even when she did meet someone she liked, it was harder to make time for playdates now that she had her business lessons to contend with.

Money made life easy; Dally knew that. She would likely never want for food, or books, or toys, and that made her very lucky. But there were a great many things that money couldn't buy: laughter, and the right people to laugh with, for example. Free time for adventures.

Dally watched Chip proudly wave his permission slip a moment longer. Then she squared her shoulders and walked to her classroom.

Adventure Club would go on for the rest of the school year. Perhaps there was still time. Regardless, this very afternoon she was going to have an adventure of her own making. For now, that would have to do.

Dally spent her quiet study time comparing Grandpa's map to the city map and deciding on an address to give the driver. First, she measured the actual distance from school to home using the small ruler at the bottom of the city map. Then she made a ruler of her own, representing ten Dally-walking minutes (at her old speed). She used that ruler to trace each leg of distance marked on Grandpa's map along the real map of the city.

For example, Grandpa's map showed three turns between "PP" and "PL," totaling fifty-five Dally-walking minutes. When Dally traced that route on the city map, she could see that it led from Peteharrington Place to the public library. She and

Grandpa had walked there many times, and it had always taken about an hour. So Dally concluded that "PL" meant public library. When she mapped the path to "AM," it led her to the local art museum.

Yes! She was cracking the code!

Excited, Dally began measuring the journey between "PP" and the X that marked the mysterious "TSL." She double-checked her work, then chose a location that she was hoping would be about three blocks shy of the X. The final destination had to remain between her and Grandpa. The letter had been clear about that.

When she walked out of school and scanned the pickup line, it wasn't an anonymous driver in a town car waiting for her but Mr. Jerry himself, in a stretch limo. He was parked front and center in the line of parents and nannies in high-end station wagons and SUVs.

"Okay, fancy-pants," one of the boys from her class called out as she approached the limo. Her stomach dropped a bit. It was things like this, exactly like this, that made her not quite like everyone else. It hadn't occurred to her to request a plainer car. Her mother might have loved a splashy exit, but Dally was trying to fly under the radar here.

Still, she smiled involuntarily as Mr. Jerry climbed out of the car and waved. Mr. Jerry's answering smile was bright and cheerful. He wore a little chauffeur's hat and a dapper black tie and vest with a gold flower stitched to the lapel. He doffed his cap to Dally and soft-shoed toward the back door with the presence of a performer onstage. She could practically hear strains of old jazz emanating from his bones as he moved.

"Well, I'll be," Dally said. "The man himself."

"Only the best for milady." Mr. Jerry tapped his hat brim again and offered a short bow as he opened the door for her.

"It's good to see you, Mr. Jerry." It was, despite her desire to keep a low profile.

"And you, Miss Delilah."

She settled in, dumping her backpack on the seat beside her. Mr. Jerry closed the door. Dally opened one of the short water bottles waiting in the cupholder. Hydration was important before an adventure.

"Where to, sweet thing?" Mr. Jerry eased the limo out of the pickup line as he spoke.

Dally gave the address she had chosen. It was a bakery, according to the city map, which seemed like a plausible place to want to go.

"You sure about that?" Mr. Jerry said.

"Yes, why?" Dally asked.

"Not really your part of town," Mr. Jerry said. "Your mother's okay with it?"

Dally hadn't expected to be put on the spot quite so directly about the issue of permission. She sipped water from the bottle and searched her brain for a true thing to say.

"There are lessons my mother wants me to learn, to prepare for being an adult," Dally said. "I get an hour after school to explore. I have to be home by four fifteen."

Mr. Jerry nodded like this explanation made sense. "Well, you're growing up right fast, Miss D."

They chatted as the car whipped past the glittering storefronts of the shopping district, then the less-glamorous strip malls, and, finally, to a stretch of blocks that had a more industrial feel. Wide sidewalks fit for window-shopping gave way to dingy parking lots, weedy fields, and chained-up warehouses. Past the warehouses, storefronts appeared again, though everything here seemed more muted and worn. The sidewalks opened up, and they were teeming with people—walking, shopping, sitting on stoops, rushing here and there, even dancing. So many people! Dally scanned the faces, in all colors from pale to dark. A Black neighborhood, one she didn't recall ever visiting on her explorations with Grandpa. That was surprising. Even though he was white, Grandpa had always worked hard to show Dally a diverse world. They'd explored Black communities much farther from home, so why not this close one?

The limo turned a corner and slowed. A large crowd filled the street.

"Dang," Mr. Jerry said. "This place is poppin'."

Music blasted from a radio that Dally couldn't see. Some people in the crowd shimmied to the beat. Mr. Jerry honked, and folks slid back toward the sidewalk in a wave to let the car pass.

"Is there a party?" Dally asked.

"New fried chicken joint opened up down the block," Mr. Jerry said. "S'posed to be good. Biscuits that melt in your mouth, whatnot."

"All these people are in line for chicken?" Dally was incredulous.

"Everyone's turning out. You know, how Black folks are gonna do." Mr. Jerry chuckled.

Dally smiled and nodded, as she knew she was meant to, but the truth was, she *didn't* know. Dally was biracial, but since her father had died when she was small and he didn't have much living family, she didn't have a lot of experience being immersed in a Black community. Dally's mother being the way she was meant Dally had lived most of her life surrounded by white people—at her school, in the business, in the community. She knew exactly what Mr. Jerry had meant when he said this wasn't her part of town, and it made her very sad.

Looking out the rear window at the spontaneous block party, Dally thought it all seemed very exciting. The sense of community, strangers making friends in the street. The laughter, the music, the dancing.

The oppression, said a tiny voice in Dally's mind. She leaned against the seat and sighed. It was her mother's voice, no doubt. Her mother, who believed that money was all you needed to overcome the problems that could come with having brown skin, that rising out of poverty and moving across town, as Dally's father had done, could insulate you from the ill effects of racism. Her mother clearly felt that was all that mattered, but Dally suspected the privilege she enjoyed came with other costs.

Moments later, Mr. Jerry pulled up in front of the bakery.

This building, too, looked rather dusty and run-down, but the lights inside the shop were bright and inviting.

"You sure?" Mr. Jerry said again. His eyes met hers in the rearview.

"Oh, yes," Dally said. She checked the clock. The drive had taken only about twenty minutes. "I'll be back in time to be home by four fifteen."

"I'll be here," Mr. Jerry said. He raised his newspaper, as if to prove that he'd be easily occupied.

Dally grabbed her backpack, hopped out, and entered the bakery. The sweet, bready scent that met her nose nearly derailed her from her mission. She made a note to purchase a cupcake on the way back, if there was time.

Luckily, the shop had a back door. It didn't look meant for customers, but it was unlocked. Dally held her breath as she tried the door, then exhaled in relief as she burst into the alley. She followed Grandpa's map from memory, skipping eagerly along the sidewalk for the final three blocks.

The destination was . . . unimpressive. Anticlimactic in the extreme. So disappointing that Dally began recalculating the math in her head. After a moment's reflection, she was still sure she'd done it correctly.

But there was nothing. Less than nothing, somehow. It was simply a field of scrub grass growing through what once might have been a patch of pavement, ugly and ordinary, with the trees of a park forming a distant backdrop beyond.

She studied Grandpa's map and the city map side by side one more time. The map he'd left her led here, she was certain. She was good with directions, and Grandpa had known that.

Dally put her hands on her hips. "Well, I'm here," she said aloud. "So now what?"

A slight humming sound filled Dally's ears. She tugged an earlobe, hoping to clear the feeling. Then she blinked. Not a special blink, but a normal, super-quick close-and-open. The kind you never even think about.

But Dally thought about this one. Because before she closed her eyes, she was staring at nothing—and when she opened them, everything was different.

A large old building, made of cut stones and sparkling glass, rose up in front of her. It stood steady, as if it had been there a hundred years. A flight of wide, shallow stairs ran up from the sidewalk where Dally stood to an ornate doorway. Carved into the stone above the pillars were three simple words: THE SECRET LIBRARY.

⋙ 5 ⋘

It was mid-afternoon, but the sun seemed to set as Dally climbed the twenty stairs toward the stately old library building. She passed between tall marble columns, shivering in the surprising early dark. Her patent-leather school shoes clicked across the landing, and she squinted through the shadows at the entrance ahead.

A sign on the wide wooden door said:

WARNING!
BEFORE YOU SET FOOT ON THE PREMISES,
THE FIRST THING TO KNOW IS THAT IT'S NOT
THE SECRET LIBRARY; IT'S THE SECRET LIBRARY.
A LIBRARY OF SECRETS. YOU CAN EVEN CHECK
THEM OUT, AT YOUR OWN PERIL.

A little shiver crossed Dally's shoulders. *Peril* had been on her vocabulary list this week, so its definition was fresh in her mind; it meant: "horrible, life-threatening danger."

Well, then. *No guts, no glory,* she thought. That had been

Grandpa's way of saying, *Have courage.* People who were brave and took risks (within reason) enjoyed the greatest rewards in life.

This seemed well within reason. It was just a library, right?

Dally reached for the doorknob. Her fingers gripped the burnished metal, and she could have sworn she felt the tiniest of jolts singe her palm. A voice in the air, possibly female, said:

> "You might think that the best place for secrets would be a vault. Somewhere to deposit deep dark truths and leave them to fester among the cobwebs for all eternity, never again to see the light of day. You would be right.
>
> "The Secret Library used to be a vault. That's what it was meant to be, just as the great pyramids were meant to be tombs for the sarcophagi of Egyptian pharaohs, sealed forever. But then a little bit of time passed, and some archaeologists decided that forever didn't really need to be forever, and the things contained in the tombs might be more valuable if they were known to the world instead of hidden away in reverence. So they cracked through the hardened sand and dug out the treasures of the pyramids.
>
> "A great wealth was contained within. The archaeologists came away with gold, silver, precious jewels, expensive artifacts, and knowledge. But such power never comes without a price . . .

"The pyramids are not the point. The point is that humans are ever tempted by knowledge that should be out of reach. They can't help but meddle in things much larger than themselves. Do you know the legend of Pandora's box? This library was once such a vault, you see, but it is no longer sealed beneath the sand. Such choices have consequences—that is the point.

"Understand, stranger: the building you are about to step into is a dangerous place. Enter at your own risk."

With that, the door swung open, revealing a cool, dim foyer. Dally folded the maps and then stuck them in her backpack. Swallowing hard, she slid inside, and the door closed behind her with an echo that faded to stark silence. She listened to the nothingness until she felt a prickle on the back of her neck.

"Hello?" she called, spinning toward the sensation. Coming here might have been a terrible idea. Perhaps she should go. But the wall behind her—which had once held the door—was smooth and white, hung with paintings Dally couldn't make out. Startled, she turned forward again.

The voice in the air whispered, *"It seems you are persistent. There is great wealth within, for those who are brave enough."*

Courage was all well and good in theory, but living it was something else entirely. The soft voice made Dally's skin crawl, and she clutched her backpack across her chest as if holding it there might afford some measure of protection. Protection from what, she could not say. And that was the crux of her nervousness.

The voice in the air said, *"Please read the letter."*

"The letter?" Dally repeated. At the sound of her voice, there was a strange curling in the air in front of her. It wasn't the sort of thing that could be described, because by the time Dally blinked, it was over. A thin piece of stained parchment unfurled as if from nowhere.

Dear Patron,

Welcome to the Secret Library. I trust you will find what you're looking for, and more. Should you require any assistance, the librarian on duty will be happy to help you.

The rules of the library are as follows:

You may peruse the stacks, but you may not remove any secrets without permission.

Secrets may not be shared.

Finally, please maintain a reverent tone. There are many secrets resting here, and you would do well not to disturb them unduly.

Thank you for your attention. Please proceed with our well wishes.

> *Sincerely,*
> *Magdalene Mitchall*
> *7th Grande Dame of*
> *the Whisper Society*

As soon as Dally finished reading, the parchment caught fire, as if lit by an invisible match. Dally's eyes widened. Her mouth formed a shocked little O as the flames crackled and licked, devouring the paper. Soon it was but a cloud of smoke that wafted into the air, leaving behind a surprisingly peachy aroma.

Grandpa, Dally thought, *did you really mean for me to come here?*

"Yes, you're in the right place," said a new voice, beside her. "Only those who are meant to find the library do so."

This time, the voice belonged to an actual body. A woman appeared, stepping forward out of the dark as if she'd been there all along, which Dally was certain she hadn't. Well, almost certain.

Dally leaped backward, clamping her hands over her mouth. She was sure she hadn't spoken aloud. "How . . . how did you—?"

The woman smiled. "I'm a librarian of secrets," she said. "I know one when I see it."

As the startled feeling dissipated, Dally stared. She couldn't really help it—the librarian was the most beautiful person Dally had ever seen in real life. She had long flowing brown hair that went down past her waist, with two thin braids snaking back from her ears and holding it all in place behind her shoulders. Her face, throat, and hands were made up of smooth, pale skin with the lightest dappling of freckles. She wore a soft-looking turquoise gown that fit every round edge of her body perfectly. The delicate, arching glasses across her nose matched her dress, and she wore a sparkling silver necklace with a turquoise stone.

After a moment, Dally realized her mouth had dropped all the way open. She carefully closed it, clicking her teeth for good measure.

"My name is Jennacake. I'm the secret librarian. How can I help you?"

Dally unclenched her hands and smoothed them over the front of her pleated skirt, attempting to dry the nervousness from her palms. She no longer felt quite as scared, now that she wasn't all alone and the voice without a body seemed to have stopped. Instead she felt awkward and somewhat silly-looking, in her uniform skirt that was a size too big (her mother said she'd grow into it, but she hadn't yet), stockings with a hole in the shin (there was always a hole somewhere), and a shirt that was missing a button (she just noticed it now, as her slightly-less-scared fingers picked at her shirt for something to do). Her hair had been neatly combed at one point but now probably looked unruly. She sensed more stray black curls leaping forward as she stood there.

"I—I'm not sure," Dally said.

Jennacake smiled, which made her even prettier. Dally tried to pull her shoulders out of their after-school slouch. "Well, that's okay," the librarian said. "We'll figure it out. Why don't you start by telling me your name."

"I'm Dally." She thought the librarian seemed strikingly pleasant. "Hello, Ms. Cake."

"Actually, Jennacake is my first name. It's unusual."

"Cake is part of your first name?" Dally smiled. "That should be more common."

The librarian clapped her hands lightly. "You are the first to put it that way. I like your logic."

"My name is also unusual." Dally had never met another Dally.

"Well, then we are two peas in a pod, aren't we?"

Dally smiled again. She would've very much liked to have anything at all in common with Jennacake. "I suppose so."

"Why don't you come inside," said the librarian. "I'll show you around."

Jennacake turned and walked—glided, really—down a wide corridor that seemed to glow with candlelight as she moved. Dally followed. The hall appeared to be made of stone or marble, and while their path was lit now, when Dally looked over her shoulder, she saw nothing but darkness behind them.

"Have you got a last name?" she asked, because talking made the surroundings seem less strange. "I hope it involves ice cream."

Jennacake laughed, a delightful throaty tinkle that made Dally's skin feel warm. "Yes, I have a last name." Dally noticed she didn't say what it was. "How about you?"

"Peteharrington," Dally reported. "My whole name together is a bit of a mouthful."

"Oh." Jennacake's steps faltered just a little bit. "Oh, my." The light around her glowed stronger, bringing the corridor from dusk toward daylight. She whirled to face Dally, her gorgeous features pursed in alarm. "Dally is a nickname? You're Delilah Peteharrington?"

"Y-yes?" Dally blurted it out like a question, which was silly, because she perfectly well knew her own name. "Yes. Delilah Richmond Peteharrington."

Jennacake sighed. "Well, then, that's enough of the theatrics, I suppose." She glanced toward the ceiling, and the air began to hum with the buzz of fluorescent lights coming on. The marble hallway shone white, ahead and behind. Its walls were etched with the most intricate pattern Dally had ever seen.

"Wow," she breathed, in spite of herself. She reached out and touched the cool wall. Even her smallest finger was too big to fit in the carved lines.

"Yes," Jennacake murmured absently. "Come along, sweetheart." She continued down the corridor, head slightly bowed, kneading her forehead with her fingertips. Her ethereal calm had been replaced with something akin to worry, perhaps even edging toward panic.

"What's wrong?" Dally's nervousness ticked back up a few notches (it had never gone totally away). She hurried after the librarian, who didn't answer.

"What is it?" Dally insisted, but then all words faded from her mind as they reached the end of the hallway; it spilled into a high-ceilinged room awash with pale golden light and lined floor to rafters with marble bookshelves packed with slender, aged volumes.

The Secret Library.

Dally spun in a slow circle, hearing a soundless sound that seemed deafening to her, a silence that could only be described as the sound of millions of voices about to speak. It made her ears pound, not to mention her heart. It made her want to listen; it made her want to scream. It made the curious corners of her mind begin to itch.

"Whoa," muttered Dally, because it was the kind of room that changed everything.

The librarian turned to her. "I'm afraid you've come to the right place, my dear." Jennacake's lovely brown eyes swam with tears. "I'm just so very sorry you had to find us so soon."

6

Dally stood perfectly still, overwhelmed. The questions on her tongue included: *What is that sound?* and *What does that mean, "so soon"?* But she found herself not saying anything. The silence in the room was far too loud to speak into. It practically immobilized her.

Jennacake drifted a short distance away, then returned. Her face had smoothed itself back to cool perfection. She held out a lightly steaming mug of pale-blue liquid. It didn't look like any drink Dally had ever seen.

"Sip this," the librarian said. "You'll feel better."

Dally hesitated. She had indeed started feeling quite awful, but not so awful that she'd forgotten the general rule of not drinking unusual potions handed to her by strangers. "No, thank you," she managed to say. It felt like she screamed it over the pounding in her head.

"I'll taste it first, if you'd like," Jennacake said. "You're really going to want to drink this." She brought forth a spoon, dipped it into the lake-like surface of the drink, and gathered a small puddle, which she raised to her lips and slurped up like soup. "See?" She extended the mug to Dally.

Dally grasped it between her fingers. It was warm. She smelled the strange steam, and it began to calm the pressure in her ears, the curious itch along the underside of her scalp. Casting her better judgment aside, she took a tiny sip.

At once, the air around her head widened back to normal, as if a great weight had been lifted.

"Oh," Dally said. "Yes, that's better." She took another sip. It tasted like a mixture of raindrops and sunshine, with a slight earthy undertone of fresh-mown grass—surprising, but delicious. Dally drank some more.

"A little is enough," Jennacake told her, "but it won't hurt you a bit if you choose to drink the rest."

Dally took a final sip, then handed the mug back to the librarian. "Thank you," she said politely.

"It's no trouble," Jennacake said. "Now, first things first. What brings you to the library today?"

Dally had a different idea about what first things should come first. "What did you mean, I've found you too soon?"

Jennacake sighed. "It's like I said—everyone who finds the library is meant to be here. So, you are meant to be here. I just wasn't expecting you yet."

"Do you *expect* everybody who comes to the library?"

"Heavens, no," the librarian said. She reached out with pale, slender fingers and squeezed Dally's arm. "You, Dally, are quite special."

Dally ducked her head, suddenly feeling sad. It was pleasant to be called special, of course, but the only other person who had ever thought that about her was Grandpa. He used to say it all the time. *Dally-bird, never forget how special you are.* Here, in the now-quiet library, she could practically hear the echo of his voice. She missed him very much.

"I've lost you to your thoughts, it would appear," Jennacake said, startling Dally out of her swirl of sad-happy memories.

"I only have an hour," Dally blurted out. "I forgot to mention that."

"We have plenty of time," the librarian said. "But if you want to dive right in, Minor Transgressions would be a good place to start." Jennacake pointed to a brightly lit section toward the front of the library.

"They're not really labeled," Dally observed, walking toward the bookshelves to get a closer look. Each book's spine had some texture on it—something like braille, perhaps—and, at the very bottom, a small row of six to eight numbers, but they were unlike any Dewey decimal labels Dally had ever seen in a normal library.

"That's right," Jennacake said. "You just choose the right one."

"*Any* one?"

"Yes."

Dally studied the rows of narrow spines. Some were thinner than others, but none were any thicker than a picture book.

Her finger traced the books on the shelf at her eye level, and then the one just below. As she touched the spines, the strangest sensations suffused her. Each book seemed to come with a *feeling*: happiness, sadness, frustration, calm. The faster she dragged her finger, the faster the emotional roller coaster.

"Whoa," Dally said, pulling back. "How do they do that?"

"Strange, isn't it?" Jennacake seemed to know what she was talking about. "But also exciting?"

Dally nodded. She moved to another shelf. Sometimes a word rang out in her ears, as though each book were speaking to her. *Locket. Carousel. Transit. Trouble.* She lingered on that last spine and tugged it out. It wasn't the word that drew her so much as the feeling of relief that surged up in her.

"Okay," Jennacake said. "Bring it here." She began walking toward a door at the far side of the room, beyond the reference desk.

Dally studied the thin volume as they went. It had a flimsy starched-cloth cover that bound just a few pages. The numbers on the spine read 202377. At the side where the book should open, a thin strip of the cloth sealed the back to the front, buckled by a tiny latch.

"It's locked," Dally noted. "Like a diary."

"We can't have secrets falling open on their own," Jennacake said. "Sometimes what is powerful has to be protected." She produced a slender key. "Come with me."

Jennacake led Dally to a stone door with the words READING ROOM above it in gold script. The door opened to a small, cramped space, barely bigger than a study carrel, with a single desk and chair and no windows, lit by a dim overhead bulb. *By rights,* Dally thought, *a reading room should be much brighter.*

"A bit dark in here, isn't it?" she said as Jennacake motioned for her to take a seat at the desk. The gentle glow of light emanating from the librarian illuminated the white stone walls, which were carved with thin gold lines like the entry hall. In one corner, several stacks of books lay, dusty and cobwebbed.

Dally set the book on the desk, and Jennacake applied her key to the tiny lock. The thin strap flopped loose.

Dally reached for the cloth lip of the cover.

"No!" Jennacake cried, slamming her hands over the book. "No, dear, you must wait until I'm out of the room. I can't come with you."

"Come with me?" Dally echoed.

There followed a slow, spreading silence, in which Jennacake's liquid brown eyes began to shimmer. "You're just so young," she whispered finally. "As it is, I can only give you a crash course in secret navigation."

Dally's pulse ticked steadily beneath her skin. She could feel it in her throat, her wrists, her knees. "Secret navigation?" Dally was beginning to feel like a cave of a person, empty of knowledge with nothing to offer but echoes and a pitch-dark heart. The nervous speed of the blood in her vessels made her skin flush. It was either that, or the anger that suddenly flooded her from the roots of her hair to the tips of her toenails. *How could you leave me, Grandpa? How could you leave me in such a mess? Why didn't you tell me about the library before you died? I hate you for leaving without telling me.*

Dally immediately felt ashamed of the horrible thoughts. She didn't mean it—she just wanted Grandpa back.

Jennacake closed her eyes.

"Each secret exists in a world of its own," she said. "A world built upon the memory of the person whose secret it is. Or a compilation of memories, if the secret is shared."

"Like a collage?"

"Sometimes. Secret navigation is . . . a bit of a journey."

"Like diving into someone's head?"

"Yes, except the world is real."

Dally's eyes widened. "Real? You mean, I will see another place?" The volume on the desk seemed too thin to contain such magic, but the possibility made her breathless with anticipation.

"Very much so," Jennacake said. "You will travel to the moment when the secret occurred, or a moment when it was revealed or shared. You may even interact with the secret holder."

"You mean, like a glimpse into the past?" Dally asked.

"Not a glimpse," Jennacake said. "It's more complicated."

"I don't get it," said Dally.

Jennacake tipped up her chin and gazed at the intricate ceiling. "You will enter the actual past."

"What?" Dally said, not quite sure she had heard right.

"We have been taught that time is linear," Jennacake said. "Because that's how most people experience it. The library is different."

"But doesn't going to the past affect the present? Or the future?"

"You're not affecting history. The why of that is hard to explain. From where we stand today, the things you do there have already happened. But for you and those you meet, it will all be happening for the first time. The secret will be revealed in time, but the bigger the secret, the larger the lead-up. Usually."

"How long will it take?" Dally had fleeting thoughts of Mr. Jerry waiting for her on the corner and her tutor waiting for her at home.

"Time is . . . different . . . in the library," Jennacake said. "It may feel like you're gone a long while, but it will be much less than an hour in real time."

"Gone?" Dally said. "It's just a book."

Jennacake shook her head. "Once you enter the pages, it's no longer just a book."

Dally's heart fluttered. "It's an adventure?"

Jennacake reached out a finger and brushed a wandering curl off Dally's cheek. Even though they had only just met, it felt like a loving touch, and it calmed Dally's racing pulse.

"You could call it an adventure," Jennacake said. "One last thing to know: Each secret has a boundary. It's white, like clouds or fog. A traveler must never cross this boundary. You must stay within the circle created by the fog, no matter what happens. No matter what you have to do. The fog is how the library keeps you safe. Do you understand?"

Dally understood Jennacake's words, but not the larger meaning of them. Nevertheless, she nodded.

"Okay, then." Jennacake's lovely frown flashed as she moved

away. "Once the door is closed, you may go." The librarian then closed it, leaving Dally alone in the shadowy room.

She waited a beat for good measure, then flipped the secret open. "Well, here goes."

Dally's head began to spin. Darkness engulfed her. She clutched the edges of the cloth-bound book until she could no longer feel it, and her hands folded in on themselves in two tight fists.

7

When the spinning stopped, Dally opened her eyes. She relaxed her fists. She was standing on grass, among bushes. Not just any bushes: the carefully trimmed and cultivated hedges of the topiary garden at Peteharrington Place. Why, it seemed she had been transported to her own backyard!

It was a rather impressive feat, but what did it have to do with any kind of secret?

Dally shook off the remnants of dizziness and took a few steps. To her left was the white fog Jennacake had described— the secret's edge. The fog swirled and billowed in place, like smoke caught behind a pane of glass. It stretched as high as she could see, like a wall to the sky.

A traveler must never cross this boundary. So Dally turned right, in order to stay inside the circle created by the fog. It must be quite a large circle, she reasoned, because from here she could not see the other side of it. Behind her, the slightly curved wall of fog ran straight through one of the six-foot hedges and disappeared beyond.

Otherwise, the gardens looked surprisingly . . . normal. This part of the hedge was a simple labyrinth leading toward the flowers and topiaries at the center. At first Dally heard only her own footsteps and a solitary chirping bird, but soon the sound of light humming and the blade-on-blade rasp of pruning shears reached her.

The humming paused. "Sí," said a man's voice. He fired off a few orders in rapid Spanish. Dally peeked around the hedge. Hector, the grounds manager, was directing a small crew of workers. He had clippers in his hands, and the others had rakes and shovels. Dally understood enough Spanish to know they were talking about preparations for her mother's annual garden party. But that had taken place months ago, in the early summer!

When Hector finished the instructions, the others scurried off into the bushes to do their tasks, leaving him alone. He walked around, humming and examining each topiary: the antelope, the giraffe, the lion, the elephant. A smattering of tools lay in the clearing, but Hector had his eyes raised to the leafy beasts. He didn't notice the rake in the grass until his toe caught it.

"¡Ay Dios mío!" Hector exclaimed as he stumbled, falling backward toward the elephant. His arms flailed and instinctively reached for something to break his fall. The closest thing was the elephant's trunk. It did break Hector's fall, but his momentum broke the trunk.

Dally's stomach sank. Seeing the now-dangling trunk brought back a memory. Not from this past summer but from the summer before.

"Oh, no—oh, madre de Dios." Hector whispered a swift and urgent prayer, holding the trunk in place as if hoping to heal it by magic. "It's hopeless."

Dally's distraction had made her careless, apparently. She had moved closer and closer while listening, and when Hector turned at the sound of her, she had no choice but to step into the clearing.

"Hello, Miss Dally," Hector said. "My, you've gotten tall, haven't you?"

"Like a weed, Grandpa says. Gotta go, Hector!" Dally skittered on by, not wanting to prolong the encounter. She was indeed much taller now than she had been two summers ago.

She ducked behind a large shrub just as her mother's shriek rang out. "Hector, what have you done? How could this happen?"

"I—I don't rightly know, Ms. Peteharrington," Hector stammered.

"Did one of your people do this?" Dally's mother demanded. "When you find out who, I want them off the property immediately. Carelessness is not acceptable."

"I—I don't believe it was one of them," he said. "I'm the only one who works on the topiaries, as you know." He quickly added, "This could easily have been an accident. Maybe an animal? Or . . . a child?"

Dally's mother's eyes narrowed. "Hector, have you seen Delilah? Has she been playing out here today?"

A surge of anger flooded Dally. She remembered this day,

indeed. She recalled the scolding, her confusion, the miserable week she'd spent banned from the garden.

"I—I don't think so, ma'am. That is, I did see her a short while ago. But I don't rightly know."

"That child treats this whole property like her personal playground," Dally's mother complained. "I shall have a word with her about her recklessness."

"As you wish, ma'am." Hector hung his head.

"The garden party is next weekend, you know. Everything must be in shape. Fix this immediately."

"Yes, ma'am."

Dally's mother stalked away. Hector let the trunk dangle once again and dropped his head into his hands.

Dally's skin began to tingle. The air began to spin. The fog swiftly darkened from white to gray to black, then billowed close and closer, from all sides. She shut her eyes.

Hector's secret would be safe with her. In fact, now that she knew the truth, she felt quite a bit better about her own memory of that day, and the undeserved punishment she had endured. Her mother might have fired Hector on the spot for making such a human error. But no matter how much her mother might want to, she couldn't fire Dally.

8

Dally opened her eyes and found herself alone in the dim stone room again, clutching the closed book in her hands as though she had simply finished reading. She dutifully snapped the slim lock into place.

"Good, you're back," Jennacake said as Dally emerged from the reading room. "That should have been a short one."

"It was amazing!" Dally gushed. "I went to—"

"Shhh." Jennacake hushed her, pressing cool fingers against Dally's lips. "It's a secret, remember?"

"Even from you?"

"You mustn't tell," Jennacake insisted. "Outside these walls, you must take care to protect what you learn here. Best to practice discretion even within the library, so you always remember."

Dally shook her head. "There's no one out there I'd want to tell anyway."

"Hmm," Jennacake said. "It seems that loneliness is something we have in common."

Dally swiftly handed over the book to hide the twinge in her tummy. Jennacake placed it on the reshelving cart.

"The secret was about someone I know," Dally said. She had so many questions about what had occurred. Maybe there was a way to ask them without revealing the secret itself.

"Secrets aren't meaningful unless you know the person, or at least understand the context," Jennacake answered. "That's part of what makes the library so dangerous."

Dally nodded. "Powerful things are always considered dangerous."

"Very true," Jennacake agreed. She paused. "Does your grandfather know you're here, Delilah?"

Dally reached into her backpack and extracted Grandpa's map. "I have this map," she said. "He left it to me when he died."

Jennacake's face folded in sadness. "Oh, I'm so sorry, my dear. When did he pass?"

"About two months ago."

"Such a lovely man," Jennacake murmured.

"You knew him?" Dally supposed that since he'd drawn her a map to the place, it stood to reason that he'd met Jennacake himself.

"Sure," Jennacake said. "He loved it here."

Dally imagined Grandpa's eyes sparkling at the sight of all the wonderful book-shaped secrets. "Can I read another?"

"Not today," Jennacake said. "Didn't you say you only have an hour?"

"Yes. What time is it? I have to get home."

"You won't be late," Jennacake said. "It hasn't been much time at all."

"Can I come back tomorrow?" Dally asked. "Will you be open?"

Jennacake's expression turned wistful again. "You can come back anytime you wish. And in your case, it's best that you go and come back another day. We must draw this out as long as possible."

"Draw what out?" Dally asked.

Jennacake's pristine forehead furrowed. "Your journey."

Cryptic much? Dally thought as she descended the steps of the library toward the sidewalk. The good news was, Grandpa had left her a way to continue having adventures. And clearly he had known she wouldn't wait until she was twenty-one. How could he have even *wanted* her to wait? Knowing the magic the library held, she was vaguely annoyed with him for not telling her sooner. They could have come together, just as they had often gone to the public library.

Mr. Jerry looked up from his newspaper when Dally opened the rear passenger door, carrying the cupcake she had procured from the bakery.

"That was fast."

Dally consulted the dashboard clock. Then she blinked hard and looked again. Only nine minutes had passed since Mr. Jerry dropped her off. But that was impossible. She knew perfectly well she'd been gone for more than nine minutes. It had taken her that long just to walk to the library and back, plus buying the cupcake! She had spent much longer than nine minutes inside the library, talking with Jennacake and reading the secret.

Time is different in the library, Jennacake had said. Different, indeed.

"Where to now?" Mr. Jerry asked.

"Home, please."

Dally asked Mr. Jerry to drop her outside the gate so that she could walk up the drive as usual and not call attention to herself.

"I need to go again tomorrow, please," she said.

Mr. Jerry met her gaze in the rearview. "Oh?"

"Yes, please. And the day after."

"Must be good cupcakes," Mr. Jerry mused.

"Oh, yes," Dally agreed. She made a note in her mind to bring him a cupcake tomorrow.

It was all she could do to concentrate on her business lesson that afternoon. She was fairly bursting with the desire to tell someone, anyone, what she had experienced. Hector rode by on the lawn mower outside Dally's private classroom window, and the very thought of his secret tickled her to distraction.

"Dally," said her tutor. "Are you with me?"

"What?" she said. "Oh, yes. I'm sorry."

Her tutor frowned but continued the economics lesson. Dally stared at the laptop screen and tried harder to focus, but his voice soon droned into a dull roar in the background. She was surprised when he ended the lesson half an hour early.

"Your mother requested that you join her in the dining room tonight," the tutor said.

"She isn't working?" Dally usually had dinner alone during the week because her mother kept very long hours in the office, typically taking the evening meal on a tray.

The tutor shrugged. "Apparently not." He winked. "But, hey, it's nice that we're off the hook for a bit, right?"

Dally respectfully pounded the fist he held out to her. She liked him all right as a person, though she did not like the concept of having a tutor in the first place.

But his words did not calm her. She could not be happy about a sudden change in plans when her mother had made such a big deal just yesterday about keeping to the schedule.

Dally marched down the hall to the formal dining room.

"How was today's lesson?" her mother inquired as she entered.

Dally tried hard to let it go—she really did. But sometimes her mouth had a mind of its own. "So, you can change the schedule whenever you feel like it, and that isn't going back on your word? *'We've signed an agreement.'*" Her tone turned mocking at the end.

It would not help anything to have such a fit, but what was done was done.

Her mother's lips tightened. "I thought we could have a nice dinner," she said. "But clearly you are still angry."

Dally thumped into her chair, crossing her arms. Jasper, the cook, bustled in and set a plate of meatloaf, mashed potatoes, and peas in front of her. It was one of Dally's favorite meals (apart from the peas, which were merely the lesser of the possible vegetable-shaped evils).

She sat up and lifted her fork. "It's not fair."

"The opportunity came up at the last minute," her mother said. She glanced at her watch. "I could have scheduled dinner for after my last meeting, I suppose. But I thought it best to let your tutor go early rather than keep Jasper an hour later."

Dally knew all about opportunities coming up at the last minute that might cause someone to want to change a plan. She shoved a big bite of meatloaf into her mouth and got an even bigger bite of potatoes ready to follow it. The surest way to keep from talking was to be chewing.

If Grandpa were here, he'd jump right in with a funny story to break the tension, something bright and entertaining that would have Dally laughing around mouthfuls and her mother rolling her eyes.

After a silence, Dally's mother spoke again. "How was your day?"

Dally swallowed. "It was good."

"Is it strange, to be switching classes and using a locker?"

"Yes, but I like it." She'd been doing it for two months now. Managing her schedule and moving through the halls made her feel important. She enjoyed dialing the combination on her locker. The door made satisfying metal sounds when opening and closing. Sixth grade had many new and exciting aspects, but Dally hadn't known that her mother was aware of them.

"I like the stickers you chose to decorate your cubby in the art room."

That took Dally by surprise. "You saw them?"

"Last night was Caregivers' Night," her mother said.

"Right," Dally said. "You went?" Usually Grandpa had gone to that type of thing. He had been treasurer of the PCTA, the Parent-Caregiver-Teacher Association. She smiled now at the thought of him in his favorite apron, manning the bake sale table at the Fall Carnival. Someone else would have to run it this year, she supposed. It wouldn't be the same.

"Your teachers seem capable." Her mother sliced a delicate bite of meatloaf and lifted it to her mouth.

"Yeah, they're fine."

"Which is your favorite class?"

"Gym and English and pre-algebra," Dally said. Math wasn't her best subject, but Mr. Datchev had a way of making it make sense. "Ms. Tompa always picks really good books for our assignments. She had us write special essays for Caregivers' Night. Did you see mine? And if you were in the art room, did you see the sculptures? My dolphin?" In spite of everything, Dally found herself getting excited that her mother had seen some of the schoolwork she was proud of.

"Hmm. I'm glad you like pre-algebra," her mother said. "It'll complement your studies here."

Leave it to her mother to comment only on the math, out of

all the things Dally had mentioned. She jammed in a huge bite of meatloaf to keep from expressing the thought out loud.

"And you went on a field trip for history class recently?"

Dally swallowed. "Yes, to a few downtown museums."

"Including the Historic Harbor Jail and the Zebediah Douglas House," her mother said. "We're major donors to both of those museums, you know."

Always back to the money. "Yes," Dally said. The docent giving the tour at the jail had made a point of mentioning the Peteharringtons' generosity several times. Embarrassing.

"What did you think of the tours?" her mother asked.

At least her mother was trying, Dally supposed. Maybe that counted for something. Plus, whether she meant to or not, her mother had proved she *was* willing to change Dally's tutoring schedule, if the reason suited her.

Dally shrugged. "They were fun. Field trips are usually fun."

"What I really mean is, do you think we should continue our contributions there in the future?"

Dally readied a forkful of mashed potatoes, vowing to be entirely non-petulant for the rest of the meal. Her mother seemed to care about her opinion, and that felt nice.

"Oh, sure," Dally said, smiling. "It's amazing what a glimpse into the past can teach you."

≋ 9 ≋

When Dally arrived at the library the next day, it recognized her. *"Delilah Peteharrington,"* the eerie-yet-pleasant voice greeted her.

This time there was no scroll, no haze, no dire warnings— just the candlelit hall with its intricate carvings. Dally traced the lines on the wall as she walked.

Jennacake was waiting with a teacup of the special blue brew. "Welcome back," she said.

"Thank you." Dally took the cup and sipped politely. Once again, it surprised her how the pressure between her ears instantly eased. "No entryway theatrics today?" she inquired.

"It's only the first time, for anyone," Jennacake explained. "The way a person reacts to the warnings tells me a lot about who they will be as a traveler."

"What did you learn about me?" Dally asked.

Jennacake continued as though she hadn't spoken. "It's important, you see, to be sure that our patrons understand the purpose of this place. Secret keeping can be serious business."

Dally could take a hint. She handed the cup back, then

strolled around the room, studying the sections. She had chosen from Minor Transgressions yesterday. There was also Guilty Pleasures. Little White Lies. Locker Combinations. Hiding Places.

Dally turned to Jennacake. "Locker combinations?" she asked.

"They're secret, aren't they?" the librarian offered.

Dally laughed to herself. In the first weeks of school, several of her sixth-grade classmates had written their locker combinations on the backs of their hands. They could be sure to remember them that way—but so could everyone else!

"It seems a bit silly," Dally said. She touched the spines. Most of them left her feeling neutral. The words that came were pretty boring. Most were simply numbers: *locker number 6, locker number 252.* Occasionally something different would come to mind, like *garage, gym, tackle box.*

But one volume in particular gave her a sharp stab of jealousy. The word that accompanied it: *forgery.* That sounded interesting. Dally pulled the volume and handed it to Jennacake, who smiled. "Ah," she said. "Very nice."

Moments later, Dally sat alone in the reading room, waiting for the door to close behind Jennacake. Then she opened the book.

Dally swirled and snapped through the darkness. The secret carried her to another familiar place—her very own school. Luckily, no one was around when she appeared as if from nowhere in the second-floor hallway outside the art room.

Dally walked ahead, nudged by the billowing white fog at

her back. She rounded the corner and saw Chip, the redheaded boy, bent over his locker dial. "Dang it," he said. He kicked the locker and began spinning the dial again.

Everything else was quiet. No voices echoing from classrooms. No footsteps or laughter in the hall. It must've been after school.

Dally stood still, unsure how to proceed.

"Oh, hi," Chip said, spotting Dally. "I thought everyone left." He looked a little embarrassed. He spun his locker dial rather pointlessly, as if waiting for her to pass by.

"Need a hand?" she asked.

"Does it go left-right-left, or right-left-right?" Chip asked. "I can't get it straight."

"Right-left-right," Dally said.

"Thanks." He spun the dial to the left.

"Your other right," she corrected.

Chip's cheeks pinked. "I'm not so good at lefts and rights," he mumbled.

Dally thought for a moment. "How about up versus down? Is that easier?"

"Well, yeah. Duh."

"Here, look." Dally put her right hand on the dial of the locker next to his. "Forget about right and left. Watch my thumb. Thumb spins up for the first number. Thumb spins down for the second. Thumb spins up again for the third."

Dally watched as he spun out the numbers: 46-22-38. Then he tugged the little tab and the locker popped open.

Chip grinned. "Hey, that works! Thanks."

"Sure thing," Dally said.

Chip reached into his locker and pulled out some papers. According to the class schedule sheet clipped to his folder, it was Monday. Just two days ago.

Among his stacks of papers, Dally noticed the Adventure Club permission slip poking out. "Adventure Club?" she asked, pointing to the form. "Didn't you turn that in already?"

"Not yet," said Chip. "It's due tomorrow. Are you joining?"

Wait, she was getting confused. The forms were due on Tuesday, which was . . . tomorrow. It was funny to realize that, at this exact moment, her two-days-ago self was walking home, nervous about making her presentation to her mother. Not knowing it was going to fail.

"I would love to join, if only my mother would let me." Dally smiled wistfully.

Chip tugged the permission slip to the top of the pile. It was blank. "Oops. I forgot to ask my parents this weekend. And they're on a business trip now."

"Too bad," Dally said. "Maybe you can join later." But . . . she was sure she'd seen his form completed, on Tuesday, in real time.

Chip pulled out a pen. "I have a better solution." He clicked the pen and scrawled his mother's name across the parental permission line.

"Whoa," Dally said. "Won't you get in trouble for doing that?"

"No one will know." He winked. "Our little secret, right? Like the thumb thing."

"Surely your parents will notice when you don't come home after school two days a week."

"Nah," Chip said. "They're away a lot. I'll say I have something after school, and my nanny will pick me up later."

Dally wished she could be so carefree. "Wow."

"Good luck convincing your mom," Chip said. "And thanks again." He waved and walked off down the hall, disappearing through the fog. A moment later, the fog swooped in close and darkened, bringing Dally back to the library.

Alone in the dim, quiet reading room, she realized: this was why Chip had said the things he did on Tuesday morning, when she'd borrowed his phone. He'd seen her and talked to her about Adventure Club the afternoon before!

Jennacake greeted her when she emerged. "You look puzzled," the librarian said.

"The people I see in the secrets already know what happened," Dally said as the realization sunk in. "I mean, it's a memory that exists in their brain today, in the present. Even if I haven't read their secret yet . . . because for them, it's the past, but for me, it's still in the future?"

"Yes," Jennacake said. "For most people, time moves in one straight line. The library lets you jump back and forth along that line, from secret to secret. So, yes. When you go into a secret, you are entering someone's past."

"So these things are really happening. They've *already* happened." Dally paused. "That's cool."

"Very cool," Jennacake agreed.

After final bell on Thursday, Dally noticed Chip and a large group of others clustering near the gymnasium. No doubt they were headed to the very first meeting of Adventure Club.

Dally searched her heart for the stake of jealousy that had pierced her only two days ago, watching Chip turn in his permission slip. She had hoped for and imagined the joys of Adventure Club ever since the school had announced the club was forming. But missing out didn't feel so bad anymore. Now she had an adventure of her own to pursue—one her classmates couldn't possibly fathom.

When she got to the library, Dally explored the section labeled Hiding Places. She chose a secret that made her feel like laughing when she touched its spine, and gave her a blast of delicious flavor on her tongue. She'd never *tasted* a secret before, but this one tasted sweet.

After the now-familiar whirl of entering a secret, she found herself in the pantry at Peteharrington Place. Outside, in the kitchen, she heard Hannah and Jasper speaking.

"You got how many bags?" the housekeeper said. "I know I didn't hear you say a dozen . . ."

"I told you, they were on sale," Jasper grumbled. "You know you're gonna go through them."

Hannah hooted. "Get those outta here. That child is gonna eat herself into a sugar coma when she finds them."

Jasper clucked his tongue. "You ask me, her momma snacks a fair bit of them away herself. Dally comes by her sweet tooth honest."

Dally heard the sound of plastic packaging rustling. "Boy, you always making work for the rest of us," Hannah huffed. "I'll take care of it."

"I knew you would," Jasper called after her, laughing to himself as Hannah bustled off. He turned up the radio. His usual jazz station was blasting holiday music. "Dally sure does love her cheer-ups," he commented to the now-empty kitchen. "It's all gonna work out."

Cheer-ups! Dally's interest was officially piqued.

She peered out of the pantry as Hannah rounded the corner, her arms laden with bags of Dally's favorite candy. Dally knew what the secret had to be about: Hannah's mystery hiding place. Dally had once spent an entire summer searching high and low, all through the mansion, looking for the secret stash. She never found it.

Dally snuck out of the pantry when Jasper turned toward the stove. She tiptoed past the kitchen island and out into the hallway, after Hannah. The fog was giving her plenty of space to move, so she followed the sound of Hannah's running commentary. The housekeeper often muttered to herself as she went about her business; you could always hear her coming.

Hannah went into the large formal dining room. Dally noticed that her usual place at the table was occupied with a booster seat. She remembered that seat, which she'd stopped using six or seven years ago.

The Dally who existed in this time frame must have been in preschool, which was only half a day. Dally glanced up and down the hallway. What if she ran into her younger self?

Well, Dally supposed, she didn't remember ever encountering an older version of herself when she was small, so hopefully it wasn't anything to worry about. Perhaps the secret or the fog wouldn't allow such a mind-bending thing to happen.

Hannah approached one of the round planters sitting on their small tables on either side of the picture window. Dally couldn't see exactly what happened next, but suddenly the leaves of the fernlike plant moved to Hannah's left. Then they were back in place, and Hannah walked into the hall that led to the sitting rooms.

Dally rushed over to the planter. It looked like it always did. Ceramic on the sides, dirt and roots in the center, leaves sticking up on top. The lip of the planter was wider than the base, and curved under. She fluffed around in the leaves and felt nothing. She curled her fingers under the lip and tugged upward, surprising herself when the plant rose up easily.

The lip was attached to a plastic bowl that held the dirt, but it was only about a third as deep as the planter base. Underneath was a cavern, occupied by a couple of sacks of individually wrapped orange hard candies.

Dally laughed out loud.

Those planters, apparently, were decorative. And there were similar planters stationed all over the house—a dozen, at least, that Dally could think of offhand. Was there candy hidden beneath all of them? Dally resisted the urge to snag a cheer-up, as she could feel that the secret was ending.

"Who's there?" Hannah's voice called. "Katherine? Is that you, honey love?" Her footsteps approached. But Dally was gone, snapped back into the darkness beyond space and time, her fingers pressed to her lips to stifle her laughter.

≷ 10 ≶

When Dally got home that afternoon, she raced to check the planters. The plants themselves had grown over the years. The stems and leaves stood quite a bit taller today, which made them harder to lift, but the bases were exactly the same.

And so were Hannah's hiding places. There was at least a whole bag of candy in each of the planter bases! Now Dally *did* take a cheer-up. The sweet, sweet flavor was intensified by the secret discovery.

On Friday, Dally journeyed to the pantry once again, this time to learn the secret ingredient in Jasper's famous chili. It wasn't merely "love," as Jasper had always claimed. It was a big old scoop of brown sugar! That rascal!

The weekend of waiting was positively interminable. She had free time—no lessons, just her homework—but she couldn't very well disappear from the property for several hours without Hannah noticing her absence. Whenever Dally felt particularly bad about being away from the library, she helped herself to a cheer-up. She was careful to take only one from each planter around the house so Hannah wouldn't get suspicious. If Dally was honest, she'd have to admit that the magic of the cheer-ups was slightly diminished when they didn't appear as if from nowhere. Still, she was delighted to know the secret.

On Monday, she once again scheduled a ride from Mr. Jerry. He nodded when she asked him to consider it a standing weekday outing.

As usual, Jennacake met Dally with tea. "Would you like to see more of the library?" she asked.

"There's more?" Dally's gaze swept over the stately room and noticed a door in the far corner with a sign that read STACKS.

"Quite a bit more," Jennacake said. "This is merely the atrium." She led the way through the door.

Everything about the library was ornate, even the winding miles of stacks. The shelves were not made of rickety metal, like the ones in the basement of the public library, but rather carved from rich mahogany or cherry wood, laden with volumes of varying sizes. Dally was surprised to see how large and thick some of the secrets here were, compared to the picture-book-sized choices in the atrium—some resembled hardcover grown-up novels, while others were huge, like dictionaries or encyclopedias.

"Family Secrets is our biggest section by far. That's all this, here . . ." The librarian walked Dally farther into the stacks, pointing out shelves dedicated to Unrequited Love, Transgressions, Deathbed Confessions, Withheld for Someone's Own Good, I'm Not Who They Think I Am, and more. The space seemed endless, peppered with quiet reading nooks here and there.

"Do people read among the stacks?" Dally asked.

"No, only in the reading room," Jennacake said, "for obvious reasons. However, we maintain a number of places to rest or reflect."

"We?"

Jennacake smiled, angling her head slightly. "I, mostly."

They emerged into a small rotunda, with more stacks radiating out in all directions.

"It would be easy to get lost in here," Dally mused, gazing back the way they'd come.

Jennacake shook her head. "The library always knows where you are and where you need to go."

Dally spun a slow circle in front of Desperate Times Call for Desperate Measures and found herself facing Small Lies That Grew Bigger Somehow.

Everything she saw—absolutely everything—activated her curiosity. "It would take forever to read them all," she said, basking in the wonder.

"No one can read them all," Jennacake said. "Remember, you may read one secret per visit."

"Is that the rule?" Dally asked. She wasn't much in favor of rules, but she did (usually) try to follow them.

"It's simply what is best. Shall we return now?"

"Okay." Dally could've wandered the stacks forever quite happily, but she was also eager to get on with her next secret adventure.

"This way." The librarian nodded toward a door in the wall that Dally was pretty sure hadn't been there a moment ago. They walked through it and emerged from the same door where they'd started, back in the atrium.

"Whoa," Dally said. "Can we go again?"

Jennacake's laugh tinkled in the air, like bells. "It's not a carnival ride, dear."

Dally wandered behind the reference desk, moving among the piles of secrets waiting to be reshelved. She spied a curtain covering another doorway. "What's back here?" she asked. The fabric was gauzy and blue, like Jennacake's dress. Dally tugged it aside.

The alcove behind the curtain was lined with bookcases. A small gold plaque on the lip of the second-highest shelf read PRIVATE: LIBRARIAN.

"What's this?" Dally asked.

"Oh, those are mine." Jennacake's voice was as calm and pleasant as ever, but a shadow seemed to cross her face as she spoke.

Dally's eyes grew wide as she studied the private shelves. "*You* have secrets of your own in the library?"

Jennacake smiled. "Of course I do. But you won't find what you're looking for there, at the moment."

It was true. As curious as Dally might be to know more about Jennacake, she found she didn't want to pull a volume. Rather, she found she couldn't.

"What's going on?" Dally protested. "Why can't I . . . ?"

"The secrets you choose are not solely up to you," Jennacake said. "The library does have some say."

"So I can't read your secrets?"

"Few people are drawn to them. Most never even notice them." Jennacake sighed. "You, Dally, are very special."

"You've said that before," Dally reminded her.

"It grows truer by the day. And soon, there will be some things we must discuss."

"Like what?" Dally trooped out from behind the desk and back toward the rest of the collection. Family Secrets might be the place to visit today. That felt right. The thought made her arm itch and twitch, where a moment ago it had been like stone. She was ready to go.

"Why can't we discuss the things now?" Dally asked.

"Because you're eleven and a half," Jennacake said.

"Eleven and three-quarters, as of today," Dally corrected, as she headed back toward the door to the stacks.

"My apologies. Eleven and three-quarters."

Dally wound past Childhood Secrets and First Crushes. The Romantic Fantasies area smelled like leather, salted caramel, and rosewater. She couldn't help but glance through the locked gate that kept visitors from wandering the Sealed in Confession aisle.

Family Secrets indeed took up a lot of real estate. Dally counted seven whole aisles, all of which stretched nearly out of sight.

"Does my mother have secrets in the library? Or my grandpa?" The idea crossed her mind in a flash. If Hector, Hannah, and Jasper did, and Jennacake did, then it stood to reason that other people she knew had secrets here, too.

"No doubt," Jennacake said. "Perhaps you'll find them when you're ready, but perhaps not. It all depends."

"I want to read a family secret," Dally said.

"Well, all right," Jennacake said. "Go ahead and choose your volume."

"Most everything about my family is secret," Dally said, running her finger along the spines. Stabs of grief, elation, guilt, and passion washed over her. "My mother says it's sometimes best that way."

"It's always difficult to know what really happened in the past. A person can live many different lives in a lifetime."

Dally supposed that was true. In eleven and three-quarters years, even she had already lived four different lives: one with two living parents in a small apartment, one with her mom and Grandpa at Peteharrington Place, one without Grandpa, and now one that included the Secret Library.

Dally felt the spines. *Blip blip blip.* Her finger landed on a slim volume that gave a feeling unfamiliar to her. A breath-stealing gut tug. *Marcus.* The word that emanated from the volume stole her breath all over again. Could it be—?

Jennacake smoothed a finger along the top of a nearby shelf, as if checking for dust, but her fingertip came up clean. "For most people, being here is about finding out who you really are, in one way or another."

Dally hugged the book to her chest. "This book is going to tell me who I am?"

Jennacake smiled. "Well, it might offer a piece of the puzzle."

≫ 11 ≪

Dally spun out of the black into a world of color. First impression: fabric for days. Floral patterns and tartans, polka dots and sheer gauzy pastels. She was standing among racks of flowing scarves and shawls. Tinkly pop music played from speakers overhead, barely loud enough to notice until you found yourself singing along with it. Beige institutional carpet underfoot. It was a department store. The accessories section. Dally could smell the leather of the belts and purses, along with the occasional strong whiff of perfume samples from the other side of a wall divider.

Dally floated her hand over the scarves. She walked around a rack of wallets and clutches into the next aisle. There stood a young Black man in a gray-and-orange Clemson sweatshirt.

Dally's heart leaped. She knew that sweatshirt well. She'd rescued it from a box of items her mother had once destined for Goodwill. Now it lived secretly in her bottom drawer, brought out on some winter nights to sleep in. It had a cozy hoodie pocket she could slip her entire forearms into. On her, the sweatshirt was very large indeed, but on the young man who wore it now, it fit perfectly.

He smiled at her briefly, then looked away.

It took all of Dally's willpower to hold herself back. It wouldn't do, she was sure, to race up to him and cry out "Daddy!"—though she almost couldn't help herself. The shock of it, in part, kept her motionless as her soul cried out to him.

Dally grasped a random wallet to give herself something to hold on to, feeling torn as to whether the library was being generous or cruel. Was she meant to talk to him? Was that allowed?

The young man—his name was Marcus, Dally knew—strolled away through the aisle of ties and belts, checking price tags on things. Dally followed his progress. After a few moments, he sighed and approached the jewelry counter.

A slim, balding clerk greeted him. Marcus asked to see some earrings. The clerk dutifully brought out several samples, reaching under the glass for each velvet box, then placing them up on top.

Marcus flicked his attention between the boxes, touching each pair and appearing to hem and haw over the options. He thoughtfully stroked the skin beneath his chin with two fingers.

"Which do you like?" he asked suddenly, turning to Dally. In spite of herself, she'd drawn quite close.

Dally pointed to her favorite of the four: a simple pair of diamond studs. They glittered in a way that felt familiar.

"Could we also see some necklaces, perhaps?" Marcus asked. The surprise of the "we" thrilled Dally. Marcus gestured down the counter toward the necklaces. He glanced at Dally, his gaze suggesting she go look at them. So she did.

The clerk nodded and turned toward the necklaces, too. Dally pointed one out, a gold chain with a heart pendant and a small clear stone. Her mother always said gold looked best on Dally. The clerk nodded again and bent with his key toward the lock at the back of the cabinet. At that moment, Marcus slipped one of the earring boxes into his sweatshirt pocket.

Dally stifled her gasp. Thief!

Marcus tossed her a wink and a grin as he closed the rest of the earring boxes one by one and pushed them away, motioning for the clerk's attention. "Thanks," he said. "Keep helping her. I'll be back in a minute."

Dally wanted to follow him as he walked away, but she was playing a role here. The role of *accomplice* to a *theft*. She hid her outrage and smiled at the clerk. He laid the glittering pendant in front of her.

"Thanks, this looks perfect. Um, what kind of stone is it?" Dally wasn't sure what sorts of questions would keep the clerk occupied long enough to let Marcus get away.

"A diamond," he said, staring at her like she was clueless.

"Oh," she said. That made sense. "A real one?"

"We only carry real ones here." The clerk's lofty tone suggested Dally should know better.

"Oh, sure, of course," she chirped. "Only the best in a store like this!" She drummed her fingers on the counter. Had it been long enough? She was too nervous to keep up the charade.

"Well, anyway . . . thanks, but I don't really have any money."

"Obviously," he muttered, putting the necklace away.

Dally pretended not to be affronted by his attitude. "I meant, I have to get my mom," she said, turning away.

The clerk was ignoring her now. He returned to the earring boxes and began putting them back. One. Two. Three. He paused, looked after Marcus. Then he picked up his phone and dialed a number.

Uh-oh. Dally scooted off in the direction Marcus had gone. Maybe she could catch him. Warn him.

There—she glimpsed his sweatshirt between some hat racks. Dally darted through the perfume section and into the cosmetics department, nearest the door. She was passing the last counter when she heard a woman yelp.

"Excuse me," Marcus said.

"Sorry!" the woman exclaimed. "I didn't see you at all." The voice was familiar. Too familiar. Dally peeked tentatively around the edge of the counter. Sure enough . . .

"My fault," Marcus said, though it clearly hadn't been. The woman—her name was Katherine, Dally knew—had several bags and was staring at her cell phone even as she apologized. Dally knew that expression awfully well, too. It was her mother's something-at-work-is-frustrating-me face.

"You okay?" Marcus said. He was inches from the door, about to make off with his prize, and yet he paused longer than necessary. *Go!* Dally wanted to warn him, but it was hard to breathe, let alone move.

"Of course," Katherine said. She raised her attention from her phone, finally, and met his glance. Then the very air locked in place around them. A frozen moment, two people gazing into each other's eyes.

"Hi," he said.

"Hi," she answered.

I loved him the moment I laid eyes on him, Dally's mother had once told her. *It was the strangest and most horrifying feeling.*

Horrifying? Dally had echoed. *Isn't love supposed to make you happy?*

Her mother had reached out then and stroked Dally's cheek. *He made me very happy.* And that was all she would ever say about how they met.

Now Dally hid behind the rack of fashion sunglasses that stood in the aisle intersection, trying to get closer.

"There!" came a shout from behind her. "That's him!" It was the clerk from the jewelry counter, pointing at Marcus. A burly security guard in a blue blazer was with him. They rushed past Dally and bore down on Marcus.

Marcus stepped away from Katherine and held up his hands. "Me?" he asked.

"Check his pockets," the clerk suggested. Marcus's face paled.

The security guard patted him down, coming up with the small earring box.

The clerk smiled triumphantly. "Told you!"

The security guard took hold of Marcus's arm. "I'm going to

need you to come with me." He tugged a walkie-talkie from his belt and spoke into it. "Coming in with a lifter."

Dally held her breath. Marcus glanced desperately from side to side, then hung his head in defeat.

"Hang on a second." Katherine reached over and plucked the earring box from the guard's hand. "That would be mine. I asked him to pick something out for me." She snapped open the box. "They're perfect," she declared, smiling hugely at Marcus. She handed the earrings to the clerk. "Shall we ring them up, then?"

The clerk shook his head. "Shoplifters! That one intended to steal this jewelry." He pointed at Marcus.

Katherine waved her hand around. "We're still in the store, aren't we? What exactly is the problem?" Her pale skin and the rings on her fingers gleamed under the fluorescent light.

The guard looked uncertain. "He was heading for the door, yeah."

"He was heading to meet me. I was by the door." Katherine's face seemed so young and smooth, yet Dally recognized the determination in her eyes. Her mother didn't know how to lose an argument; Dally knew that much for sure.

The clerk looked unconvinced.

"My family is well respected here," Katherine said. She reached into her purse and pulled out a credit card. "I think you'll agree that there was no need for us to steal anything."

The clerk's mouth formed a small O as he studied the card. "Oh, why yes, Miss Peteharrington. Yes, of *course*." He fumbled over himself. "I can ring you up right here, in fact." He bustled to the nearest makeup counter and began logging into the computer behind the register.

"Please release him," Katherine said to the guard in a tone only the very richest of the rich can manage. Dally had heard her mother use it many times to get her way. The guard let Marcus go.

"Sorry for the confusion, sir," the guard muttered, and ambled off.

Katherine walked over to complete the transaction, leaving Marcus standing in the doorway, looking relieved and confused.

"Thank you," Katherine said to the clerk, with melodramatic sweetness. "I trust you'll get a commission for your help today?"

"Yes, ma'am. Certainly." The clerk practically bowed.

"Excellent." Katherine grabbed Marcus's hand, and together they dashed out the door.

≋ 12 ≋

You don't really seem like the shoplifting type," Katherine said. She set her bags down by the fountain in the mall corridor. It was a large, old mall, its huge, wide hallways lined with glass-fronted shops. The area bustled with people, from parents pushing strollers to clusters of giggling teens to elders in tracksuits power walking through the crowds. Dally lurked beside a tall potted fern, listening.

"I've never stolen a thing in my life," Marcus admitted.

"Must be why you're no good at it." Katherine smirked.

"Wasn't quite the thrill I was hoping for." He smiled self-deprecatingly, then clasped his hands in front of his chest, as if in prayer. "You saved my life, you know. They'd have sent me to prison."

"Probably not for a first offense," she said. "You look like some kind of honor student."

"To them I look like a Black guy in a hoodie." Marcus laughed it off, but underneath he seemed quite shaken.

"I know." Katherine sat on the fountain ledge and crossed

her legs. "Whereas I could've told them I already paid for it earlier and they'd probably have let us go. I know about privilege."

"Well, good for you," Marcus said. He glanced around as if unsure what to do next, then resumed smiling brightly. "Anyway, thanks for the assist. Couldn't have gone better if we planned it. Next time, I'll be sure to have a beautiful accomplice waiting in the wings to save me from my own recklessness." He offered her a courtly bow, then started to move away.

"Hey, aren't you forgetting something?" Katherine called. The tiny bag that held the earrings dangled from her finger.

Marcus looked alarmed. "I . . . I'm sorry. I don't have that much money on me."

"But you need them for something, right?" Katherine said. "I doubt you woke up this morning and randomly decided to commit petty larceny."

He frowned at her. "Are you a lawyer or something?"

"It sounded fancier than 'shoplifting.'"

Marcus spread out his hands. "You don't know what I woke up thinking. Maybe I'm studying to be a cat burglar."

She made a face. "Try again."

"Maybe this is how I woo beautiful women." He winked.

Katherine nodded thoughtfully. "It's a novel approach, I'll give you that."

"Seems like it's working, too." Marcus grinned and moved closer. "We've known each other, what, five minutes? And here you are, offering me a fine piece of jewelry."

The package still dangled from Katherine's finger. "You'd have been long gone by the time they got there if I hadn't bumped into you. It's my fault you almost got caught."

"Sure," he agreed with a laugh. "Let's remember it that way. In the meantime, I'll be rethinking my future as a jewel thief."

"Probably wise." Katherine patted the fountain ledge beside her. "Before you disappear into the night, you at least owe me the whole story . . . ?"

"Marcus," he said, filling in the gap she'd left open.

"Kate," she answered, beaming up at him and tossing her hair. Dally struggled to reconcile this carefree young version of Katherine Peteharrington with the austere mother she knew.

"I told you, cat burglar."

Kate threw him a look that said, *For real, though . . .*

"I'm pledging a fraternity," he admitted, perching on the ledge beside her.

"So?"

"So, it's a hazing thing. We do all this ridiculous stuff, like a series of challenges, to prove we're worthy or whatever. Annoying but harmless." He waved his hand. "Swim naked across the lake; first one to reach the island gets a towel and a kayak for the return trip. That kind of thing."

"Don't you think there's a better way to prove you're worthy than that?"

Marcus shrugged. "Look, I'm trying to seem debonair, or whatever, but the truth is, I was planning to sneak the earrings back into the store later on."

"Why not buy them and pretend you stole them?"

He laughed. "Cash flow. Not everyone can whip out a charge card at a moment's notice."

Kate regarded him seriously. "I don't completely buy that."

"That people can be poor?" Marcus made a face.

"No, that you, specifically, couldn't find a way to buy some earrings that you plan to return in a few days anyway. You seem smart enough to solve that problem."

He raised his gaze to the ceiling, painted to mimic a bright-blue sky. "I thought I could do it, okay? I thought it might be fun. And if I returned them, what would be the harm?"

"It was all fun and games until the mall cops showed up?"

"Basically." Marcus looked sheepish. "I guess I bought into the hype too much."

Kate fingered a strand of her hair. "What hype is that?"

"The rich-white-boys-get-away-with-anything hype." He punched his knee. "*They* can do stuff like this because there's no extra scrutiny on them."

"So maybe you tell them that," Kate suggested. "Maybe you ask them to accept you on your own terms."

He blew out a breath and dropped his chin. "Or maybe stuff like this is why, in all these years, they've never had a Black member before."

"Seriously?" Kate raised her eyebrows.

Marcus nodded. "Right? Welcome to the twenty-first century."

"So you're trying to prove something?"

He tilted his head thoughtfully. "The guys in this frat, so many doors open to them. The connections. The influence. I could list out the alumni and you'd see. The governor. One of our congressmen. Lots of high-powered people, not just in this region but around the country."

Kate shrugged. "So you want your piece of the pie. Nothing wrong with that."

Marcus seemed agitated. "I want to break down walls. This is the wall in front of me."

"Or is it just what you *think* you're supposed to be doing?" she said softly. "What do you really want to do?"

Marcus smiled slightly. "I want to explore. I want to have adventures and be able to go where I want and experience life to the fullest. But you have to have money to live like that."

Dally's ears perked up. Explore? Adventures? She'd always thought those qualities in her came from Grandpa. She'd always assumed her father was like her mother: quiet and staid and generally indoorsy.

"You can get rich by pretending to be something you're not," Kate said. "But true wealth comes from knowing who you are and figuring out how to make the most of it. That's what my father says, anyway." Dally had never heard Grandpa say those words, but the idea rang true to her. Wasn't that why she was here, in her parents' secret, to begin with?

Marcus stared up into the seemingly endless indoor sky. "I want to know what it feels like to have an advantage in life, for a change."

"Probably gets harder if you go to jail for shoplifting."

He dropped his face into his hands. "God."

She nudged him gently. "I'm messing with you."

Marcus looked pained nonetheless. "We're all supposed to meet back at the food court with something we stole that's worth over a hundred dollars."

Kate removed the earring box from the shopping bag and held it out to him.

Marcus was confused. "What?"

"I was right. You need it. To get into your frat?"

He shook his head. "I can't afford to pay you back for those. It will take me quite a while, I mean."

"No biggie. I can be patient."

Did her mother really just say "no biggie"? Dally stifled a laugh as Kate pulled out a business card and handed it to Marcus.

"Consider it a loan. Interest-free."

The earring box still lay in Kate's outstretched palm. Marcus hesitated. "I was supposed to steal it. Feels like cheating."

She grinned. "Please. If you're not willing to cheat a little, you're not going to last too long in rich-white-boy world. Trust me."

Marcus appeared thoughtful.

Kate's grin grew. "Well, well, well. An *honest* cat burglar."

"You're having way too much fun," Marcus said, the slightest of smiles on his lips. "You don't even know me."

They exchanged a glance that spoke volumes. Even from

behind the fern, Dally could feel the sparks of connection flying.

"Okay, fine. Steal it from me." Kate closed her eyes and turned her head away. "Oh, dearie my, those brand-new precious earrings have disappeared!" she exclaimed in an affected, high-pitched voice. "Someone strong and handsome should take me out to dinner tonight to cheer me up."

Dally closed her eyes, too, feeling a cross between amused and grossed out. Her mother was *flirting*.

Marcus took the earring box and slipped it back into his sweatshirt. "Thanks," he said softly, standing up to leave.

"Don't mention it."

"Could I really take you out later?" he said. "I bet you've never been to the Grease Pit."

Kate grinned again. "Are they going to tune up my car?"

Behind the fern, Dally giggled. The Grease Pit was a restaurant in one of the Black neighborhoods downtown. It did have a silly name.

Marcus laughed, too. "Dinner," he said. "Best fried chicken you've ever eaten. Guaranteed."

"'Come for the chicken, stay for the hush puppies,'" Kate said, quoting the slogan on the menu.

"You've been there?" Marcus looked surprised.

"My father likes it."

"Tonight, seven p.m.? See you there?"

Kate nodded and Marcus strolled away.

"By the way, I like *She-Ra*, too," he tossed over his shoulder. "Used to watch it all the time."

"The cartoon?" Kate said. "I loved *She-Ra*. How'd you know?"

Marcus spun around. "'Oh, dearie my!'" he quoted. "Never question my savvy with pop culture references."

"Really dated ones, at least," Kate shot back with a grin.

Dally came out from behind the fern. As Marcus walked away, the fog billowed along with him. She knew she had to follow.

Her mother had returned her attention to her phone and didn't even notice as Dally swept by, fairly close. Kate wouldn't have recognized her anyway, Dally realized with a start, so she slowed long enough to study her mother's young face. It was odd and delightful. Dally didn't know what to think of the magic that could make them strangers and yet leave her feeling she knew more about her mother now than she ever had before. The truth was, they were strangers in her own time, weren't they?

Dally got *too* close then, accidentally kicking one of Kate's shopping bags. "Oh, I'm sorry," she said, catching the young woman's eyes as she looked up.

"It's okay," Kate said, meeting Dally's gaze with a bright, friendly smile. "It's such a perfect day, don't you think?"

"Truly perfect," Dally replied. She was close enough to see the phone screen.

I met someone, Kate's text read.

Tell me everything was the response.

Dally stared a moment longer, until the fog became too pressing. Then she scooted on down the hallway. Soon, the savory smells from the food court overtook her. She rode an escalator, glancing over the railing in time to see Marcus—the young man who would one day become her father—join his frat brothers. He waved the earring box in triumph and they cheered.

Dally step-step-stepped down the escalator, keeping ahead of the fog. As she reached the ground floor and turned to approach Marcus and his friends, the secret ended. The fog darkened fast and hard and claimed her, tossing her across time and space amid a slightly sick-making mix of love and happiness and sadness and regret.

13

I saw my father," Dally said as she strolled out of the reading room. She blurted it out without thinking, but hopefully it wouldn't hurt to confess that detail to Jennacake. It would be nice to talk about it with someone.

"Oh?" The librarian unfolded her hands and beckoned Dally closer.

"It was weird." *Weird* didn't begin to describe it, Dally admitted to herself. But she didn't have words for the rest.

"It's not always easy to learn the truth about people we love," Jennacake said. She wrapped a comforting arm around Dally's shoulder.

"It wasn't a bad thing." Dally decided it as she spoke. She allowed herself to lean against the librarian, if only for a moment. "Just strange."

"As we grow, we learn to know our loved ones differently," Jennacake said thoughtfully. "With or without help from the library."

Dally wasn't sure that was true if the person in question

was dead. Sometimes, then, who they were—or who you *thought* they were—became kind of frozen. Dally's real-life memories of her father were only fleeting: The feel of his hand under hers and the rumble of his chest behind her back when they sat together to read stories. His bright smile and the taste of the cinnamon muffins he used to feed her piece by piece. Sometimes he'd "forget" where her mouth was and feed a piece to her belly button or her armpit to make her laugh.

She had seen many pictures, of course, scattered about the house in frames and in a few printed photo albums someone had ordered from the internet: Her parents' wedding. A trip to Europe. A beach vacation. Dally's first year. Dally's second year. And her third. But then nothing.

"Are you all right?" Jennacake said.

"Oh, sure," Dally said. And she was. Such melancholy came and went; that was how it was after losing someone. But the twinge of sadness was far surpassed by her excitement. Jennacake's comment about the library showing you who you are made sense now. The library could show her much, much more than mere secrets.

It wasn't *entirely* unusual for Dally and her mother to dine together, but it had been happening less and less since Grandpa died. Tonight, Dally was actually excited to see that her mother's place was set. (That, to be sure, was a bit more unusual.)

"Hi," Dally said when her mother appeared. "You're not working tonight?"

"I may have a late call," her mother said, sliding into the chair across from her. "Time zone juggling."

Dally nodded as though she understood the pressures of running a major corporation.

"I hope it's not *too* late," she offered. She held herself taut, working hard to present herself in a way her mother would approve of. It wouldn't do to start gushing and hurrying the conversation she hoped they could have.

The dinner consisted of pork chops, a beet salad, and warm, buttery dinner rolls. Once Jasper brought the dishes to the table, they served themselves and dug in.

"This is all right," Dally said, a bit grudgingly, of the beet salad. Those were two words she didn't like on their own, let alone put together. But the beets were sweet, and the dressing added a light fresh flavor that wasn't awful.

"Thank you for trying something new," her mother said. "I'm glad you like it."

If only you knew all the new things I've been trying! Dally thought. They ate in silence for a few minutes.

"I'm glad you're here tonight," Dally said when she couldn't hold it in any longer. "I have some questions."

"Oh?" Her mother seemed interested. She cut her pork chop into neat slices and made her way through them, bite by bite.

Dally took a deep breath. "Yes, I'm in the middle of a lesson on family history." That was stretching the truth a bit, but it wasn't actually a lie. "I'd like to know more about my father."

Her mother stirred the sauce on her plate. "Oh."

Dally wished she could stay quiet and wait, but the excitement grew unbearable. "I remember a little, but I want to know more. What was he like? How did you meet him? You've never really told me the story." She held her breath then, hopeful.

"You know the story," her mother said, which hadn't been true at all, before the secret.

"Only that you met in college. Tell me again," Dally begged.

"There's not much more to tell," her mother answered.

"There must be," Dally insisted. "It's not fair, you know."

"What isn't?"

"That I have to live without a father."

Her mother's face flashed with an unusual expression, possibly sadness. *Over Marcus,* Dally wondered, *or over Grandpa?*

"Grow up without one, I mean," Dally amended. It was different, she thought. Or maybe it wasn't.

Dally's mother laid down her fork. "Life isn't fair."

"Why do you have to be like this?" Dally blurted out. It was on the tip of her tongue to add, *You used to be so carefree.*

"Delilah, this isn't the sort of question you spring on someone over dinner." Her mother picked up her fork and speared a beet wedge.

With Jennacake's admonitions about secrecy ringing in her ears, Dally couldn't say anything to prompt her mother about the story. Anyway, she was sure memory wasn't the problem.

"Why won't you tell me about him?" she asked, feeling her voice grow small.

"You know plenty about him."

"The things I remember are little. I want to know the big things. Things he'd have told me if he could have."

Dally's mother touched her earlobe. Dally's eyes followed the motion. The small pair of earrings were the same ones her mother always wore. She might change them up for a particular outfit now and again, but not often. They were basic diamond studs. Nothing especially fancy compared to some other things she owned, but they had long been her favorites, Dally realized. Looking closer, she wondered—were those the same earrings her father had "stolen" the day they met?

Dally's lips parted in wonder. For all her refusal to speak of the man she'd married, her mother wore this talisman daily.

"Did he give you those earrings?" Dally asked.

"These?" Her mother paused for a long moment. "He—actually, I bought them." She shook her head slightly. "They do remind me of him, I suppose."

Dally wanted to toss a roll at her in frustration. "Is that why you wear them every day?"

Her mother stood, wiping her mouth with a napkin. "I have to get back," she said. "Let's talk about this another time."

Her mother shot her one final glance, then strode out of the dining room, chin tipped toward her chest.

Dally grabbed a roll and took an angry bite. Then—she couldn't help herself—she pounded her fists on the edge of the table. The dishes rattled loudly.

Jasper burst in from the kitchen. "Is everything all right?"

Dally pulled her hands back into her lap. "Yes, I'm sorry, Jasper. Everything's fine." She smiled politely, tucking her feelings away. She was still her mother's daughter, apparently, when push came to shove.

14

Dally's mother did not appear at breakfast. Perhaps she guessed (correctly) that her daughter's line of questioning from dinner might continue. Dally quietly ate her scrambled eggs and fruit and stuffed down her disappointment, which she was exceedingly used to doing. Her disappointment place was downright *over*stuffed at this point. She packed her backpack and went to school.

After school, as was usual now, Dally approached the empty, scrubby lot three blocks from the bakery and announced her presence. As usual, once she blinked, the library appeared.

After that, things became unusual.

Someone was coming out! Two people, actually. One was a short, elderly man—barely taller than Dally herself—in a top hat and vest, its buttons strained across his portly chest. The other was a slightly younger, slightly taller, slightly less portly woman in a smart skirt suit with an elegant top bun and moon-shaped spectacles. They appeared to be in the throes of a heated conversation, though Dally couldn't hear a word. And when they caught sight of her ascending the steps, they froze.

"Hello," Dally said politely as they met on the stairs.

"Good day, young one." The man doffed his hat.

"Indeed." The woman tipped her chin so as to peer at Dally over her spectacles.

Neither stepped aside to make way for her, as passersby naturally might. Instead, they stared curiously at her, blocking the path up the steps in the process. "Excuse me, please." Dally scooted around them.

"That must be her," the woman whispered after Dally passed. "Gracious."

"Well, I say," answered the man, in an even softer voice.

As Dally reached the door, a third person emerged: a nervous twig of a man, carrying a satchel. "Oh, my," he said at the sight of her. "My, my."

"Good afternoon," she said.

"My, my," he muttered, and flitted along.

Dally caught the door and burst inside, eager to find out why the library was so popular today.

Jennacake was standing near an open set of wooden double doors, talking to yet another person. Gold script above the doorway read CONFERENCE ROOM, and inside was a large wooden table surrounded by elegant leather chairs.

They paused and looked over when Dally rushed in.

"It's on the reference desk." Jennacake gestured to where Dally's cup of calming tea was waiting. "Have a sip, and then come meet Ms. Mitchall."

The woman was about as old as anyone Dally had ever seen,

but she moved almost as smoothly as Jennacake. Her face was a topographical map of wrinkles, her eyes bright and curious and wary all at once. Dally found herself looking closer, as there was something intangible about the woman that slightly reminded her of Grandpa. Ms. Mitchall was dressed in jeans and a blouse in a style that Dally's mother would have called "hippie," her gray-white hair done up in a stylish crown of braids.

She extended her hand. "Delilah, it's a pleasure." The handshake was firm and businesslike. Ms. Mitchall's skin was soft and papery, her fingers strong and sure. "Magdalene Mitchall, at your service."

"Pleased to meet you as well, Ms. Mitchall," Delilah answered. "Grande Dame of the Whisper Society, if I do remember correctly."

Ms. Mitchall looked delighted. "Why, yes, indeed. You are familiar with us?"

"No, not at all," Dally said. "But I believe you wrote one of the notes in the entryway. How do you make it appear as if from nowhere?"

"Ah, well, I suppose you won't be surprised to learn that such things are—"

Let me guess, Dally thought. "Quite secret?" It was rude to interrupt, but sometimes she couldn't help herself. Grown-ups could be so frustrating.

Ms. Mitchall smiled. "You're getting the hang of the place, I see. You mustn't worry. The library reveals much to its patrons over time. It's a matter of trust, of course."

"I'm very trustworthy," Dally assured her.

"I'm sure you are, dear. But no one tells all their secrets to a person they've just met, do they?"

Dally supposed not.

"We've just adjourned a meeting of the Whisper Society," Jennacake interjected. "Why don't you browse the stacks and choose today's secret while I finish up with Ms. Mitchall?"

Dally herself wasn't quite finished with Ms. Mitchall.

"Why did you have a meeting today?" Dally asked.

"We meet regularly to take care of library business," Ms. Mitchall said. "We're essentially a board of trustees. It's important that we be active."

Maybe it was all the time she was spending in the library, but Dally felt the strong presence of a secret lurking behind Ms. Mitchall's words.

"So, this was a regularly scheduled meeting?"

"Well, no. Something came up that warranted examination. A bit of an emergency."

"Was the meeting about me?"

Ms. Mitchall hesitated long enough for Dally to grow even more suspicious. "Our meeting discussions are many and varied," she answered.

"I can only imagine," Dally said. "And was I one of the many variations discussed?"

Ms. Mitchall smiled. "Your name may have come up." To Jennacake, she said, "The child is very much as described."

Jennacake nodded.

One of Dally's least favorite things in all the world was the way grown-ups sometimes talked about her as though she wasn't there.

Ms. Mitchall hitched her hip onto a low stool near the door, bringing herself down a few inches closer to Dally's eye level. "You see, Delilah, this library is a very rare and special place. The society discusses everyone who finds their way here. And when a member of the Whisper Society dies, we meet to discuss and appoint their replacement."

Dally's brain worked through this information like a logic puzzle. "Grandpa?" He was a member of the Whisper Society? If that was true, why had he never brought her here when he was alive? That question had been lurking in the back of her mind for several days.

"Yes, indeed." Ms. Mitchall paused. "Your grandfather was one of our longest-serving members. The youngest we'd ever appointed, in fact, up until . . ."

The air around Dally began to feel full and weighty.

Jennacake picked up the explanation. "Dally, membership in the Whisper Society is a lifetime appointment. The typical procedure is that current members each designate a successor for their chair. But the rest of the society must accept and approve the recommendation, of course."

A slowly looming weight pressed down on Dally. "And Grandpa recommended *me*?" She raised her chest and evened her shoulders against the pressure. She was eager to accept the new challenge and responsibility. To have a formal role in this magical place? What could be better?

"You are an incredibly bright young lady, and I can see why he thought highly of you." Ms. Mitchall tapped her knee. "But we've never had a . . . society member of your age. The committee is not in full agreement that it should be allowed."

"Is there a rule against it?" Dally felt steamed. It seemed no matter where she went, there were always a handful of grown-ups trying to dictate what she could and couldn't do. If Grandpa, who knew her better than anyone, believed in her, why couldn't they?

Ms. Mitchall and Jennacake exchanged a glance. "It doesn't seem as though there is," Ms. Mitchall said.

"Then what's the problem?"

"It's not so much a problem as a . . . concern," Jennacake explained. "We don't want you to have to take on such grown-up work so young."

"What is it that you do?" Dally asked.

The women glanced at each other again. After a brief silence, Jennacake spoke. "They oversee the business of the library."

"We fundraise for its upkeep, support the librarian, and, well . . . perform other duties as assigned." There was an undeniable twinkle in Ms. Mitchall's eye as she said the last bit.

"Other duties?" Dally echoed. "Like reading secrets?"

"Oh, yes," Ms. Mitchall said. Again with the twinkle.

"There's something else," Dally said. "You're not telling me everything."

"That's true. You're a very perceptive young lady."

Jennacake said, "Everyone who comes to the library has a purpose, you know. The society members are no exception."

"You could say we are guardians, of a sort," Ms. Mitchall said. "Protecting the library, and its secrets, from those who'd wish to do it harm."

Dally felt a surge of energy at the thought. "I could do that."

Jennacake shook her head. "You have school and things to occupy you for now, so your induction will likely need to wait."

"Do the meetings last longer than an hour?" Dally asked, suddenly feeling discouraged.

"Yes," Jennacake said. "And there are other commitments."

"Oh." Dally folded her hands. "I'm afraid the earliest that I can renegotiate my schedule will be summer vacation. My mother is very strict."

The women appeared relieved. "There, you see. Perhaps we can revisit the discussion in a few months," Jennacake said, patting Dally's shoulder. "Go ahead and pick your secret, love." She turned back to Ms. Mitchall.

Feeling dismissed and at an impasse, Dally headed toward the stacks.

"Delilah," Ms. Mitchall said, causing Dally to turn back. "We're all so sorry for your loss, my dear. Your grandfather was a special man, and we all enjoyed him very much. We will miss him."

"Thank you," Dally said politely, despite the storm of thoughts pounding through her. She wished she could run home to Grandpa right now and demand he tell her the whole truth—about the library and the Whisper Society and why exactly he waited to share the news of this wonderful place until it was too late for them to enjoy it together.

Dally pushed thoughts of Grandpa aside and wandered toward Family Secrets. *Most everything about my family is secret,* she had told Jennacake. That felt truer than ever. Dally blipped her finger over the spines, searching for a particularly elusive feeling. A carefree energy, the light of a certain haphazard grin. But none of the options felt right. She turned away from Family Secrets, toward the rest of the stacks.

Withheld for Someone's Own Good seemed interesting. Dally chose a volume that gave her a whiff of wood smoke and the sound of a keyboard clicking. It wasn't a family secret, but the feeling it gave was surprising and warm. A feeling that reminded her of Grandpa.

≋ 15 ≋

Dally found herself standing in a familiar room: the library at Peteharrington Place. She rushed to the window and looked down into the yard. Was it two summers ago again? Like when she'd seen Hector in her first secret trip? No, it appeared to be late fall or early winter, based on the gardens. The flowers weren't blooming and the hedges looked small, Dally thought, as though some of their leaves and branches had yet to grow in.

Past the gardens, the lawn stretched out, down the slight hill toward Dragonfly Lake. Dally smiled at the sight of its surface glowing in the afternoon light.

"You needn't worry, my dear. It's handled."

Dally spun around. That was Grandpa's voice!

He had spoken from the next room. The den and the library were separated by a wall with a fireplace, one that used to burn wood but had long since been turned into a gas unit. It was framed by identical sculpted metal grates on each side, one in each room. Dally turned to run into the den, to greet him—she had so many questions! And surely now that they both knew about the Secret Library, it would be safe to discuss it. But she froze midstep. The fog was blocking the path to the hallway. So instead of joining Grandpa, Dally knelt beside the fireplace grate and peered through it.

Grandpa stood in the den, opposite Dally's mother. She was older than college age, but still much younger than she was in Dally's present.

"You're not worrying *enough*, Dad. These numbers"—Kate brandished a sheaf of papers—"they're catastrophic."

"Katherine, dear, Peteharrington Enterprises has seen rough quarters before."

"This is more than a quarter. This is years of decline. Haven't you been paying attention?"

Grandpa held out his hands. "These are my problems to solve, honey."

"Dad, the salary overhead is tremendous. You have to stop raising salaries at this rate. The bonuses alone nearly put us in the red last year."

"Generosity is what's missing in business these days."

"It's not like you're paying minimum wage," Kate insisted. "These are competitive white-collar and blue-collar jobs. Even the cleaning crews are drawing twice the market rate for their services. I've done a full breakdown." She smacked the papers onto the desk. "We would save several million dollars if you froze salaries for a year or two."

"Kate, I appreciate your diligence, but we have plenty,"

Grandpa said. "We should be thinking about more than the bottom line."

"Try telling that to the shareholders," Kate retorted. "They do expect to make a profit at some point."

"How about I reduce your entry-level salary to minimum wage for a year, and you can do a breakdown on how it feels to live below the poverty line?"

"Dad!" Kate exclaimed. "The market values certain skills and roles at certain rates. I didn't make the rules or invent the economy."

"Why follow rules when you can break them?" Grandpa said.

Kate spread her hands wide in frustration. "Maybe if you spent more time here and less off gallivanting God knows where, you'd know what it takes to keep this place up and running."

"Now you're just channeling your mother." Grandpa sounded grumpy.

"This is serious."

"Darling, I'm as proud of your brand-new MBA as you are, but I don't need you checking up on me."

Kate stood silent for several moments. "We need to tell Mom about this. And Marcus."

"No," Grandpa said sharply.

She crossed her arms. "So you do know how bad it is?"

"Of course I do." He rubbed his forehead.

Kate softened her tone. "The entire business is in jeopardy. The estate. So when we tell them—"

"I wish you wouldn't," Grandpa said. "Please keep the financial details between us."

"But—"

"Look, honey, it's a temporary setback. The business will bounce back. We always do." Grandpa rubbed his forehead again. "Frankly, I used to be able to solve such problems more easily, but it's gotten a bit harder for me to travel on my own. I've told you about my offshore holdings—"

Kate rolled her eyes. "Dad, money doesn't grow on trees, not even on a tropical island."

"I've told you before, if you would only see fit to come with me . . ."

Kate's response was drowned out as the fog rushed in and closed the secret.

"That one was too short," Dally said as she emerged from the reading room. She frowned at the thought of Peteharrington Enterprises being in such big trouble. It had all started as one small dry goods store, but today, the family business operated successfully across many lucrative industries: construction, real estate, shipping, investments. The dry goods store had evolved into a big-box retail empire, and they even had a chain of luxury hotels under their umbrella. The argument she witnessed must have taken place years before her mother fully took over the company.

She turned to Jennacake. "Did my grandpa . . . when he came here, did he ever talk about his life outside? His normal life?"

"Not much," Jennacake said. "We had a fair bit of business of our own to attend to."

"Like what?"

"Everyone who comes to the library has a purpose, remember. That includes your grandfather. He spoke of you, though. You were the light of his life, Delilah, dear."

"I'm tired of you not telling me the things I need to know," Dally declared.

"I tell you *only* what you need to know," Jennacake countered. "Try not to worry about the rest." Her words echoed what Grandpa had said to Dally's mother inside the secret.

"That's not enough," Dally whispered. Why did she feel this way? She ached at the mere *thought* of leaving the library, let alone when it came time to actually go. There was something more here for her. She was sure of it.

"I'll see you next time," Jennacake said, nudging her toward the door as usual.

"That'll be tomorrow," Dally said. "I come every day now." At least, every school day. On the weekends it simply wasn't possible to slip away unnoticed, unless perhaps she could get Mr. Jerry to pick her up down the block from home. Something to think about . . .

"Tomorrow, then," Jennacake agreed. "I do look forward to seeing you," she added. "In case you were worried."

"I wasn't worried."

Buoyed by the prospect of weekend visits, Dally was all smiles on her way out the door.

That night, over bowls of Jasper's secret-recipe chili, Dally asked her mother, "Was Grandpa good in business?"

"He was a Peteharrington," her mother answered. "We're all good in business."

Dally wasn't quite sure that could be true. "If it's automatic, I could probably do without quite so many lessons."

Her mother smiled, and Dally swore there was a hint of the old carefree Kate in that smile. "Oh, I see," she said. "The campaign continues."

"I want to know more about the business," Dally said. "Our real business, not abstract ideas about economics."

"Your lessons are meant to prepare you for exactly that." Her mother stirred a scoop of sour cream into her second bowl of chili. "There will be a lot for us to go over one day."

One day. Far in the future. Dally sighed. There was absolutely no winning with her mother, it seemed. Even when she asked about the very thing her mother loved most, she met with resistance.

"Was Grandpa a good businessman? Like Great-Grandpa?"

"Your great-grandfather built all this from scratch," Dally's mother said. "He was a visionary."

"And Grandpa?" Dally pressed. She supposed she was walking on thin ice. But it was a burden, carrying the truths of the library alongside the version of reality her mother tried to present.

Dally's mother stirred her chili quite a bit longer than

necessary. "Grandpa meant well, but he wasn't always the most practical. He cared much more about the employees than he did about success."

"Don't you care for the employees?" Dally asked.

"Of course," her mother said, sounding surprised. "We pay higher than our competitors in nearly every job we offer. It's how we guarantee that we attract the best workers."

"So, it's always about the bottom line?" Dally felt disappointed in a way she couldn't explain.

"Being the best is a bit more complicated than that," Dally's mother said. "There are a lot of considerations to balance and a lot of big decisions to make. Grandpa tended to be more of a teddy bear than a shark. But that's not how you get ahead."

A teddy bear—soft and comforting and often perfectly still? Dally thought she'd much prefer to be that than a shark—slick, mean, and constantly swimming for its life.

Jasper burst through the swinging door from the kitchen. "Ladies, are we ready for dessert?" He collected the serving dishes as Dally and her mother finished their portions.

"It's delicious, as always, Jasper," her mother said, scraping the last bites of chili out of her bowl. "The perfect balance of spicy and sweet." She patted her lips with her napkin.

"As sweet as your love," Dally told Jasper, sugaring her voice right up. "The super-secret ingredient."

"Nice try." Jasper chuckled. "But that's my story and I'm sticking to it. It's a family recipe."

Dally giggled.

"What's so funny?" her mother asked as Jasper swung back to the kitchen.

"Oh, you know," Dally said. "Jasper will never reveal his secret ingredient."

Her mother nodded absently. "He makes anyone else who's in the kitchen leave while he adds it. I remember."

"Jasper has a whole box of secret recipes passed down from his family," Dally mused. "The business is what gets passed down to me." It was strange and a little scary to imagine herself in her mother's shoes. Sitting behind a desk all day, making decisions and phone calls, managing accounts, leading meetings, hiring and firing people. The idea of running the company felt like wearing her one-size-too-big school uniform skirt: an outfit chosen for her that didn't quite fit. Maybe she'd grow into it one day—but did she really want to?

≋ 16 ≋

The next day, Dally was pleased to see that she was once again not the library's only patron. Jennacake was speaking with a man in a brown tweed suit and cap.

"Why, I look fit as a fiddle, my dear. You really have quite the eye," the man was saying as Dally entered.

Jennacake laughed her twinkle of a laugh. "Mr. Horatio, you're nothing but a tease."

"Ah, we have company, it appears." The man turned toward Dally, who had gone straight to the reference desk for her sip of Jennacake's brew.

"Yes." Jennacake waved her over. "Mr. Horatio, may I introduce our delightful new patron? Miss Delilah Peteharrington."

Dally stepped forward and stuck out her hand. "Pleased to meet you." And she was, indeed, curious to meet another traveler.

"Miss Peteharrington." He took her hand. "The honor is mine." He bent formally and dropped a delicate kiss on her knuckles. "Ah, yes," he said, meeting her eyes again. "You've really caught the spirit of the place, haven't you?"

"You can tell?" Dally asked.

"You are radiant with it," he declared. "And rightly so. We are living quite the life, you and I!"

Dally couldn't help but agree.

Turning to Jennacake, he added, "Miss Peteharrington's going to keep you on your toes, isn't she?"

"I daresay." Jennacake released another peal of her tinkling laugh.

"My volume, then!" Mr. Horatio exclaimed, reaching for a table with nothing on it. "Ah, where in the devil have I set it down this time?" He ambled off in the direction of the stacks.

Dally smiled. "He's a character."

Jennacake smiled, too. "Hardly anyone uninteresting comes to the library."

"And he has a purpose here?" Dally chose her words carefully, hoping for a better answer than usual.

"Yes." Jennacake gazed toward the stacks. "Mr. Horatio is about to befriend someone of importance."

"How do you know?" Dally felt excited.

"He already chose his secret. As librarian, I know something about what is contained in each volume. When I pick one up, a fair bit is communicated."

Dally nodded. It sounded like a next-level version of what she felt when she touched the spines. "So the library already knows what's going to happen?"

"What's past is past," Jennacake said. "It's already happened, remember? Just not for Mr. Horatio."

He strode out of the stacks then, carrying a midsize secret.

"Most of our patrons are looking for something," Jennacake added. "And, likely as not, they're needed for something."

Mr. Horatio made his way to the reading room. "Ladies, I bid you a pleasant afternoon." He offered a slight, stiff dip of a bow, then disappeared inside. Jennacake followed.

"Good luck, Mr. Horatio." Jennacake stepped back out of the reading room and closed the stone door behind her. Dally expected she'd come over to resume their conversation, but instead, Jennacake took a few steps away from the door, turned around, and waited.

Dally was about to ask what she was doing when the door burst open again and Mr. Horatio strolled out, looking rather windblown and exhilarated. "Bully!" he exclaimed. "Mighty fine day." He tipped his hat to the two of them and headed for the front door.

"Wow," Dally said as he left. "Is it always so fast?"

"Time is different in the library, remember? From here, it's always the same. They go and come right back. Unless they don't." A wave of sadness crossed Jennacake's face. "It's a relief, every time, when it goes as we hope it will."

Dally thought about the dusty piles of secrets on the floor in the reading room. "Sometimes people don't come back?"

Jennacake's expression turned sad again. "Yes, some secrets are lost when the reader is unable to return with them. If they die in the past, they are dead. If they fall through the fog, they are lost to history. Many, many things can go wrong, I'm afraid."

"If you're needed for something, and you fail, what happens then?"

"It varies," Jennacake said. "Depending on what happened, there are sometimes remedies. Our Whisper Society members do a bit of work in that area, on occasion. It's more of an art than a science. Our travelers' purposes range widely, but it's rare for a mistake in one person's journey to have world-transforming consequences."

Dally considered this information. "Do my travels have a purpose?"

"Absolutely," Jennacake said. "But you'll have to keep reading a while longer to find out what. Shall we?" She waved her hand toward the stacks.

Dally wandered eagerly among the miles and miles of books. It seemed, though, that wherever she turned, Family Secrets was always on her left.

One particular shelf drew her hand to it. She allowed her fingertips to *blip blip blip* over one spine after another until they landed on a thick hardcover tome, the sort of book that would shake the tabletop no matter how gently you set it down. The word that emanated from it was *treasure*. The feeling: exhilaration, like a hearty rush of wind.

"Whoa," Dally said as she found herself tugging it free. "That's a big one."

"Let me see." Jennacake peered at the spine: 1850416. "Hmm. This is further than you've gone yet." She looked Dally over from head to toe. "No, that won't do."

"What won't do?" Dally asked.

"Come with me. A quick peek into the closet should solve it." Jennacake strode purposefully across the library toward a pair of double doors that Dally had never noticed before. They were gloriously tall and wide, but the carved wood blended in perfectly amid the glamorous shelves.

Jennacake swung open the doors. Dally gasped in awe. The large room was lined from floor to (high) ceiling with clothing racks and shelves. It was an explosion of color, in sharp contrast to the muted browns and golds of the library bookshelves. Every shelf and hanging bar was bursting with hats and gowns and suits and finery. Rolling ladders lined the walls. It was the closet to end all closets, a veritable library-within-a-library of clothing and accessories.

"Wow," Dally breathed. She hadn't expected to find such a thing in the library. Was there no end to the wonders it contained?

Jennacake flipped through a rack of dresses and skirts. "Something simple, I think," she murmured. She came up with a small brown skirt and pressed it against Dally's waist. It fell to her ankles. "That should do." Then she spun away to a nearby rack and pulled a creamy beige shirt with buttons.

Dally fingered the skirt. It looked rough at the edges, the

seams uneven. The shirt, too, was a bit coarse in style.

"Shoes," Jennacake murmured. To Dally, she prompted, "Go on, get dressed now."

Dally removed her pleated skirt, shoes, and tights and slid into the brown skirt. She took off her uniform vest and slipped her arms into the bodice. "This is very weird," she said as she buttoned herself in.

"Trust me, you don't want to waste time trying to explain the concept of spandex to people who've probably never seen a sewing machine."

No sewing machines? Dally examined the hem of the shirtsleeve. Sure enough, it looked hand-sewn. Neat! Sewing machines were nearly two hundred years old. Was she really going back so far? It was both impossible to imagine and electrifying, though she did also feel a twinge of sadness to know she wouldn't be seeing her parents this time.

Jennacake produced a pair of brown leather shoes. "Do these fit?"

They did, though they were awkward to tie. The laces were small and on the side of the shoes.

"I really have to wear this?" Dally asked.

"Today, yes," Jennacake said. She retrieved the large volume Dally had selected and handed it back to her. "You're going all the way to 1850, my dear."

"This one's going to be quite different, isn't it?" Dally said, her voice a nervous trill of energy. In 1850, no one she'd ever met would be alive yet. Whose secret could this be?

"So it seems," Jennacake agreed. She drew out her secret-opening key, hung on its chain around her neck.

They walked to the reading room. Though the stone walls were thick and Dally was entirely alone, she thought she heard Jennacake's voice drift at her through the door.

"Be safe, dear Delilah."

≫ **17** ≪

When the spinning stopped and the black fog turned to gray, then white, then pushed outward, Dally found herself swaying uneasily in the belly of a ship, surrounded by the worst foul stench she'd ever experienced. It smelled like the portable toilets at the annual Fourth of July festival, only far, far worse.

Dally gagged and held her breath as she gained her sea legs and sought her bearings. The hold of the ship was a maze of packed wooden crates. She dared a shallow breath, then fumbled toward the nearest porthole to peer outside. Water sloshed against the round window, and there was nothing but blue and white as far as her eye could see. No landmass. No port. No other boats or ships. She was at sea.

Dally pushed away from the window, unsure what to do. Hide? She didn't know how long she would be here, nor how to conceal the fact that she'd appeared as if from nowhere on a ship in the middle of the ocean.

In the center of the hold, there was a small wooden table with crates for chairs. Several hammocks lined the sides, and a cluster of simple fishing poles were gathered in a corner. Even at a glance, Dally could tell the poles were old-fashioned. She had been fishing with Grandpa many times, and even his oldest poles were fancier than these. And the hold appeared to have no proper bathroom, hence the smell. Life in 1850, so far, was stinky and strange.

She heard a stirring from across the hold. Someone was asleep in one of the hammocks! A blanket moved and a snort of a snore burst out of it, then the hold was quiet again but for the constant lapping of waves.

A retching sound close behind her startled her. She whipped around and saw a boy six inches taller and perhaps a few years older than she was. He edged his way around a stack of wooden crates full of bottles and jars. She braced herself for him to raise a hue and cry about an intruder.

"This is unreal," he said. "Have you ever smelled anything this bad?" A lock of sandy hair flopped into his eyes, and he fluffed it back with practiced fingers.

"No," Dally said.

"Well, come on, then," the boy said. "Let's get topside and see what's up." He wore gray-brown pants with suspenders over a pit-stained short-sleeved blue shirt with buttons and a pocket.

While Dally was glad that she wasn't wearing her usual clothes, she felt self-conscious in her period costume. She wasn't dressed for boating. But at least she looked like she belonged in this era—Jennacake had been right about that.

The boy headed for the ladder that led out of the hold. When

Dally didn't follow, he looked back. "What are you waiting for?"

"You go ahead," Dally said. She badly wanted to breathe fresh air, but she also needed a moment to think. She glanced out the porthole again, seeking the line of the fog. But she couldn't discern it.

The boy paused, narrowed his eyes at her. "I'm Jack. Have we met?"

"I'm Dally."

She waited for him to ask what she was doing there. Surely it wasn't common for girls to be on a boat like this. But he didn't press her. Maybe the crew was big enough to fool him into thinking she belonged. Still, whoever was in charge was going to notice eventually.

Jack grinned hugely. "Well, we can't sit around down here all day, can we?"

"I—I don't want to be seen," Dally admitted.

The boy smirked. "Nice try, but you can't really hide on a ship this size."

Dally didn't see another option, so she joined Jack at the base of the ladder. He climbed first, and she followed. They emerged into a wash of sunlight so blinding it forced Dally to close her eyes.

The scent of the sea was fresh and familiar. Dally sucked in deep breaths, turning her face into the briny wind. It blew hard enough to lift her twin puffs of hair off her neck, cooling her clammy skin. She opened her clenched hands and let the air massage her palms.

Being on the water reminded her of summers with Grandpa. They often took day trips to Welleston Harbor to sail his boat. Dally had always loved the salt on her skin and the wind in her hair. But whenever she wanted to leave the hard part for Grandpa and float along with her eyes closed like this, he would call her attention back to the work of sailing. *This will be useful to you someday,* he'd say.

Dally had never been at sea without sunglasses, but there was no help for that now. She opened her eyes to a squint, and they began to adjust. Once they did, she glanced around to get her bearings. The ship was much larger than any Dally had personally sailed. It had two masts, both with their sails raised.

The mainmast had a large triangular sail occupying most of its height, plus a smaller square sail on top. The foremast, in front, had three square-rigged sails, with the largest at the bottom and the smallest at the top. The elaborate maze of ropes holding the sails in place was quite the sight to behold.

"*Not a 'rope,' Dally-girl.*" Grandpa's voice echoed in her memory. "*On a sailboat, they're called 'lines.'*"

"*I know, I know,*" Dally remembered responding. It had taken her quite a while to get in the habit of using proper sailing terms.

"*What is this line called?*" Grandpa quizzed her, pointing to a line stretching from the corner of the mainsail.

"*The mainsheet,*" Dally recited.

"*And this one?*" He'd pointed to the line that controlled the sail at the front of the boat.

"*The jib sheet!*" The jib had always been Dally's favorite sail. It was a fun word to say.

"*Excellent. I'll make a sailor of you yet, Dally-girl,*" Grandpa had declared proudly.

Dally blinked away the warm flash of memory and zoomed in on the action taking place around her. Four large-muscled crewmen held the sheets, as though preparing to adjust the tilt of the sails.

The sun's position told her they were traveling southwest. She could feel the wind coming from the west. Dally guessed this meant the ship's destination was also to the west, but since sailing straight into the wind was impossible, the ship had to set a course that included tacking. She had done it with Grandpa many times. To move straight west against the wind, you had to sail at a forty-five degree angle to the *south*west for a while, then turn quickly and sail at a forty-five degree angle to the *north*west. The sails could still catch air that way, and the ship would move west—though in a zigzag pattern instead of a straight line.

This exciting maneuver was happening right now! The four crewmen faced forward, their backs to Dally and Jack, all attention captured by the wind and the sheets they controlled.

"Ready about," called a voice from slightly above.

Dally turned and gazed with awe upon the man who was surely the boat's captain. He stood in command at the helm, behind the large wooden wheel. His picture could have illustrated the Wikipedia entry for "Pirate." His face was a suntanned white, with chiseled features. He wore a tricorn hat trimmed with glittering coins or jewels. His undershirt was black and ragged at the neckline. The sleeves of his overshirt had been ripped off, and if there had ever been buttons down the front, they weren't operational now. He had a wide green cloth belt around his middle. His pants were loose at the thighs and around the knees, but tapered at the ankles. His low-heeled boots looked like they'd been carved out of mud.

Beside him stood a muscular, dark-skinned man with a seafarer's bandanna covering his head. His shirt, too, had the sleeves ripped off, with nothing underneath but a pair of rock-like pecs. He had rope for a belt, short pants that stopped below his knees, and bare feet. He had the lanky-yet-muscled appearance of a sprinter or a running back, and when he knelt to coil a loose line, his hands moved with precision and expertise. Perhaps a first mate?

When he stood, he steadied himself by widening his stance again. His hand went toward one of the wheel handles—one already occupied by the captain's hand. Dark fingers entwined with light and gave a quick squeeze.

The captain's bright, blue-eyed gaze cut toward the first mate, and a smile flicked the corner of his otherwise stern lips. "Tacking!" he shouted, and the brief sizzling touch ended. The captain rotated the wheel, and the ship began its ninety-degree turn through the oncoming wind.

It looked to Dally like the beginning of a very interesting secret, indeed.

≋ **18** ≋

Jack waved up at the pair at the helm. The first mate waved back, then gave a little motion toward Dally with his hand that implied a question: *Who is that?* or maybe *What is going on?*

The captain spoke, and the first mate responded. They conferred a moment, and then the Black man stepped into the captain's place at the helm and took over shouting orders from on high. The captain slid down the ladder.

Up close, he was slighter than he had seemed from below. He was barely taller than Jack.

"Hey, Eli, look what I found in the hold," Jack said.

"What the devil?" Eli said. "What are you doing, Jack? And you brought a girl?"

"I didn't bring her so much as she was just here," Jack said. "This is—"

"Dally," said Dally.

"Stowaways?" the captain grumbled. "Just what we need."

"Negative, sir," Jack said quickly. "Extra deckhands, ready, willing, and able."

"Trim to course!" shouted the Black man at the helm. Eli

glanced up, then at the horizon. The deck crew adjusted the sheets and called out commands and warnings to each other. When the sails were in position, they cleated them off, tying each line in place so the sails would not shift.

When Eli returned his attention to Dally and Jack, his eyes flashed with an emotion Dally could not identify. "A pirate ship is no place for a girl," he said. "Get her back below before she's noticed."

Dally shuddered at the thought of being stuck in that stinking hold, hidden away from the crew. How long would she have to stay down there?

"No," she said. When the captain frowned at her disobedience, she quickly added, "I know how to sail. I can help."

Eager to prove herself, Dally studied the rigging. Truthfully, she didn't know the proper names for *everything* on this ship . . . but she did spot a slight ripple at the base of the forwardmost sail. She pointed it out. "That jib sheet looks a little slack, don't you think? The sail is luffing a bit."

No sooner had she spoken than the first mate called out an order to address that very issue. Jack chuckled. Eli let out an amused grunt himself.

Dally beamed. "See, I'll be a good crew member."

"Not in that getup," Eli said.

"I—I would change," Dally suggested, "but these are the only clothes I have."

"You should have thought of that before you stowed away." Eli turned to Jack and said, "I'll take her."

Eli grabbed her roughly by the arm, such that Dally had no choice but to accompany him. But he didn't take her below. He opened a door beneath the quarterdeck, where the wheel stood, and pressed her into the small space.

It was dark and stuffy in here, but cooler than the deck. The room had a single bunk and a foot-wide desk with a journal strapped to it. The ceiling was barely high enough for Eli to stand. A taller man would have had to stoop, but still, these were likely the best digs on the boat.

Captain's quarters.

Eli rummaged in a small satchel and came up with some gray fabric. He thrust it at Dally. "Here, girl, put these on." It was a pair of short pants. "You need to look like a boy. Don't let them have any question, you hear?"

"Okay." Dally pulled the pants on under her skirt. Then she unbuttoned the skirt and shimmied out of it.

A corner of Eli's mouth twitched up. "I would have stepped outside so you could change without worrying."

"Oh." Dally felt embarrassed. She hadn't thought anything of making the quick change, since she'd been fully covered the whole time. But what was proper was bound to be different in this day and age.

Eli shrugged and tossed her a newsboy cap. "This, too."

"That's not going to fit." Dally touched her twin puffs of hair. She had never been good at wearing hats that couldn't be pinned on, because her hair refused to cooperate with such things.

Eli studied her. "Can you make your hair any smaller?"

"Not really." Soon enough, the humid sea air would make it bigger.

The captain sighed. "Kneel down so I can reach your head."

Dally did. To her surprise, Eli's fingers plunged into her hair.

"You know how to braid?" she said.

"I've lived an interesting life," he answered. His fingers were not as smooth and practiced as Hannah's or even Grandpa's, and Dally gritted her teeth through quite a bit of pulling, but Eli got the job done. Dally ran her hands over her crown a few minutes later and found two even braids running from her hairline to her neck. She tucked the tails inside the cap and tugged it down over her forehead.

A pirate captain who can braid? Is that the secret? Dally wondered.

"Not too bad, I daresay." Eli tweaked Dally's cheek. "If anyone asks, you braided it yourself. Now we must return and make sure these ruffians haven't sailed my ship into a reef."

As Eli slid out of his quarters onto the deck, he turned back. "Do you truly know how to sail?"

"Yes," Dally said. She'd certainly never sailed on a ship like this one, but she understood the wind and she could tie any knot you ever asked of her. She could handle this challenge, for sure. It would be fun.

"Then I need you in the crow's nest for a spell. There's a knot of weather on the horizon."

"Sure!" Dally followed him out the door and looked up to locate the nest.

"Watch and report if those clouds are moving toward us or away along the horizon."

"Okay." Eagerly, she skipped toward the mainmast, then adjusted her gait as she neared the other crew members, reminding herself to look and act like a boy.

Dally climbed up the mast's rigging carefully, moving from grip to grip as the ship rocked and rolled with the water. *Eeep!* She made the mistake of looking down. The crow's nest was a lot higher than it had seemed from the deck. Dally clung to the rigging and returned her gaze to the sky. *One rung at a time,* she instructed herself . . . *and Don't. Look. Down.*

Dally understood her role in the nest. What worried her most was the secret fog's boundary. From this high up, she finally spotted it in the distance. But the lookout had to be able to see all the way to the horizon, and if she couldn't, what would she do? She couldn't put the crew at risk, so she'd have to climb back down and admit she was no help at all.

As if the fog had heard her thoughts, it thinned, then receded, then cleared. On the horizon, a blurred spot indicated rain in the distance. Dally watched the spot for a few minutes and determined that, for the time being, the weather was moving parallel to their ship's course, not toward it.

"Oof." A head of tousled, sandy hair poked up over the edge of the crow's nest. Grunting like he'd been through an ordeal, Jack flopped into the basket beside her.

"Can I help you?" Dally asked, scooting to the side to make

room. The crow's nest was not all that big for two. Jack might have been skinny, but he wasn't exactly small.

"Rightly so, I think." Jack grinned. "Since we're not on duty, I fancied a chat. How's it going?"

"It's fine." Dally felt that she was, in fact, on duty. Being the lookout was an important role, wasn't it?

Jack flicked his hair off his forehead. Something about the motion felt familiar to Dally. She started to relax, even in the awkwardness of him being so close.

"Sure went better than it could have," Jack said. "That's a relief."

At first Dally didn't know what he was talking about, but then it clicked. He was referring to the introduction to the captain, how Eli had taken her under his wing so immediately. She supposed a random stowaway could easily be sent to walk the plank, or thrown into the brig, or otherwise punished.

"Thanks for covering for me," Dally said. "How long have you been with the crew?"

Jack grinned again. "I met Pete and Eli on their last sail."

"Pete," Dally echoed. The way he said their names like a unit made her picture the Black pirate who stood alongside the captain. "Is he the first mate?"

"Something like that," Jack said.

Dally looked out over the ocean. The storm in the distance seemed no closer but no farther away, still moving parallel to their course.

"Eli told the guys your name is Dal, by the way."

"Okay. That makes sense, I guess. Do I have a backstory?" Dally asked.

"A what?"

"You know, like, did he tell them I'm an orphan, or an escaped circus performer, or something?"

"What is this, the theater?" Jack laughed. "They don't care where you came from, as long as you're small enough not to eat through too much of the rations."

Uh-oh. Dally had an appetite like a horse, according to Grandpa. She made a note in her head to keep that fact to herself and eat only what she was offered—if she was here long enough for it to matter.

"Where are we going?" Dally asked.

"What do you mean?"

"The ship. Where are we headed?"

"We're pirates," Jack said. "We're headed to wherever there's a ship we can attack."

"Attacking a ship?" Dally felt suddenly nervous. She loved sailing, and the idea of an adventure at sea seemed fun, but she had less of a taste for cannons and broadswords and plunder. She peered over the side of the basket. The ship had three cannons—one at the bow, one at port, and one at starboard. "If we find another ship, what happens then?"

Jack shrugged. "Before Eli was captain, how it went was pretty ugly. They'd sail close and storm aboard the other ship. If they looked scary enough, the other crew might hand over the goods without too much bloodshed." Jack peered down over the side of the basket, too. "But usually there'd be bloodshed. You'll hear the guys tell those tales soon enough. Most of them don't mind the fighting part."

Dally watched the crew far below. Even from here, they looked rough enough to do some damage in a fight. "You said 'before Eli was captain.' What about now?"

"Now, I don't know. We haven't taken a ship since Eli took over."

Dally scanned the horizon, new ideas stirring in her mind. "Eli sent me up here to watch for weather. Did he really mean watch for ships we could attack?"

"Maybe," Jack said. "But I get the sense that Eli and Pete aren't your ordinary pirates."

≋ 19 ≋

Dally and Jack climbed down from the crow's nest when Pete called up that it was time to eat. The cook, who the crew called Doughy, could have gotten his name from his job or from his soft-looking physique. He wore red pants, a rope belt, and a sleeveless floral jacket as he clambered out of the hold carrying a pot of stew. Behind him came a second man with a stack of earthen bowls and a plate of biscuits.

"Food," Doughy said simply, brandishing a ladle.

"Fellas," Jack said as the crew gathered round. "This is Dal. He's new." Jack pointed at each of the guys, spitting their names so fast Dally had trouble keeping up. Bradley, Vern, Cork, Sparky... The crew eyed her in return.

"Didn't see you in port when we set sail this morning," grunted Vern, a squarely built Black man with hair in locs like vines.

"That's because he was hiding in a barrel," Pete said dryly. He was using a small knife to whittle a piece of wood. The scraping punctuated his words.

For a moment, Dally worried about this admission. But the

circle of brutes merely nodded. It was a pirate ship, after all, she reasoned. Perhaps they'd each stowed away a time or two themselves.

Vern studied her as he sipped his stew. His clear eyes seemed to notice everything. Dally began to wonder how much he had seen of her original appearance. But he said nothing more.

"You're a mite small to be at sea, lad," said Bradley. He was the tallest of the group, with long spindly legs.

"A right powder boy," Sparky agreed. He was short, round, and solid and looked like he could carry just about anything. "You been on a gunship?"

"Sure," Dally lied. "You name it, I can powder it."

"Really?" Jack sounded surprised.

"Of course," she said. Luckily, she knew the term "powder boy." Boys around her age sometimes served on warships, carrying gunpowder from the stockpile to the cannons. You had to be small, lightweight, and fast to do the job well. Dally had read a novel with a powder boy character last year: *Daniel at the Siege of Boston, 1776,* by Laurie Calkhoven. She had liked the book, and now she was extra glad she had read it. Of course, if the time came to actually fire the cannons, she'd need a proper lesson. But that was a problem for later. Right now, she was quite hungry. She picked up her spoon and dug in.

They sat on the deck in a loose oval, Eli at one end and the crew at the other, with Dally and Jack in the middle. The separation between the crew and the captain was more than physical. Pete had returned to the helm, steering the ship. Without him to bridge the divide, Eli seemed to be a bit of an island.

Dally wanted to talk to the captain, but no one was talking to him. So Dally worked on remembering the crewmen's names. Cork wore a tan hat and had ruddy cheeks. His laughter always came a beat behind the rest of the group. Not the brightest bulb in the box, as Hannah might say, but he seemed friendly enough . . . right up until he started telling war stories.

"I slashed him and I bashed him!" Cork exclaimed, slicing his stew spoon through the air, mimicking swordplay.

One by one, the crew members regaled each other with horrible tales of their past exploits. Ships they'd taken, men they'd fought, destruction they'd caused in one way or another. *Yikes!* The violent tales turned Dally's stomach. These pirates had a strange idea of what made good dinner conversation, that was for sure.

As the meal ended, the men made their way back to their stations, leaving Jack, Dally, and Eli resting together.

"Well, that was a lot," Dally muttered.

Eli cracked a smile. "They were in rare form tonight."

"I'll say," Jack agreed.

Eli stared up at Pete, manning the ship's wheel. Dally turned her gaze to follow the captain's. Pete had his eye on the horizon, calmly scanning the sea. He raised a hand and absently stroked two fingers beneath his chin.

Dally sat up, taking closer notice. That small motion struck her as an echo of something she'd seen before. She struggled to place it . . .

Marcus! In the mall, her father had made a similar gesture. This was a family secret, after all. Pete must be their ancestor! Dally felt a fresh trill of excitement. She turned back to Eli.

"Thank you, Captain," she said softly, breaking the silence. "For your hospitality." She couldn't thank him directly for what she truly was grateful for—the chance to touch base with one more piece of her history.

Eli shrugged a shoulder. "You can call me Eli," he said. "I tend to think we end up in the places we do for a reason."

The sunset scattered the water with glorious colors. As the sky darkened, Dally found herself yawning uncontrollably. She scooted toward Jack and they sat back to back, giving each other something to lean on. Jack and Eli chatted on about fishing and other things, and soon Dally closed her eyes.

Then a hand shook her knee. She blinked hard to regain focus. "I'm awake," she lied. "I'm awake."

Eli leaned forward and whispered, "Dal, you can sleep on the floor in my quarters."

Beside her, Jack raised his eyebrows. "Hey. I'll look out for Dal."

Eli dressed him down with a glance. "You're clearly up to no good, lad. Get your behind into the hold."

Dally stretched and smiled. Having spent the day with Jack, she was pretty sure he wasn't up to anything other than covering for her, but Eli still believed that Jack had snuck her onto the ship on purpose. He probably assumed Jack was her boyfriend. *Ewww.* The thought almost made Dally giggle aloud.

Eli assigned the two crewmen who'd slept through the afternoon to keep watch and hold their course. Then he led Dally into his quarters and lit the single short candle on the desk. It hadn't felt strange to be with the captain in this small room in the daytime, but in the dark, Dally understood the awkwardness of her presence on a ship full of men.

She reminded herself that in this time and place, entire families had sometimes shared a single bed. The whole idea of privacy had been different. Maybe this seemed normal to Eli.

The captain removed his overshirt. "I brought you in here to protect you," he said with a sigh. "I'm aware that the proper thing to do with a young lady on the ship would be to give you this room to yourself, but I can't do that. It would raise too many questions for the crew, and I can't afford that."

"You're new to being captain," Dally said, recalling what Jack had told her.

"But if I send you down to the hold like a proper lad, you'd be sleeping alongside Jack, and that would be far less proper, I'd say."

"I suppose." Dally knew there came a certain age when boys and girls weren't trusted to stay friends only. She had no interest in such things herself, but someone at school had hosted a multi-gender sleepover last year, and the parents had gotten riled up about it. Dally didn't see what the big deal was. One of the kids invited was nonbinary and used they/them pronouns. Another was trans. She and her classmates understood that gender was a social construct, even if some of their parents were too old-fashioned to get it.

Eli continued. "You're safe with me. I'm no threat to you, do you understand?"

"Yes," Dally said. The captain seemed gentle and kind. Plus, she remembered his and Pete's fingers entwined.

Eli handed her a blanket and motioned to the narrow slice of floor beneath them. He took off his boots and shoved them into a corner. "I can't say the same for all of my crew. This bunch is untrustworthy in the best of circumstances."

The bitterness in his voice inspired Dally to ask, "If you don't like them, why did you choose them?"

"I didn't choose them."

"Oh."

Eli blew out the candle and rolled into his bunk. "I more or less inherited them. The old captain died, and someone had to take control. It should have been Pete, as he'd been in the crew longest, but . . ."

"But this crew would rather listen to a white man?" Dally wrapped herself in the blanket and lay down.

"That's what I told myself," Eli whispered. "But they respect Pete. Maybe I was wrong. Maybe I just took what I wanted."

Dally could hear Eli shifting position on the bunk above. She supposed he was now gazing down at her in the darkness. "I was always taught that power is the most important thing," he said. "That having people subject to you was the path to getting your way in the world. I left home in the first place because I didn't want to believe that. I didn't want to do what was expected of me. And now, here I am, doing it in a different way."

Dally wasn't quite sure what to say. "You seem like a good captain."

Eli sighed. "I remember how simple the world seemed when I was your age. I don't even know why I'm telling you all this."

"Maybe you just need someone to talk to," Dally said. "I know what it's like to feel alone even with people all around you."

"You do, do you?" Eli's laugh was surprisingly light and bell-like for such a rough-and-tumble pirate. "All right, Dally-girl. Tell me all about it."

Dally's eyes prickled. The way Eli said "Dally-girl" reminded her too much of Grandpa. "I had someone who took care of me," she said into the darkness. "He was my grandpa, but also the perfect friend. We talked every day and had a lot of adventures. He's the one who taught me to sail. And then he died. Now there's no one else who understands me."

"I'm sorry," Eli said.

"Do you have a perfect friend?" Dally asked. "Someone to take care of you?" She wanted to draw him out about what she was sure was the secret she was here to learn.

Eli didn't answer.

"Pete, maybe?" she prompted.

He blew out a soft breath. "Pete is the ideal first mate. And, yes, a good friend."

Dally was about to say something more, when Eli continued. "Look, you can't understand what it's like to be at sea, among these rough men. I'm small, and I may be the captain, but it hasn't always been easy to hold my own. So when you find someone gentle, like Pete, it's a breath of fresh air."

"That sounds nice."

"In a perfect world, maybe it would just be Pete and me, sailing a ship for two. Maybe we'd leave the pirate life behind and find a new way. Be fishermen for a spell, perhaps."

"That's your secret? That's your dream?"

"A dream, yes. My secret, Dally, is so much bigger."

20

Dally sailed with Eli's crew for four whole days. She helped trim the sails and learned to climb to the crow's nest in half the time. She earned the grudging respect of the crew when she never failed to follow directions to the letter, never failed to tie the perfect knot. She wasn't strong enough to handle the big sails on her own, but working together with Jack, it was easy. Laughing with Jack was even easier.

Whenever she could, Dally studied Pete. She hoped to glean as much as she could from him, but there was so much going on that it was difficult to catch a moment to actually speak to him. From afar, she determined that he was patient, kind, observant, and highly attentive to Eli. Were his feelings for Eli his secret? If so, how would Dally ever confirm it, when it was clearly an unspoken truth?

The days went by so fast and were so full of challenge and delight that Dally barely paused to wonder if she was being missed at home. Time worked differently in the library, she knew, but could she really be gone for days without a moment passing in her home world?

Dally did not miss being at home. Not even a little bit. Every morning, she awoke grateful that the adventure hadn't ended. She hadn't known the library could take her this far, for this long, that it could plunge her into a hands-on adventure— something more than a sneak peek behind the scenes of her own life. And it was exhilarating.

On the fourth morning, she woke on the floor of Eli's cabin, alone and shivering in the chill predawn. The barest hint of light filtered through the cracks around the door. She crawled up and out and found herself staring into a gorgeous sunrise in the east: a stunning array of pinks, oranges, reds, yellows, the warmest of colors. And through the remnant shadows beyond the masts, she saw the outline of Pete and Eli sitting side by side at the bow, heads turned toward the horizon.

Above her, Jack stood alone at the helm. Dally clambered up beside him.

"Wow, they let you steer?"

Jack grinned. "First time for everything."

"Can I have a turn?"

"Heck, no," he said. "I'm the captain for now."

Dally didn't care. She let her gaze drift over the water, glancing down occasionally to peek at Eli and Pete. "What are they doing?"

"Breakfast," Jack said. "Anyway, isn't that the most perfect thing you can imagine? Sunrise at sea with someone you care about." He leaned down and bumped her shoulder with his. His eyes remained on the horizon, but she caught the corner of his friendly smile all the same.

Dally nudged him back and smiled, too. "Pretty perfect, I guess."

Jack kept one hand on the ship's wheel and tossed the other arm around her shoulder. She let herself lean back against his taller frame. It felt quite nice to have a sort of hug. Dally had always wondered what it might be like to have a big brother. Maybe this was how it would be. Four days on this ship, and she had a stronger feeling of friendship and belonging than she'd had in her real life in the months since Grandpa had died. It made her happy and sad all at the same time. For a moment, she had forgotten that it was going to come to an end.

Dally pushed away thoughts of the inevitable. It would be too easy to let that get in the way of enjoying the now. She breathed in the sea air and the slightly ripe scent of Jack and closed her eyes, letting the first warm rays of sun wash over her face.

"Have you ever seen such a sunrise?" she asked.

"Only every morning, sleepyhead." Jack chucked her chin with his fist. "Glad you finally made it out to enjoy one."

"Har, har." Dally rolled her eyes and play-punched him in the stomach. Jack pretended to stagger back a step.

"Whoa, Nelly," he said. "Someone's cranky in the morning."

They laughed.

The sliver of sun inched upward, rounding itself as it grew. Once the air brightened and cleared, Pete and Eli unfolded themselves from their cross-legged positions, stood, and stretched. They waved up to Dally and Jack, who waved back.

Then they moved to the foremast and raised the jib. The night of slow drifting was over, and it was time to catch the wind. A brand-new day.

That morning and into the afternoon, Dally worked the sails, first with Jack and then with Pete. She cherished this rare opportunity to be close to Pete. He was so often up at the helm, either alone or with Eli, and he was invariably quiet over meals and with the group. The other men laughed and joked in a bawdy grown-up way, but Pete remained set apart somehow. Dally wondered if being one of only two Black men on the ship had something to do with it, or if it was simply his closeness to Eli that put him in an odd middle ground between captain and crew. When Dally smiled at him, he always nodded kindly. But his eyes moved warily over the crew, and he never seemed quite relaxed, even at rest.

Now, as they stood side by side coiling loose lines, perhaps it was a good moment to find out more.

"How long have you been with the ship?" she asked. "Eli said longer than him, so that must be a long time."

"A few years," he said. "Three, I reckon."

"And how long have you been with Eli?"

Pete caught her in his thoughtful, piercing gaze. "Eli joined the ship, oh, about two years back."

"I meant, how long have you been . . . friends?" Dally asked. When Pete's stoic expression did not change, she forged on. "I mean, it seems like you're friends. And not necessarily everyone in the crew becomes friends. I mean, it seems different. A little. Or, you know . . ." Dally forced herself to stop rambling. "I just wondered," she finished awkwardly.

Implacable. Another of Dally's vocabulary words perfectly described Pete's face. Immovable, unchanging. Like a rock. She couldn't think of anything else to say, so she kept coiling in the silence that Pete seemed to prefer. They finished that task and headed toward the foremast to repeat the exercise.

"You could say we are friends," Pete said as they walked. Dally nodded, pretending not to be surprised by his delayed response. He glanced back at the helm, where Eli stood. They were farther away now, certainly out of earshot. The light spring wind was so gentle that it was just the two of them on deck; Jack and the others had gone below to nap. The cardinal rule of sailing was to rest when you could, because you never knew when the wind might turn and Eli would call for all hands on deck.

For now, they were sailing with the wind at their backs, a glorious straight shot toward the horizon.

"Eli is an unusual person," Pete said. "He likes things to be complicated. But it keeps life interesting." The expression on Pete's face seemed to be a mix of amused and confused. He shrugged and resumed coiling.

"He cares about you, too," Dally said. "It's obvious."

Pete nodded, then looked away.

"Where I come from, there are men who love other men," she said.

Pete glanced at her. "Where I come from, too," he said. And then nothing for a while. "But you shouldn't speak about such things."

The water lapped against the hull in its soothing, now-familiar rhythm. Far in the distance, the sky met the sea with a thin line of white. Above it, the field of blue was dotted with fluffy clouds.

Dally marveled at the expanse of glittering water. The fog had receded out of sight, as if the whole ocean was part of the secret. She decided not to press the issue any further at the moment. If she convinced Pete to say it out loud, the fog beyond the horizon might close in. The secret might end, and she didn't want it to.

You keep your secret, Dally thought. *And I'll keep my adventure.*

As if he'd read her mind, Pete said, "If you'd be so kind not to share those thoughts elsewhere? A lot of people wouldn't understand us."

"Yeah," Dally said, gazing at the sky. She was but a guest in their world, not here to right the wrongs of history. "I just thought you'd like to know that some people would."

Soon Pete joined Eli at the helm, and Dally climbed into the crow's nest. She loved it up there, in the quiet and the breeze, where she could cast her eyes over 360 degrees of ocean.

The line at the horizon had thickened. The clouds rolling toward them were no longer a pleasant, fluffy white, but a roiling gray with hints of black. It wasn't the fog. Not at all.

"Ahoy!" Dally called, pointing at the approaching storm.

Pete glanced up, then rushed to the open hatch to the hold and shouted down at the crew. The clouds were coming in fast and strong, closing the distance more rapidly than Dally would have thought possible. The crew came up from below and scurried to secure the ship and adjust the sails. All hands on deck.

"Can we get around it?" Eli shouted.

"Not completely," Dally shouted back. She was not entirely certain, because no one could be certain of such things, but the lookout's job was to make the best guess. "Cut to starboard?" she suggested.

The storm was quite large. From her perch, Dally thought they could stay near the edge of it, if they were lucky and the winds didn't shift too suddenly. "Harder to starboard!" she shouted, but she wasn't sure if Eli heard. Already the air twisted and pulled around her, practically tearing the breath from her throat.

Dally took off her borrowed hat and tucked it into her shirt. The wind whipped her hair so hard that it yanked strands from her once-neat braids. The ship listed as Eli executed the swift turn to starboard, hoping to skirt the weather.

"Dal, the topsail sheets!" Eli called. Behind her, the small, square sail at the top of the mainmast was taut with air. She climbed out of the nest and scooted along the topsail yard, gripping the wood beam as she balanced on footropes below it. It was the smallest sail and one she could manage, but if the wind picked up further, the task might become impossible.

"Lower the sails!" Eli shouted when it became clear they couldn't outrun the storm. "We'll have to ride this one out!"

The deckhands began lowering the mainsail and securing it. Winds this strong could send the ship careening in the wrong direction or drive it into a wave too tall to weather. A nasty storm, indeed.

Plump drops of rain began to fall, leaving circles the size of quarters on the skin of Dally's arms. The waves picked up and the ship began to rock.

"Come on down, my little crow!" Eli called.

"Coming!" Dally yelled. But as soon as she moved, she knew she wasn't coming. The topsail had captured her attention these last few minutes, causing her to stop looking all around. Had she not been distracted, she'd have realized that the storm clouds weren't alone in their approach. The boundary fog was also rolling in, closing around the ship.

"No," Dally whispered. The secret was ending. "No!" She spoke firmly to the fog, as if it were a puppy in need of training. As if there were a chance it might do her bidding. But the fog had a mind of its own, and rules to follow. The darkening air pressed against her, then there was a snap like a rubber band, and everything went black.

21

I have to go back!" Dally blurted out. She burst from the reading room and nearly collided with Jennacake right outside. Dally grasped the librarian's arm to catch her balance. "Is there any way to go back?"

She'd just disappeared from a ship in the middle of the ocean. Jack, Pete, Eli, and the crew would wonder forever what had happened to her. Or worse, they'd assume that she'd been tossed overboard in the storm.

"I'm afraid not, dear," the librarian said.

"It was a terrible time to leave," Dally reported. Her head pounded anew. The silent voices of the library pressed against her eardrums. "Ach!" she cried out, drawing up short. She jammed her fingers over her ears. This had never happened upon returning from a secret before. But she'd been gone much longer than usual. Days, for her body, even if only moments had passed in the library.

"Here, I'll get you a sip of tea," Jennacake said, steering Dally toward the reference desk. "The long trips do require a bit of adjustment."

"Mm-hmm," Dally agreed. She still felt like she had her sea legs.

"My, you got some sun, didn't you?" Jennacake said.

Indeed, Dally's skin prickled with exposure. It was extremely noticeable now that she was back in the cool, dry air of the library. She was going to return home with a slight sunburn that would have to be explained, but it was well worth it for the adventure she'd just experienced.

"So it seems," Dally murmured, stroking her reddened arms. She felt slightly sick, in spite of the tea—sick from the feeling of abandoning Jack, Pete, and Eli. "Why would I leave right in the middle of things?" she asked.

"There are a few possible reasons," Jennacake answered. "Did you learn a secret?"

"Yes," Dally said, "but I was there for a while afterward, too."

Jennacake nodded. "Often when it takes longer to reveal the secret, the exit is also longer. And the library doesn't want you to be seen entering or leaving a secret, if at all possible, so sometimes it waits for a more opportune time to bring you back."

That makes sense, Dally thought, though still she hated the idea of Jack, Pete, and Eli believing she was lost in a storm at sea.

Jennacake handed over Dally's school clothes, folded and stacked. Dally looked down. She was dressed as she'd been on the ship, in Eli's hat and short pants. Her costume skirt must still be tucked away in the captain's chambers, some two hundred years ago.

Dally sulked on the ride home. She sulked through eating her daily cupcake. She sulked through her business lessons. By dinnertime, she was tired of sulking, so she brooded through her chicken piccata, flicking the unwanted capers one by one into her empty salad bowl.

Her room at Peteharrington Place certainly smelled better than the hold of Eli's ship. A hot shower and a toothbrush didn't hurt terribly, either. Her warm, soft bed was night and day from the hard wood floor below Eli's bunk. But to be pulled from the adventure right when the crew needed all hands was still a blow too big to handle. Dally turned her face into her pillow to try to stop the tears that threatened to leak from the corners of her eyes.

She had glimpsed something she desperately wanted on the deck of that ship. Something she needed. Jack's smile and his arm around her shoulders. Pete's reluctant sharing. Eli's semiskilled hands working through her curls. The trust. The teamwork. It was well worth the gross closeness of the hold if it came with a different kind of closeness.

But, like so many good things in Dally's life, it had been snatched from her before she was through.

≋ **22** ≋

Dally traced her pinkie finger along the lines in the hallway's engraved walls as she made her way into the library. She picked up the pace when she heard a loud yelp from the atrium.

A man staggered out from the reading room, nearly collapsing in Jennacake's arms as the door swung shut behind him.

"Almost . . . didn't . . . make . . . it," he panted, cringing in pain.

Jennacake tucked herself under his arm and helped him walk a few paces. He yelped with each step.

"What happened?" Dally cried, rushing forward.

"Oh, Dally," Jennacake said with urgency. "Good. Quickly— behind the counter there is a small satchel."

Dally dashed to the reference desk. It was quite a long desk, but somehow she looked in exactly the right spot. She spied a brown-and-tan satchel, like an old-fashioned doctor's bag. It was heavy. Her cup of tea was waiting on the counter right in front of her, so she took a quick sip to stop her head from pounding. First responders, Dally knew, were supposed to make sure they were fit to help before plunging into an emergency. There was only the one mug, but the traveler might need some tea, too, Dally figured, so she brought it with her.

She tried not to spill the tea as she lugged the satchel over to Jennacake, who was aiding the man in lying down on a cot that Dally swore hadn't been there a moment ago.

Jennacake bent over the traveler. Dally recognized him as Mr. Horatio, whom she'd seen teasing and laughing with Jennacake a few days ago. No, it had been just yesterday, in real time, Dally realized. Her four days on the ship didn't count. How odd.

"What happened?" she asked again.

"A secret gone wrong, I'm afraid," Jennacake said.

Mr. Horatio cried out in pain, doubling forward. He clutched at his leg. It was bleeding rather profusely, soaking his baggy brown trousers.

"Do you need some tea?" Dally asked, extending the mug toward him.

Mr. Horatio simply groaned.

"He's not going to need that," Jennacake said absently as she snapped open the bag. "That's only for you."

"Oh." Dally took another sip, then set the mug aside on a table. *Why?* she wondered. *Maybe everyone gets their own blend?*

Jennacake dug into the satchel and removed a wicked-looking pair of metal scissors—long, skinny, and evidently quite sharp. "There's gauze in there as well," she said.

Dally foraged and came up with a beige roll and a stack of individually wrapped white squares.

"Open a few of those squares," Jennacake said as she deftly snipped the leg off Mr. Horatio's pants. She studied his wound. "Well, it didn't get the artery. You'll be fine."

Mr. Horatio groaned again. A mix of pain and relief, perhaps.

"What happened to you?" Dally really wanted to know.

Mr. Horatio grunted.

"He can't say, of course," Jennacake explained, rather cheerfully. "It's a glorious mystery. But that's a knife wound; I can tell you that much."

"He was stabbed?" Dally cringed. She had known a secret could be dangerous, in theory—that someone could be hurt or killed in the reading of one. The stack of lost secrets on the floor of the reading room spoke for itself. But seeing the possible effects with her own eyes felt quite different.

Jennacake pierced Mr. Horatio's thigh with a small injection and swiped antiseptic over the deep cut. "That painkiller should take the edge off."

"Are you a nurse?" Dally asked, watching Jennacake's fingers move swiftly and surely over the wound. She layered white gauze squares over the cut and wrapped the beige bandage around his leg to hold them in place.

"Not at all," the librarian answered. "This is nothing more than basic first aid. He'll be on his way to the hospital once we get him up and walking."

"She's being modest," Mr. Horatio commented. A bit of the color had returned to his face. "What Jennacake does is much more than basic."

"Even in this state, sir, you're too kind."

Mr. Horatio swung his legs off the cot. Jennacake and Dally helped him stand up. He plopped his fedora back on his head. "Well, I'm off, then. Thank you, ladies."

Dally giggled. "Um . . ." Mr. Horatio made quite the amusing picture, with one half of his trousers missing and a giant bloody bandage on his thigh. The jaunty angle of his hat completed the ensemble.

Jennacake smiled. "Perhaps a wardrobe change is in order?"

Mr. Horatio looked down, then joined them in laughter. "Quite right, my dear. As ever, you're quite right."

Jennacake brought him a pair of loose corduroys from the closet. He donned them over his ruined pants, tipped his hat to the two of them, then limped away toward the door.

"Well, that was about enough excitement for today, don't you think?" Jennacake said.

"What do you mean?" Dally asked. "I only just got here."

Jennacake gazed upon her with concern. "But now you've seen. Things don't always go smoothly."

"So?" Dally said. Her voice sounded a little bit braver than she felt. It *was* scary to see firsthand that the library's secrets came with a side of danger. But some things were worth the risk. "It wouldn't be much of an adventure if it were completely safe."

"Many of my patrons feel that way," Jennacake acknowledged. She followed Dally into the stacks and toward Family Secrets. "Will it do any good to suggest we try something more innocuous today?"

Dally didn't bother to reply. She moved to the shelf that had drawn her yesterday and blipped her finger over the spines. They all felt similar and looked similar, too.

"Got one?" Jennacake asked. Dally nearly giggled, because the phrase sounded so casual coming from Jennacake's elegant person.

"Yes."

It was nearly identical to yesterday's secret in size, shape, and binding. Maybe a tiny bit thicker was all the difference, but Dally wasn't sure.

She hesitated with the book in her hand. "Can you pick up the same secret twice?" she asked. She suddenly worried about appearing beside herself in the hold of Eli's ship.

"I've never heard of it," Jennacake said thoughtfully. "But the library still occasionally surprises me."

Dally turned the book over. She'd already chosen. Was it too late?

"If that was going to happen, I suppose I'd have already run into myself there," she theorized.

"True." Jennacake ran her finger along the spine. "Some volumes have companions," she said. "This is a new secret. Let's get you dressed."

Minutes later, Dally felt the familiar rush of dark air carrying her into the secret. Then the rush became unfamiliar, replaced by a feeling of falling.

Dally screamed.

⩘ 23 ⩗

The harsh wind ripped Dally's scream away. She plummeted through the air, flailing her limbs. When her wrist hit something firm and flat, she twisted toward it and grabbed on with both hands. She held on for dear life, her legs dangling over the seeming nothingness.

The boundary fog whitened around her and pushed back, leaving Dally suspended in the storm-dark sky. Rain pounded her skin. She gasped, breathing in the raging sea air.

"Dal!" Pete's voice rang out. "Hold on!"

It took a moment to get her bearings, but getting them did little to help the fear. She knew where she was now: Back on the ship. Back in the storm. Climbing down from the crow's nest, as she'd been about to do when she disappeared.

Sequel, Dally thought as her feet sought purchase in the rigging. She struggled downward. The fierce wind tore at her clothes and tugged her hair from its freshly washed and smoothed puffs.

"Get down!" Pete was yelling.

"I'm trying!" she shouted.

Her curls plastered themselves against her face and neck like swimmers seeking shore. Dally reached the deck only to find herself nearly washed overboard by the surge of a wave. She saved herself by clutching the rail, then Pete's strong arm caught her around the waist.

"We thought you went over," he said. "You didn't come down and we couldn't see you for a minute."

"I'm here," Dally said. "I'm sorry." There was no way to explain.

"We have to get below," Pete said. "Come on, Jack. We have her."

"It came on really fast, didn't it?" Dally asked. Or had it only seemed that way because she'd gone away for a while?

Pete didn't answer. He was gazing at an empty spot on the deck behind him. "Jack?"

"Help!" The sound was like the ghost of a scream, loud for an instant, then snatched away on the wind.

"Jack!" Pete shouted. His arm was still around Dally's waist, but he twisted toward the rail, tugging her with him. Jack's head bobbed in and out of view among the waves. Overboard!

Dally gasped in horror.

"Help!" Jack coughed and waved, but each dip and swell of the sea carried him farther from the ship.

"We have to get him!" Dally shouted.

Pete looked up at Eli, lashed to the wheel and fighting hard to keep the ship on an even keel. Pete shook his head. "Can't swim so good," he said, which left Dally no choice.

"I'll go." She could swim as well as anyone her age—better, after years of racing Grandpa to the basking rocks and a summer of junior lifeguard training at the rec center.

"Help!" Jack cried again.

"It's too risky," Pete shouted, grasping her arm. "This is life at sea, sometimes."

But Dally refused to accept that. "We have to try."

Pete hesitated no more than a beat, then nodded. His agile fingers loosened a length of spare rope, made a loop around Dally's middle, and secured it with a good strong knot.

Dally held the rope around her waist and leaped into the icy, churning water. She tried to keep her eye fixed on Jack's bobbing head the whole time, as she had learned in junior lifeguards, but the sea was rough and the valleys between crests were deep. The ocean tried its best to suck her in. When she surfaced, she caught a wave smack in the face.

"Jack!" she shouted.

"Help! Dally!" His voice was coming from a little to her left, ahead. She powered through the water, trying to reach him.

She was inches away when the tenor of the air around her changed. Through the rushing wind and the pelting rain, in the darkness of the vast sea, Dally suddenly perceived a wall of white. The fog! Jack flailed at the edge of it, oblivious to the nightmare before Dally. If he passed through, she couldn't follow. Jack would be out to sea, an arm's length away but unreachable. She was still tethered to the boat, yes, but was it enough? Jennacake had said never to breach the boundary, no matter what.

"Dally! Help! Don't let me go," he called.

Dally surged forward. "Swim to meet me," she cried. "Hard as you can!" Her stroke was powerful for her size, but she was ultimately no match for these angry waves and the current.

She lost sight of Jack again. Had he been dragged beyond the fog? Was he right there in front of her but invisible? How would she forgive herself if she let her friend drown? How would she explain to Pete and Eli why she hadn't gone the extra few feet to save him?

"Jack!"

"Here!"

His voice came from her left again. Dally pivoted and swam hard, stretching out her arms as she kicked for dear life. Her fingers met Jack's. But no sooner had they touched than they began slipping.

"Grab my wrist!" she yelled.

Jack's fingers circled the bones at the base of her palm. The grip felt good, much more secure than a hand clasp. His other hand grabbed her forearm, and suddenly it felt as if he was climbing her like a rope.

The rope.

"Pull us in!" Dally screamed, but the wind ripped her voice to shreds. Could Pete hear her? Could he see them? She looped her arms and legs around Jack's body. It meant she had to stop swimming, but at least she wouldn't lose him again. She closed her eyes and prayed to whatever god ruled the ocean.

The next few moments felt like an hour. Jack kicked to try to keep them at the surface. Each time her head broke the waves, Dally choked and gasped and pulled in as much air as she could. She fought the rising instinct to release Jack to the sea and swim for her own life. She told herself to trust the rope, trust Pete, trust the power of the secret to buoy her. She tried to put out of her mind the knowledge that some readers of secrets had never returned.

When she felt the hull of the ship slam against her back, the remnants of air whooshed out of her lungs. Jack wriggled free of Dally's starfish grip and fumbled his way up the rope ladder. Dally's muscles were just about spent. Pete hoisted her by the rope until she was able to grasp the ladder and begin dragging herself up. She sprawled on the deck beside Jack.

"Cough it up while you batten the hatches!" Eli shouted from the helm. "It ain't over by a long shot."

24

When the sea had settled and the rain dialed back to a fine mist, they sat on the quarterdeck under the stars, eating hard biscuits and salted fish. On the main deck, the crewmen cleared away their plates and went below again to rest. Dally remained with Jack, Pete, and Eli. They sat calmly in a square, practically knee to knee. With the intensity of Jack and Dally's ocean plunge behind them, Dally sensed a new, unspoken bond between the four. Life-or-death moments could do that, she supposed.

"We're miles off course," Pete said, pointing up at the night sky. The position of the ship in relation to the stars had changed. "That storm stirred up a wicked current."

"They were overboard," Eli said. "It took precedence."

"Appreciate that," Jack said.

"It's a miracle we didn't strike the reef," Pete said. "We could turn back, though navigating it again will be just as much of a risk."

Eli shrugged. "Or we could explore."

Pete's face conveyed his uncertainty.

"What does it matter where we go?" Jack said. "I thought y'all were pirates, just living for the sea."

Pete cleared his throat and chewed on a biscuit.

Eli brushed crumbs off his hands and folded the cloth that had served as their table. "South of this particular reef, we're in some treacherous waters."

"Where exactly are we?" Dally asked. She knew they were in the Northern Hemisphere—the bright spread of stars above looked similar to the view from the coast of South Carolina, where she and Grandpa had sailed. But the Atlantic Ocean was a very big place and she had been having so much fun with Jack and the others that it hadn't occurred to her to wonder where in the world they were sailing. Like Jack, she had figured the pirate life didn't require a destination.

"We're in the vicinity of Bermuda," Pete answered.

Bermuda. Something pinged in Dally's memory. Grandpa had once spoken of dangerous waters in this area. *Only the bravest sailors are willing to enter the Bermuda Triangle,* he'd said. *According to some old legends, at least.*

"The shoals near Bermuda?" Jack looked trepidatious. "Isn't that the place where ships and . . . well, lots of ships disappear?"

"That's a myth," Dally said, recalling Grandpa's explanation. "Sailors' lore."

Eli shrugged. "Some people say. But it's true that the waters here pose a great many dangers. We could encounter many more reefs, as well as endless shoals and sandbars. Even in the depths, I'm told, there are strange and swift currents to contend with."

"A ship much bigger than ours would struggle," Pete agreed. "But luck got us this far; maybe it'll take us farther."

"Or maybe we'll disappear," Jack said.

"Maybe we have already," Dally countered. "How would we know?"

Eli smiled. Jack turned his head toward the invisible horizon. Pete grunted a laugh and said, "Fair enough."

"After a storm like that, how can you even tell where we are?" Dally asked.

"The sky is as good as a map." Pete cast his hand toward the speckled blanket above.

Dally gazed up at the glittering stars. It was incredible how much she could see, even compared to being on a sailboat at sea with Grandpa. The ambient light of her modern world had dimmed the entire sky. "It's beautiful here."

Pete pointed out several constellations. "There's Cassiopeia, the Dragon, Big Bear, Little Bear."

They still looked much the same as usual to Dally.

"I recognize those," she said. "But they look just like this on land."

"Not exactly. I'll show you," Pete said. He retrieved a strange metal object from Eli's cabin. It was the size of a dinner plate and bronze-colored, with many dials and levers and lenses. One part looked like a small telescope, and the rest was curved like a gear from some giant, old-fashioned clock. It reminded Dally of a machine she had to look through at the eye doctor's office.

"This is a sextant," Eli said, taking it from Pete. "When you've been sailing a long time, like we have, you can tell a lot with just your eyes. But this little fella can tell you exactly." He explained how it worked, then Dally and Jack took turns peeking through the telescope part and measuring the distance between certain stars and the horizon. Soon they had a set of numbers that they could use to find their true position on a nautical map. Very cool!

They kept the sails down and lay head to head, like a four-pointed star. Pete told stories he had been taught about the constellations and the people who named them and the people who followed them. Then Eli told some, too. Dally recognized several of the stories, ones Grandpa had told, and it made her so joyfully glad.

Even out there on the water, the early-morning weather was tropical warm. The foursome dozed on the deck to the lulling rock of the gentle, lapping waves. Near-death experiences aside, of course, Dally couldn't have imagined anything more perfect.

The sun rose, stunning the water with rainbow reflections. Dally stretched and stared at the horizon, grateful that the adventure had lasted through the night. She wondered briefly why this particular secret had two volumes, because she was sure she already knew the secret. It was lying right in front of her.

In their sleep, Pete and Eli had turned toward each other, their hands so close it was hard to tell if they were touching or not.

"Land, ho!" Jack shouted from the helm. "Looks like an island."

Eli and Pete stirred, and Dally hopped to her feet. "Looks like a toucan beak," she said. The island's jutting hills formed a hump and a point that from this angle resembled the bird.

"So it does," Pete agreed. Together, he, Dally, and Jack scrambled to adjust the sails.

"There could be a reef," Eli said, taking the wheel. "Or rocks. We don't have a chart for this water. Maybe it hasn't been charted at all."

Pete pounded on the hatch to the hold to alert the crew of the landing. They staggered out one by one and helped guide and slow the ship as it approached the shore. The island appeared to be relatively narrow, with no visible signs of a dock or any settlement.

Eli dropped anchor about a hundred yards offshore, so as not to risk running aground. The water shone with the glare of the sun, so they could not see much of what was below.

Eli sent the four crewmen ashore first to check out the island, and they went eagerly, glad for an excuse to leave the ship, if only briefly. Doughy, the cook, rode along, carrying a large empty crate to collect any fresh fruit or shellfish that might be available.

"Why can't we all go?" Jack asked, staring after the dinghy. The small craft fought a choppy ridge of waves as it approached the shore. The strong men rowed through the splashing surf, unfazed, as if they'd done it a hundred times before.

"Because you never send a whole crew onto new land," Pete said. "It could be occupied."

"It doesn't look inhabited," Jack said.

"Looks can be deceiving," Eli said. He winked at Dally. "Right?"

"Right," she agreed.

"Not just people," Pete added. "Predators, natural threats . . . If it's uninhabited, there may be a reason."

Dally studied the expanse of beach and trees. "So what do we do?"

Eli spread his arms out under the sun. "Relax. Have a nap. Take a swim."

"Listen for screaming."

Jack and Dally laughed at Pete's dry addendum.

"A swim sounds mighty pleasant," he continued.

"Easy for you to say," Jack muttered. "You weren't in on the last swim."

A shiver cut through Dally even as they laughed together now, safe in the sunshine. Remembering how close she'd come to crossing the fog made her look for it now. There it was, at the edge of this stretch of beach, jutting into the ocean, arcing a wide loop around the ship.

Pete removed his shirt and climbed onto the deck rail, looking ready to jump into the water. Instead, he balanced there for a moment. He stood lean and strong, peering down at the sea, one fist clenched around the mainmast rigging. His dark skin glistened.

Dally stared. She couldn't help it. Pete's wrists bore the scars of chains, and three sharp lines across his back told another part of his story. Pete's quiet strength had been tested somehow.

Dally studied the crisscross lines, a mix of ache and awe rushing through her. She'd known it was likely that some of her ancestors had been enslaved, but putting Pete's face on that knowledge now gave her chills. It had always felt rather abstract, reading about it in books. Movies brought slavery to life but made it all a little too shiny, sometimes. Pete, though, was very, very real. She had felt the gentleness of his hand on hers while pulling in a sail, known the kindness of his gaze, and witnessed his leadership among the crew. She had admired his loyalty and affection for Eli, too, and it pained her to imagine him being chained or beaten.

"There's something below us," Pete said. "Look, there." He pointed at a spot in the water that looked as wavy and blue as every other part of the ocean.

"Where?" Eli bent over the deck rail.

"There's a glint, or something. Just there. You don't see it?"

Dally didn't. Eli stared a moment longer, then shook his head. "No. But if you're certain, I'll take a look." He clambered up onto the rail, one hand on the rigging. He pointed. "Just there?"

"Yes, and not very deep, so don't—"

Pete's sentence was punctuated by the smack of Eli's hands meeting overhead, then the swooshing splash of his dive.

Pete cringed and banged his fist on the rail. "I say there's something under the surface, and Eli dives, headfirst."

A tense few moments followed as they waited for Eli to

emerge and be all right. Dally held her breath, imagining she was underwater, but she could not hold out for as long as Eli was gone.

Finally, he burst through the surface and waved.

"You'll break your neck that way one of these days!" Pete shouted.

"Not today, though!" Eli shouted back. "But you're right: there's something down there."

"What is it?" Pete called.

"See for yourself! You're not going to believe it." Eli plunged downward again, disappearing below the swirling tide. And there *was* a slight swirl to it, Dally noticed now. The waves rocked steadily toward the beach, as was typical, but there was a subtle curve or break at the place where Eli was exploring.

That was all the incitement Jack needed, apparently. "Let's check it out!" He kicked off his shoes and leaped overboard (feetfirst, thankfully), then surface-dove after Eli.

Dally hesitated. She wasn't sure if it was worse to go home with sopping wet shoes or to lose them in the past altogether.

"Don't you want to swim?" Pete asked, noticing her slow reaction.

"Yeah," Dally said. She peeled off her shoes and clambered over the rail. The fog was holding its distance, creating a clearing that encompassed the entire island in front of her and stretched well beyond the ship behind her, so she hoped she had time. The secret, she now suspected, was somewhere under this water.

25

The cool Atlantic enfolded her, toes first, then rushed up along her body like a giant liquid glove. After the heat and sweat of sailing, the water felt amazing. It stung a bit to open her eyes against the salt water, but Dally had been practicing all her life. Grandpa had always said that a good sailor must know how to be at one with the sea. A little salt spray in the eye couldn't stop you from steering responsibly, he said.

Under the surface, the water was clear blue and rippling with refracted sunlight. Dally wasn't sure what Pete had seen from on high, but now she could see it all clearly. The swirl in the water was caused by the mast and crow's nest of a sunken ship. It was an old wreck, so old that the wooden hull was half buried in sand, the other half covered in barnacles and thick seaweed. It was like a reef, teeming with ocean life—jarringly foreign and yet so much a part of the landscape that its full size was impossible to discern.

It was a very large vessel, no doubt European in origin, and would have had a crew of dozens. Perhaps it had been a cargo ship or a clipper, bringing supplies to the colonists or exploring in search of land to conquer. Dally counted at least three masts, all broken.

She surfaced and looked up at Pete. "How did you see that?"

"I don't know," he answered.

Eli broke the surface and kicked toward Dally. "Feast your eyes on this!" His hands were full of something that glittered. Gold!

Dally grinned. Jack came swimming from behind Eli, cupping a similar handful. Dally gathered her shirttail into a pouch, where Jack and Eli dumped their finds. She treaded hard to stay afloat, waiting at the surface as they dove down for more.

Pete lowered a rope ladder, and the three climbed back onto the ship. They spread out the treasure on the deck. A heap of gold coins glittered in the sunlight. There was also a mound of slimy platters and goblets, turned black by time and the tides, but likely silver underneath, according to Eli. Several seaweed-encrusted pouches contained colorful jewels and gold chains. Pete unwrapped a pair of daggers ensconced in decaying leather sheaths, tucked in what must once have been a fine cloth or garment. All in all, it was a trove of Spanish doubloons, silver, jewels, and finery.

"There's more?" Dally guessed.

"So much more," Eli said. "A roomful."

"We're rich!" Jack cried, swooning onto the deck.

The current around the ship was a bit too strong for Dally, so she hovered at the base of the ladder, helping Pete bring the treasure to the deck, while Eli and Jack dove down again and again. Dally swam to meet them when they came up gasping, and traded empty pouches for full ones. The sacks became instantly heavier when she tried to lift them out of the water, so instead she lugged them to the ladder, then scooped handfuls of gold into a leaf-lined crate that Pete had prepared. When it was full, Pete dragged the crate up to the ship deck using a make-shift pulley.

They worked for an hour and filled five whole crates. It was exhausting. No wonder people had switched to paper money and ultimately to digital systems for tracking currency. It was difficult to imagine having to physically carry all your money around the world with you as the sailors on this ship apparently had done.

After the hour of hard labor, Eli crawled up to the deck and collapsed, utterly spent. When Jack surfaced, he treaded for a moment, gulping air, then propelled himself to the ladder as well. Dally retrieved his final bag, then climbed up and helped Pete haul the last full crate to safety.

"There's more." Eli gasped for breath. "There's so much more."

"When the crew comes back, we can have them help," Jack suggested. "We could do twice as much in half the time."

Pete and Eli exchanged a meaningful glance. "That may not be the best idea," Eli said.

"Why not?" Dally asked.

No one spoke for a long moment. Dally sensed a great deal of tension in the silence.

"There's only so much this ship can carry," Pete said finally. "We need to be strategic."

Eli nodded. "We've emptied out some food stores on this journey, so we can fill more of those crates, but there's too much treasure down there. I can't see our way clear to getting it all."

That wasn't the whole story, Dally could tell. Something important was going unspoken.

Jack clued in before Dally did. "Finders, keepers?"

"What?" Pete asked.

"Finders, keepers," Jack repeated. "You found it, so you want to keep it. Just you. Not the crew."

"This kind of treasure is what we always dreamed of," Pete said. "A fabulous find, all ours. No taking a ship, no fighting."

"It's a fortune," Eli said. "And money like that can go to people's heads. It makes them do things. Sometimes bad things."

Dally was getting the picture now. "You don't want to tell the crew about the treasure because of what they might do?"

"Their respect is tenuous at best," Eli said. *Tenuous* was one of Dally's vocabulary words. It meant tentative, at risk, iffy, with a side of "could fail at any moment."

"We'll be sleeping with one eye open the rest of the way back to port," Pete said.

"But you're the captain," Dally argued. "They have to listen to you."

"Ever hear of a mutiny?" Jack said, pantomiming a punch to his own face.

Eli tossed him a glance. "In a fight, the four of them are stronger than the four of us," he said. "No question."

"Plus," Pete added, "the more people who know the location of the treasure, the more risk that they could tell other people. We could lose everything, or end up in a fight for it one way or another."

The foursome sat on the deck and stared at the treasure.

"Our secret, then?" Eli said.

"Agreed." Jack stuck his hand into the middle of their circle.

"Agreed." Dally laid hers on top of it.

Pete and Eli joined, hand over hand. "Agreed."

"Let's continue working," Pete said, getting to his feet. "They could all be back pretty soon."

"How do you know?" Dally asked.

"We have a system," Eli explained. "They'll go off in pairs and explore for an hour or two in opposite directions and then turn around. If they're not back within three to four hours, we know there's a problem."

They worked together to tuck the treasure-filled crates away beneath other supplies in the hold. It looked pretty good, if Dally did say so herself.

"Doughy's already back," Jack observed when they returned to the deck. The cook was now wandering along the near beach, lugging a crate full of food treasures.

Eli stretched. "Let's head over, then." He started toward the ladder. Then he paused. "We found this place by accident, in the storm. How will we find it again?"

And that was how it happened. Pete laid a scrap of canvas on the deck in the sun. He retrieved a well of ink and a steel-tipped pen from Eli's quarters. Then he bent over the canvas and drew the rough lines that represented landmarks they'd passed along the way. Eli joined him, took the pen, and added a few simple words here and there in a lovely, practiced script.

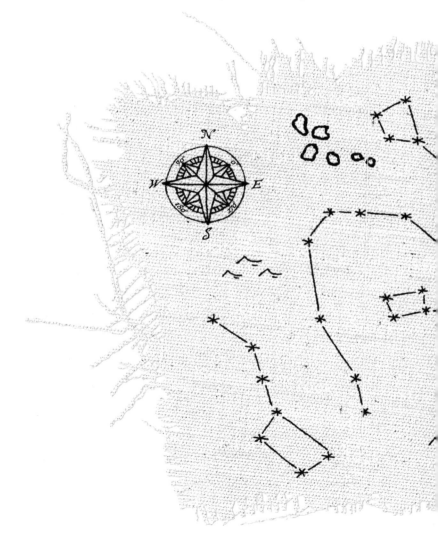

Jack rested his elbow on Dally's shoulder. "Amazing," he whispered as Pete and Eli worked.

Amazing, indeed. Dally watched a familiar map—the treasure map framed on the wall in Grandpa's study—come to life before her very eyes.

26

S o, that's it?" Jack said. "All someone needs is that map, and they'll find their way to the island? Isn't that a bit risky?"

"Not exactly," Eli said. "Every map has a key. Only those who know the key can decipher the map."

Jack and Dally studied the canvas. Nothing about it seemed overly secretive. "What's the key?" Jack asked.

"The key is in your mind already. That's why the map seems clear," Pete said.

"What *isn't* on the map?" Eli prompted.

Dally knew the answer, because of Grandpa's stories. "The map doesn't tell you where to start. It's full of landmarks that are relative to something, but if you don't know the *something*, you could be sailing the ocean in circles for years."

"Exactly," Eli said. He dove into the sea again and began swimming to shore.

Dally carefully tucked the treasure map away in Eli's quarters, then joined Pete and Jack in the ship's second rowboat.

When they arrived on the beach, Doughy was chasing crabs

in the shallows. Pete and Eli disappeared around a large rock. Jack and Dally lay on the sand, sunning and resting with their feet at the edge of the lapping waves.

"They're coming back." Jack pointed down the beach. Cork and Vern were now in sight in the distance, walking along the shore.

Dally hopped up and trotted toward the rock where Pete and Eli had gone. They were still right there behind it, apparently. She could hear their voices as she approached.

"They really *could* mutiny," Pete was saying.

"There's not a leader among them, or they would've already," Eli answered.

"That gold is a few hundred thousand reasons."

"There's more than enough gold to go around. We'll share it with them when we reach port."

"And tell them it came from where? We haven't taken a ship in weeks. They're already concerned about why we're not cruising the shipping lanes, out for blood."

Eli grunted in acknowledgment. "Maybe we found reserves hidden in the hold. Maybe the old captain was holding out on them."

"So . . . lie, to earn their trust?" Pete laughed, but in a not-very-amused way.

"That's pirates for you. They're here for the money. What do they care where it came from?"

"You want to buy their loyalty?"

"Or give them the means to choose a new direction." Eli's

words were punctuated by a soft sound Dally couldn't place. "We have to have faith."

"If either of us knew how to have faith in how things were, we wouldn't be here."

"That was before." The soft sound again. Dally peeked around the rock.

It was the sound of *kissing*. Dally clamped a hand over her smile. She'd won her bets!

She ducked out of sight again and made ready to announce herself loudly.

"There's no place we can go," Pete said.

Eli sighed. "You've never had money. But you'll see. This, all this, can buy us any kind of life we want."

"You haven't seen what I've seen," Pete countered. "They hate you even more when you're free."

They'd spent a pleasant night on the beach and enjoyed a meal of roasted crabs and juicy island fruit before heading for a port on the mainland. The sooner they got to shore, Eli said, the sooner they could distribute the treasure and part ways with the crew. The port they had in mind was considered a safe haven for thieves, brutes, and scalawags. With a pocketful of treasure, each man would have many options there.

The crew worked the sails, Pete and Eli stood at the helm, and Jack and Dally bent over the bow, gripping the rail as they leaned out to get a look at the ocean floor below.

The Bermuda shoals had had some of the most beautiful water

Dally had ever seen. Clear and glittering blue, rife with colorful corals, darting fish, leaping dolphins, undulating jellyfish. As they'd sailed westward, away from the shipwreck island, the water had remained shallow for quite a while, and they'd moved slowly so as not to run aground on any unexpected obstacles. Dally had wished for a glass-bottomed boat, or scuba gear, or even just a snorkel and mask to get up close with all the beauty. The hair on Jack's arm tickled hers, the salty wind pressed at her cheeks, and every cell in her body was alive with adventure.

But now their trip was ending. After several days' sail, they were arriving at the port, and the water wasn't nearly as clear. Even though the beauty of the shoals was behind them, Dally strained to take in the last drops of adventure before the fog closed tight and whisked her home. She tried to turn her mind away from sorrow and embrace the gratitude for this moment, right now, but it wasn't easy.

"What's wrong, Dally?" Jack asked quietly. He tugged her arm, pulling her away from the rail, and wrapped his arms around her. He was just enough taller and just enough warmer that she felt quite safe, and the fullness behind her eyes overflowed.

"It's all so beautiful," she said. "I don't want it to end."

"Dally," Jack said, "we can sail forever if we want to."

Dally shook her head. The fog was close. It was ending. "Once we drop anchor," she whispered, "we'll go our separate ways."

"Never," Jack said. "Do you believe me? You're my best friend, you know."

Dally had the impulse to smile, but it felt like it took days for the corners of her mouth to rise.

"Land ho!" Pete's voice shouted. "Make ready to anchor!" They had reached the port. But Dally could no longer see Pete and Eli at the ship's wheel, or the crew, or the towering twin masts. All she saw was a ripple in the fog that might have been the remnant shimmy of a sail in the wind. All she felt was the boards beneath her feet and the firmness of the bow rail. Just a fading scent of salt breeze. And Jack.

Jack, all warm and close and ready for endless adventure.

You're my best friend, too, Dally wanted to say. But the fog filled her throat and snapped her back to the cold stone room, all alone.

⋙ 27 ⋘

The cold reading room air hit as sharply as ever after the coastal sunshine.

She tried not to let her heartbreak show as she emerged into the atrium and greeted Jennacake once again. Instinctively, Dally knew that there was not another volume in the pirate treasure secret. This one had carried her all the way to port—no more disappearing and reappearing on the ship at sea.

"A tough one?" Jennacake asked, reading Dally's mood.

"It's amazing to get to travel," Dally said. "And sad whenever it ends."

"That's a feeling shared by many of our patrons, I'm afraid." Jennacake gazed at her thoughtfully. "Do you feel it's worth it, Dally? The experience, in spite of the pain?"

"Oh, yes," Dally said. And never had she meant anything more.

The next morning, Dally and her mother stared at each other across the width of the very large dining room table. Sun streamed in through the floor-to-ceiling window that looked out over the lake.

The table could seat twelve, which didn't happen often, and without Grandpa between them at the head of the table, everything about the room felt cold and quiet. For some reason her mother still preferred this space for their shared meals. Dally much preferred to eat in the kitchen, amid the hustle and bustle and the chatter and noise of people who were easier to talk to: Hannah and Jasper. On many mornings, Dally crunched down a bowl of cereal in the kitchen, listening to Jasper prattle about his grocery shopping plans and their dinner menu. Sometimes he'd let Dally choose what she wanted for dinner, or he'd say something like "Soft-shells are in season—how does that sound?"

Dally tried to be generally agreeable, because Jasper, like everyone in the household, worked very hard. Case in point, her mother sat across from her now with a stack of business files alongside her place mat. She'd been reviewing them when Dally walked in but had set them aside to greet her daughter.

"What are you looking forward to at school today?" her mother asked.

Dally willfully pulled her meandering, back-of-the-mind thoughts away from the library and its mysteries. "Um. At school?" she echoed.

Her mother raised an eyebrow. "You do plan to attend?"

Dally laughed. "Unfortunately, it's required."

Jasper set down a plate of scrambled eggs and bacon for

Dally and eggs Benedict for her mother. He placed a large bowl of berries between them. Dally's plate already had the dollop of sweet cream he knew she enjoyed with them.

"Thank you, Jasper," Dally's mother said.

"Thank you, Jasper," Dally said, too.

Dally's mother flourished her napkin and laid it across her lap. Dally did the same. Dally's mother picked up her knife and fork. A fork was all Dally needed, but she mirrored her mother once again.

She had been quite well-behaved around the house lately, if she did say so herself. But it wouldn't hurt to get even further onto her mother's good side. Dally's trips through the library had made her hunger for more chances to explore in the real world, and for adventurous friends to explore with. Maybe soon she could broach the subject of Adventure Club with her mother once again. *If at first you don't succeed . . .* right?

"The berries look delicious," Dally said.

"Yes." Her mother moved the top file off the stack, as if to peruse the next one.

"Anyway, you asked about school? I don't think much of excitement is set to happen today . . ."

"Mm-hmm," her mother said. She raised a mug of coffee to her lips.

A flood of heat struck Dally's throat, even before she sampled the steaming eggs. It was a bit unusual for her mother to show interest in her activities at all, and Dally supposed she should have appreciated the effort, but if she was going to have her mother's attention, she deserved more than a half-hearted listen.

Dally raised her voice. "Today we'll have gym and no art class, so that's good."

Her mother's gaze flicked back up. "You don't like art class anymore?"

"We are drawing a lot of fruit."

"I see."

"We did collage at the beginning of the year, which was fun. And I liked the sculptures we did a couple of weeks ago." Dally preferred the art that made a bit of a mess. You had to sit still a long time for pencil drawing—not exactly her strong suit.

"What about your academics?"

Boring, Dally wanted to say. Truth be told, she loved to learn, but surely there were more interesting ways to do it than droning lesson after droning lesson, worksheet after worksheet.

"I don't like always sitting behind a desk," Dally said. "I don't really know how you do it."

They both regarded the stack of work on the table.

"I consider myself lucky that I don't have to do hard labor for a living," her mother said. "Many people do truly backbreaking work, all day every day."

"Some people prefer that."

"Some people don't have a choice."

The flood of heat struck Dally again. She jammed a bite of eggs into her mouth to stop herself from blurting out something she shouldn't—something about how her mother always thought her own choices would be anyone's preference. And to think, she called *Dally* stubborn.

"Didn't you ever want to do something else?" Dally asked.

Her mother was quiet for a moment. "It's our family business," she said. "It was my obligation, as it will be yours one day."

Maybe it was being around all these secrets all the time, but Dally could sense that her mother wasn't answering the question. "Is it what you always wanted, though?"

"It didn't matter what I wanted," her mother said. "It was my destiny. And it was a rude awakening when the day came to take responsibility. I don't want that to happen to you. I want you to be ready."

"Grandpa didn't make you take business lessons?" Dally asked, surprised.

Her mother looked equally surprised. "No," she said. "He traveled so often for work. I didn't learn much about the business from him at all."

"Wow."

"I grew up thinking it would be a breeze," her mother said. "Because when he was here, he was all fun and games. I never saw him pick up a pen, hardly."

"Sounds like him," Dally said, smiling at the thought of Grandpa's goofy ways. "So you went to business school to learn everything?"

"Yes."

"And you met Daddy there?"

"A little before that, actually. He was a sophomore in college and I was a senior when we met. But we did end up in grad school at the same time." Her mother hesitated. "It makes sense that you want to know more about him, Dally. I suppose it's hard to know where to begin."

"Any random facts about him would be okay," Dally said. She thought for a moment. "What fraternity was he in?"

Her mother frowned in confusion. "He wasn't in a fraternity."

"Really?" Dally now felt confused, too. "But I thought . . . Well, I don't know what I thought," she finished awkwardly. Secrets.

"He considered it," her mother said. "He even had the opportunity to pledge at one point, but in the end he decided he would rather be himself than bend to fit certain social expectations."

"Cool." Dally felt surprisingly proud of Marcus.

"Very cool," her mother said. "He was quite brilliant. He could make anything make sense and he could make anything funny. When you were little, he took you absolutely everywhere with him, you know. Do you remember any of that?"

Dally shook her head. She thought about the wall of pictures in her sitting room. Skiing. Riding in his hiking backpack. They were snapshots, frozen in time. She'd never considered the stories behind them. She and Marcus had adventured together?

"He hated to wear hats, and he never met a challenge he wouldn't face head-on with a great big smile. You're like him in that way," her mother said. "When you want something, you go after it with your whole self."

Dally was delighted to imagine herself being like Marcus in any way at all. "Thank you," she said softly.

"Do you have a favorite project at the moment?"

It was the perfect opening to ask about Adventure Club, but suddenly Dally didn't want the fight.

"I've been spending a lot of time reading," Dally said. She sipped her orange juice to hide her secret smile.

28

D ay after day, Dally read secret after secret. Some were quick, quiet whispers, like Hector and the topiary or Hannah and the cheer-ups. Some were fuller adventures, like the ship, though none quite as long or delightful. Often she saw someone she knew—even Kate or Marcus, occasionally—but the secrets were briefer and at more of a distance than before. She cherished each short glimpse of them, and she always longed for more.

Once, she landed in a neighborhood park. She perched atop the slide and looked toward the sound of a little girl laughing. There was Grandpa! He was pushing a five- or six-year-old Kate on the swings.

"Not so high," she shrieked as her toes brushed the clouds.

"My cautious girl." Grandpa laughed, allowing the swing to settle. "Someday you'll learn to love flying, like I do."

"No, don't fly away this time," Kate begged. She slid off the swing and ran to him. "Stay longer."

"It's a big world, darling. Someone has to see all of it."

"I'll swing as high as you want," the little girl pleaded. Her voice caught. "I can be brave."

"I don't want you to be anyone but who you are, my dear Kate." Grandpa scooped his daughter up in a bear hug so tight it made Dally's heart twinge. The memory of his affection was so strong in her. "If you find the courage to do that, you've found the true secret to happiness in life, my darling."

Dally started down the slide toward them. Young Kate and Grandpa wouldn't know Dally yet, so there was no harm in saying hello, right? She skidded down the sun-warmed plastic and leaped to her feet just in time to be swept back into the fog.

In another secret, she found herself high atop a carnival Ferris wheel in late autumn. As the ride lurched her slowly over the crown of its circle, then started back down, she could see the couple in the carriage in front of her. The dark-skinned man had his arm around his lighter-skinned date. He pulled his arm away and they turned to face each other.

Dally gasped. Marcus and Kate!

"I have something for you," he said, reaching into his pocket. He handed her a small jewelry box. "It's a year to the day since we met, you know."

"I know," Kate said, opening the box. "I wasn't sure if you remembered."

"How could I ever forget?"

Kate gasped with joy at the sight of the same diamond

earrings. "You paid me back for these months ago," she said. "I thought you'd returned them."

"Surprise," he said. The Ferris wheel swung to a halt, suspending them halfway down.

Kate yelped as the carriage bounced beneath her. Marcus put his arm back around her. "Want to know a secret?" She laughed. "I'm terrified of heights. I can't believe you got me up here."

"But it was worth it, wasn't it?" Marcus asked. "The view alone . . ." He was looking at her, not the landscape, as he spoke.

Kate looked back at him. "The view is pretty amazing."

They were both smiling when they kissed.

From each and every trip, Dally returned breathless, with wind in her hair and joy in her heart.

"So, I can just keep coming here and reading secrets forever?" she asked Jennacake one day as she was selecting her volume.

"Ah, well . . ." Jennacake looked troubled. Her unlined face crinkled slightly at the brow, like a crease appearing in a freshly stretched bedsheet.

"There's something you're not telling me, isn't there?" Dally said. She'd seen that expression fall over Jennacake's face before.

"Nothing truly lasts forever, does it, dear?"

"I suppose not." Dally had the feeling that it wasn't the whole truth.

The librarian's expression softened into a smile. "I know a great many secrets. I've told you very few."

"That isn't really an answer to my question, though, is it?"

Jennacake was an expert in deflection, Dally well knew.

Perhaps that was what made her the perfect secret librarian. But it was frustrating to be on the receiving end of so many half-truths.

"Yes, there is something I'm not telling you," Jennacake said, surprising Dally with her directness. "It's a rather big thing, in fact, so I'm waiting for the right time."

"Why can't now be the right time?"

Jennacake shook her head. "It's just too soon."

Dally thought about that for a moment. Patience was definitely *not* her strong suit.

"I think you should tell me now."

"Dally..." Jennacake paused. "There are some things... once you know them, you can never unknow them, and it changes everything. It changes your whole life."

"Like finding out your parents aren't really your parents?" Dally asked.

Jennacake let out a tiny bursting laugh. "That's quite an example! What made you think of that?"

Dally blushed. The words had come out sounding different than she meant them. She loved the parents she had, but that didn't stop her from occasionally wishing *some* things were different. She often wished she could see eye to eye with her mother, for example. And as a small child, she'd fantasized that her dad was really alive and would someday come rescue her from Peteharrington Place, that he would turn out to be a fabulous explorer who would whisk her away into a dream life as good as one of the library's most adventurous secrets. Seeing him through the library had only heightened the fantasy, if she was honest.

"Well, is it like that?" Dally said, by way of deflection. She would be embarrassed to admit such wishful feelings to Jennacake.

"I suppose," the librarian mused. "Though, I'm certain your parents have always been your parents, Dally."

"Do you always know things like that about people?"

"No," Jennacake said. "Many people who come here do learn surprising things. But John—your grandfather—knew a great deal about your lineage."

"Did he?" Dally asked. She knew family was very important to Grandpa, but she didn't remember hearing him talk about the specifics. Maybe in his travels through the library, he'd seen his own ancestors. Other than Pete, Dally had yet to meet any far-back family, but he had made her feel connected to something much bigger than herself. It took away some of the sting of missing Jack, Pete, and Eli, to imagine that Pete, at least, was still a part of her. Just like her dad, and like Grandpa.

Dally sighed. She had been selecting lighter secrets of late, but perhaps it was time to return to the part that felt like it truly mattered. She wandered into Family Secrets. The volumes on some shelves seemed quite a bit older than those on other shelves. As if they had been bound according to their time. That made sense, Dally supposed. The secrets that had taken her to Pete and Eli's ship had been old and well-worn. The ones on the shelf in front of her now looked more like the books in her local library. The numbers on their spines all started with 200, she noticed. There were a handful of 2004s, several 2005s, a 2006, and a whole fleet of 2009s, among others.

The lone 2006 was a fairly thin volume, standing all on its own. When Dally touched it, she was overcome by a feeling of goofy affection. The word it emanated: *kite*. Well, okay then.

Dally pulled it. "These numbers," she said, turning to Jennacake. "Is this a date?"

"You're very perceptive," the librarian answered. She tapped the number, which was 2006619. "Year: 2006. Month: six, which is June. And day, the nineteenth."

"So I can pick my secret based on where I want to go in time?" Dally found this delightful.

"If you like," Jennacake said. "You can pick it however you want to. Is this the one for today?"

"Yes," Dally said. The feeling, that goofy affection, was one she wanted to lean into forever. She had to see where it led.

29

Dally popped out of the darkness into a bright afternoon in a park. It didn't look familiar. There was a playground on one side of her and a large expanse of grass on the other. Straight ahead, at the far end of the field, stood a set of pavilions with picnic tables and public grills. Dozens of people were gathered there, chatting, eating, and laughing. It looked like one giant picnic, and whatever was grilling smelled great.

Dally turned at the sound of voices behind her. There was a small cluster of children on the grass, surrounding a dark-skinned man flying a kite. The kite was blue on the bottom and red on top, with a white bursting star in the center.

"Who's next?" the man asked, lowering the kite handle so a child could grasp it.

Dally gasped at the voice. It was Marcus! Her heart leaped with joy.

"Me, me!" shouted the chorus of children, clambering toward him.

"Deion, then Jazz."

The chosen child grabbed on and darted off across the

grass. Marcus wore a bright red T-shirt with a large orange sun on the chest. Should she talk to him? Oh, how she wanted to. The decision ceased to be hers when Marcus turned to her and spoke.

"They've all had a first turn already," he called. "Did you want to try next?"

"Okay, sure," Dally said, stepping closer.

"You look familiar," he said. "I'm sorry I can't place your name. Remind me?"

"My name's . . . Lilah," Dally said.

"Marcus." He smiled at her. He seemed about the same age as when she'd seen him the first time. Maybe he remembered her from the jewelry counter. Or maybe he simply recognized her from looking in the mirror each morning. That smile was Dally's own smile.

Marcus beckoned to Jazz and Deion to return to the group. They raced across the field in a snaking pattern, the kite dipping and swirling through the wind behind them.

"Is that your kite?" Dally asked.

"Yeah, it belongs to the Soul Center," Marcus said. "We bust it out every Juneteenth for the picnic."

Dally didn't know what the Soul Center was, but she didn't dare ask. Marcus's tone suggested it should be common knowledge. Now that she was closer, she could see that the sun on his T-shirt read *Soul Center* in the middle. The sun's rays were filled with words as well. *Pride. Community. Solidarity.* His arm was blocking the lower three, so she couldn't read them.

Jazz's beaded braids bounced against her shoulders as she landed beside Dally. "Again?" she asked.

"It's Lilah's turn," Marcus said, passing her the string.

There was just enough breeze that the kite stayed aloft during the handoff. Dally understood how to play the kite off the wind, so she didn't have to run across the field to keep it flying like the smaller children had done. She tilted the handle to and fro. The kite swirled a figure eight above them.

"Hey. Looks like you've done this before," Marcus said, sounding impressed.

Dally's heart glowed at the praise. "Maybe I'm naturally talented," she countered.

Marcus chuckled. "I don't doubt it."

Dally grinned, gazing into his warm, attentive face hovering beside hers. A dream come true.

When the kite finally started to dip, Marcus tapped her wrist to guide the string. "Try this." The kite resumed its happy swirl.

"Cool," Dally said. "Thanks." She supposed it was time to give the other children a turn, but with Marcus alongside her this way, she never wanted the moment to end. If he had lived, this could have been real.

It sure felt real.

A young woman in box braids and a matching Soul Center shirt crossed the field toward them. She was carrying a huge bag over her shoulder, Santa Claus style.

"Who knows what's in my bag?" she called.

Like a flock of birds, the children soared across the grass. "I know! I know!" they shouted.

Marcus retrieved the kite from Dally, then began to wind up the string. Dally raced out and caught the kite before it stabbed into the ground. She held it while he wrapped up the last of the string.

"Thanks," he said. He waved to the woman, who was now supervising the children in unwrapping a large, colorful parachute from the bag. Dally had played with a similar parachute in gym class many times.

Marcus tucked the kite under his arm and started toward the picnic tables. Dally followed.

"That was fun," she said.

"It was," he agreed. "We can fly it again later if you want. I'm going to get a bite to eat for a minute, though."

Marcus was moving away as though the conversation was over, but Dally didn't want it to be. She searched for something more to say.

The crowd around the picnic tables was mostly adults. A cluster of teenagers hung out at one side of the gathering, and a few small children raced among everyone's knees. Marcus headed for the grill area, where a couple of guys in Soul Center T-shirts were flipping burgers and brats and corncobs still in their husks. Beyond them, a portly fellow in a dashiki stood over a boiling vat of seasoned water. Marcus and Dally arrived right as he was pulling the boil basket out of the water. He lugged it over to a picnic table lined with newspaper and poured it out. A delicious-looking pile of shrimp, sausage, corn, and potatoes tumbled out, steaming hot and smelling like Old Bay.

Dally's stomach growled. "Couldn't have timed that better."

"You know it," Marcus agreed, handing her a sturdy paper plate. They joined the line of Black folks who had materialized in front of them—not a line so much as a scrum, with everyone on top of one another, shoving and sharing with equal enthusiasm.

"Mmm, that shrimp is on point, Calvin!" one older man called out. He tossed a wave to the cook in the dashiki, who offered a small salute in return.

"Oh, Lord, yes," a woman answered. "Pure as a Sunday morning." A chorus of murmurs and amens rose up around her.

Everyone was laughing and chatting as they jostled one another to get to the hot food. The jovial, celebratory mood was infectious. Dally soon found herself grinning along, bumping shoulders with the crowd, and stepping aside with Marcus as he allowed several senior citizens to get first dibs.

It felt like everyone was talking all at once. Dally could barely follow any conversation as her attention blipped from face to face. Nearly everyone at the gathering was Black—young and old, light-skinned and dark, tall, short, round, lanky, and the whole range in between.

She filled her plate and continued to hang near Marcus as he chatted. He seemed to know each person by name, and they all seemed happy to exchange a few words with him before they drifted along on their way.

Upbeat music pumped from a speaker somewhere. A banner on the pavilion bore the Soul Center logo and proclaimed, JUBILEE DAY PICNIC: HAPPY JUNETEENTH!

"There you are," said a familiar voice. Dally whirled around, her eyes wide. Kate emerged from the crowd and stepped into Marcus's arms.

"Hey, you made it!" He grinned.

Kate smiled back. "I was promised fireworks."

"Not until dark," Marcus said, glancing at the pre-sunset sky. "But you're just in time for the low-country boil."

"I'm nothing if not well organized," Kate answered.

Marcus kissed her cheek and plucked another paper plate from the stack. "You better get in there before the elders clean it all out."

Kate studied the crowd around the table, looking hesitant to shove her way to the front.

"I could get some for you," Marcus offered. Kate nodded, appearing relieved. He slid easily among the people.

Kate's gaze flicked to Dally, who was still staring. "Hi."

"Hi."

"I'm Kate."

"I'm Lilah," Dally said, remembering the version of her name she'd told Marcus earlier. Idly, she wondered when her mother had gone from Kate to Katherine, even around the household. Dally didn't recall ever hearing her called Kate in real time.

"Are you part of Marcus's youth group from the Soul Center?" Kate asked.

"No," Dally answered. "I'm visiting."

Kate smiled. "Me too. It's my first time at a Soul Center event." She looked around as though feeling uncertain. Dally herself felt a bit like a fish out of water in this vibrant Black community, but at least she looked like she belonged. It must have felt strange to Kate to be one of the only white faces in the crowd.

"Mine too," Dally assured her. "Everyone seems really nice."

"Yeah," Kate agreed. "I'm excited to be meeting the people Marcus always talks about from work. That must be Calvin," she said, pointing to the man at the boiling station.

"Yup. I think so," Dally said.

Marcus returned then with a plate of food for Kate. It was generously piled.

"Whoa," she said. "I'm already at my fighting weight."

Marcus laughed. "I wanted you to have choices."

Kate accepted the plate. "This isn't so much choices as . . . *all* the food."

"Only the best for the best," he said, and kissed her cheek again. Kate blushed. They were positively adorable, Dally decided.

The couple moved toward an empty corner of one of the picnic tables. Dally could not help but trail behind.

"Is it okay if I sit with you?" she asked. Other people shifted down to make room for the trio.

"Of course," Kate said, sitting beside Marcus and opposite Dally. "Is your family here with you?"

"My parents are here," Dally said. "I mean, they will be. I came a little early." She smiled to herself. "It seemed like so much fun."

"The whole neighborhood turns out for this party every year," Marcus said. "I guess we're doing something right."

"Calvin did this shrimp right, that's for sure," Kate mumbled around a mouthful. Dally ate more of hers, too. It was truly delicious—salty, seasoned, and perfectly textured.

"So, Lilah," Marcus said. "What grade will you be in next year? We have a youth group that meets at the center every Saturday afternoon. We do all kinds of fun stuff."

"That sounds great," Dally said honestly. "But I'm only visiting."

Marcus nodded. "Well, lucky for you, you're here on the best day of the year. Celebrating our freedom with food, families, and fun."

"And fireworks, to round out the alliteration." Kate grinned. "Can you tell he wrote all the flyers for the party?"

Dally laughed.

Marcus seemed amused, too. "And fireworks." He glanced at the sky. "It's nearly time to get them ready, actually. Kate's going to help."

"Not a chance, buster." Beneath her smile, Kate's face flashed with genuine discomfort. "I prefer to be far from where things are exploding."

"Well, that's because you're no fun at all," Marcus said, though his tone made it clear that he was teasing.

"Or because I'm smart like that," Kate responded. "It's the little things that bring me joy, you see. Like having fingers."

Marcus wore a pained expression. "It hurts that you assume I'll be inept at blowing things up."

"You lost me at 'blowing things up,'" Kate quipped.

"See?" Marcus said. "No fun at all."

Dally couldn't help the grin that split her face. Her parents, both alive. And together. Having fun. Being silly. It was a dream she hadn't known to dream, and yet it was coming true.

Kate pouted. "This man made me jump out of an airplane with him on his birthday, and now he's saying I'm not fun? I'm made of fun."

"You're made of hummus and homework," Marcus joked.

Kate laughed. "That's uncomfortably accurate."

"You went skydiving?" Dally asked, incredulous. Her afraid-of-heights, risk-averse, desk-job-loving mother had jumped out of an airplane?

Kate winked. "Anything for an adventure, right?"

Dally sat speechless. It was all she could do to hold her corn-cob. "You like adventures?" she asked once she got a bit of wind back in her lungs.

Kate smiled. "As Marcus likes to say, you've gotta take life by the horns, Lilah. It's especially true as a woman, in the world we live in."

Marcus beamed. "Aha!" he cheered. "Finally, my influence is paying off."

"He's always dragging me off to do some wild thing or another," Kate said. "Case in point: skydiving."

"Can we go skydiving in the youth group?" Dally asked.

Marcus laughed. "Pretty sure you have to be eighteen. Sorry."

"Looks like you have another recruit for the cause," Kate said. "Adventurers of the world, unite!"

Marcus kissed her cheek. "You mean that?"

Kate raised her chin loftily. "No, I have serious pursuits."

"My pursuits are plenty serious," Marcus said. "I'm only getting started."

"So you won't always work for the Soul Center?" Dally asked.

"I love it there, but it's only until I graduate," he said. "I'm studying to be a climate change scientist. We don't fully understand the global impact that's coming. I'm going to travel all over, study icebergs, coral reefs, volcanoes . . ." His voice trailed off and he stared into the sky.

"You want to be an explorer?" Dally whispered.

"Oh, yeah," Marcus said. "Especially if Kate will come along."

Dally's eyes widened. "You're going to adventure together? And save the world?"

"I already work for a nonprofit, so I'm in the general field of trying to make the world a better place." Marcus smiled.

"Mmm, you're quite the knight in shining armor." Kate brushed away a stray corn kernel clinging to Marcus's cheek.

He let out an exaggerated sigh, grasping her hand and

clutching it to his chest. "Exactly—all suited up and ready to storm the castle and rescue the lady."

"The lady is perfectly capable and not in need of rescue, thank you very much," Kate retorted.

"And yet she refuses the invitation to tour the globe with me, doing science." He made jazz hands. Dally giggled.

"I can support your research from the comfort of my own home through the magic of the internet, you know." Kate shrugged. "I like facts and data."

"Two feet on the ground and her nose in a book." Marcus sighed.

"That's me. No fun at all," Kate reiterated.

"You're fun," Dally said. "We're having fun."

Kate laughed. "Finally, someone who truly appreciates my charm. Thank you, Lilah. Hey, I need to get a soda," she added. "Do either of you want anything?"

"Water," Marcus said.

"I would take a root beer or a Sprite," Dally said. "Thanks."

"Coming right up!" Kate swung out of the bench and sauntered toward a row of coolers in the near distance.

"Want to know a secret?" Marcus mused, staring after Kate.

"Always," Dally said.

"I'm gonna marry her someday."

≶30≶

Dally snapped back to the library as Marcus was walking away. Her heart was full, but her stomach was slightly uneasy. Maybe it was a side effect of time travel, but she suspected it had more to do with her feelings. She tried to shake them off as she strode out of the reading room. Feelings could definitely put a damper on an adventure.

"You okay?" Jennacake asked. Perhaps Dally wasn't as good at shaking off feelings as she tried to be.

"I saw my mom again," Dally said. "Long before I was born."

"And?" Jennacake said. Since the librarian was the one who'd asked Dally not to talk about the secrets, the question annoyed her. It was a question entirely about the very feelings she was trying to avoid.

"If that day is one of my mother's memories still, why doesn't she remember meeting me?" Dally asked.

"She does remember meeting someone," Jennacake said. "But she doesn't know it was you. Memory is a funny thing. It's imperfect."

Dally nodded slowly, trying to understand. "So she remembers me, but not that it was me?" That was confusing.

"We remember the people we love in great detail. But we don't remember people we meet casually in the same way. For example, do you remember the exact face of the person who sells you your daily cupcake?"

Dally thought about it. "It's not always the same person. One of them is blond and kind of tall. The other is shorter. A brunette."

"See?" Jennacake said. "Five or ten years from now, you might not remember even that much."

"I see," Dally said. "But it's odd." So much about this was odd. Most especially that her mother, long ago, had been an entirely different person. A person, perhaps, who was a lot more like Dally herself.

When Dally arrived home that afternoon, she marched straight up to her mother's office. She pushed through the large double doors into the outer office and strolled confidently down the long runway of a carpet.

"Oh, Miss Peteharrington. Hello," said the receptionist.

"I don't have an appointment," Dally said. "But may I see her anyway?"

"She's not in," the receptionist told her. "I believe she's taken her laptop down to the gardens this afternoon."

"Really?" That struck Dally as unusual.

"I'm always encouraging her to get a bit of fresh air. No one should be cooped up in an office for so many hours a day."

"That's for sure," Dally agreed. "Thanks anyway."

She left the office and ventured out into the gardens. She moved among the winding hedge-lined paths, letting her fingers drift over the leaves as she walked. As much as she loved the Secret Library, it was refreshing to be back in these familiar gardens. It had been weeks since she'd properly played in the yard. Months, if she was honest. Because nothing about Peteharrington Place—nowhere she could be and nothing she could do—was quite as good without Grandpa.

But today, after the most recent secret, Dally felt a tiny glimmer of something she hadn't felt much since losing him. A tiny glimmer of . . . hope. Maybe there was a chance that things could get better.

Hope, it turned out, was one of the feelings stirring up Dally's stomach. She had tried to push it away because hope could be quite a scary feeling. It terrified her to imagine something great happening when the likelihood of it being possible felt very small.

Dally smiled as she passed the topiary garden. She tossed a little wave at the elephant with the too-small trunk that was still growing back. *I know your secret,* she thought.

Through the hedge came the sound of water flowing. And there was another sound—the click-clack of a laptop keyboard. Her mother must be sitting and working on one of the benches near the fountain.

Dally took a deep breath and wound her way over there.

"Hi, Mom."

Her mother looked up from her laptop, surprised. "Hi, honey."

"Hi," Dally said again. She felt strangely awkward, face-to-face with the mother she'd always known, with the memory of the Kate she'd just met lingering in her mind. Those two images floated in front and in back of each other with all the blur of a time-lapse photo.

"Were you looking for me?" Dally's mother asked.

"Adventure Club," Dally said simply. There was no point in beating around the bush. This version of her mother wasn't much for subtlety or nuance.

Her mother's eyes clouded. "Oh," she said. "This again?"

"There's something I forgot to say, with regard to the permission slip," Dally said.

"Oh?" Her mother seemed curious in spite of herself.

"There was a box on the form for parents to check if they are willing to be a chaperone for some of the outings," Dally said. "Maybe it's something we could do together."

"I—"

"Even if it's not until next school year," Dally rushed to add. "It really sounds like fun, don't you think? So far, they've gone rock climbing and to a ropes course and to help with animals at the zoo . . ." She bit back the rest of the ramble that threatened to flee her lips.

"I couldn't possibly," her mother said. "And you still have your lessons."

"You said that for next year, we could renegotiate the timing," Dally reminded her.

"Right," her mother said. "Well, we'll talk about it next year, I guess."

"So that's a maybe?" Dally could hardly believe it. "To being one of the Adventure Club chaperones?"

"No," her mother said. "I doubt it."

"I bet Dad would have done it with me," Dally blurted out. "Don't you think so?"

Her mother looked surprised. Her closed expression softened a bit. "There are lots of things he would have wanted to do with you," she said gently.

"Will you think about it?" The tiny roil of hope in Dally's belly was not going down without a fight.

Her mother hesitated. "I suppose I could think about it," she said. "If it means that much to you."

Dally leaped forward and threw her arms around her mother. "Oh, it does!" she exclaimed. "Thank you."

The hug was awkward, due to the angle. Dally was standing. Her mother was sitting and also trying to keep her laptop from falling to the ground now that it had been bumped by Dally's enthusiastic knees. But Dally didn't care.

One tiny bit of movement was one tiny bit of movement.

Dally was all smiles as she skipped away through the garden.

Hope. What a concept.

31

Dally carried that hope along with her to the library the next day. In turn, hope ferried her back toward *Family Secrets* with a buoyancy that reminded her of sailing on the pirate ship. She hoped for her next great adventure. She hoped that the questions she carried in her heart truly had answers somewhere.

When the spinning stopped and the fog lifted . . . well, Dally thought the fog was lifting, anyway. The air around her stilled and went from black to gray-white, then back to dark, dank black again. She could see nothing. A rank, ripe scent filled her nostrils, causing her to gag and cover her mouth. It was the worst odor she'd ever experienced—worse than the odor of a hold full of pirates, something Dally wouldn't have thought possible. It felt like she had been dropped into a giant toilet that hadn't been flushed in years. She held her nose and tried to pretend she couldn't taste the filth around her.

She blinked slowly until her eyes began to adjust. She was in a room with damp, bumpy walls. There was barely a hint of light, and she could see only a few inches in front of her face.

A cave, perhaps? She put out her hand and felt along the slimy wall, gauging the room's dimensions.

"Ow," she cried as her fingers found the lip of something harder and sharper than stone. Metal. "Where the heck am I?" She felt around the metal. It formed a loop, a rod curved such that the ends were embedded deep in the stone. Hooked to the wall loop was another, thinner metal loop, leading to a series of even smaller loops, linked like sausages all the way to the floor.

A chain.

A sinking feeling struck Dally's core. She grasped the chain, which rattled as she lifted it and passed it through her hands, searching for its natural end.

"Who's there?" whispered a voice from the other side of the room.

"Um. Hello?" Dally answered. "I've only just arrived. Where are we?"

The voice laughed gruffly. "What's the matter, kid? You never been thrown in jail before?"

The sinking feeling turned into a roller-coaster drop. She found the end of the chain, and sure enough, a chunky pair of wrist cuffs dangled there.

"Well, that's a load of codswallop," Dally muttered.

"Dal?" said the man's voice. "Is that you?" Soft stirring.

Dally's eyes were still adjusting, but she turned toward the sound and sensed a long, thin shape hovering at the base of the far wall. It wasn't all that far, really—maybe six or eight feet. There was barely a body's length between them.

"Pete?"

"That's a hell of a coincidence," Pete said.

"Not a coincidence at all," Dally admitted, thinking of the Family Secrets shelf and feeling a trill of satisfaction. Pete *was* her ancestor. Despite the horrible circumstances, her heart flipped with joy at the sound of his voice.

As Dally moved toward him, she discovered that the fourth wall of their hole was actually a thick wooden door.

"How did you find us?" asked Pete.

"Us?" she asked. "Is Eli here, too?"

"Somewhere. They separated us."

"How did you end up in jail?"

Pete shrugged. "Pirating."

"What happened to taking the treasure and sailing away together?" Dally asked. They were already speaking softly, but she lowered her voice even further on the word *treasure*.

"Ironically," Pete said, "pirates happened."

"You got robbed?"

"Finding a safe place took longer than we hoped. We were good for almost a year, then we lost that first run of the treasure at sea to a boat full of scoundrels. We've been trying to get back to the island ever since, but things keep getting in the way." Pete shook his handcuffs. "For example."

"Hard to believe it's been over a year," Dally said. Her heart ached for Pete and Eli, trapped on the run in a world that refused to understand and accept them.

"It's been quite a few years," Pete said. "You disappeared

without a word when we reached port. Without even taking your share of the treasure."

It had been four years, Dally recalled, according to the secret spine. "It just doesn't feel like that long, I guess," she explained, in hopes of covering her gaffe. "I really liked sailing with you."

"Then why did you leave?"

"I always hoped to return." Dally dodged the question. "Some things are out of our hands, you know?"

Pete shook his chains by way of answer. After a pause, he said, "It was a pleasant dream, sailing off and maybe having a patch of land to ourselves someday. A dream worth chasing."

"Don't lose faith, Pete," Dally insisted. "There must be someplace."

"It's too late now."

"It's never too late."

"You do understand—we're to be hanged, Dal."

"Hanged?" Dally echoed, horrified.

Pete rubbed his forehead, rattling his chains. "That's what they do to pirates. This is Welleston, after all, not some haven for thieves."

Welleston? This was her own city? Dally was surprised to learn they were so close to home. Last she knew, Pete and Eli were destined to roam freely through the ocean, hopping from smugglers' port to smugglers' port until they found their plot of land. How did they get to South Carolina?

"I have to get you out of here, then," Dally said.

"There's a chance they'll spare Eli." Pete's voice was quiet, but it carried the energy of hope. "When they realize . . ." His words trailed off.

Dally was already on her feet. It was one thing to sit and keep Pete company in jail, but it was entirely another to let him die. She didn't have all the time in the world, but she had to do *something.*

"We have to find a way out." She moved to the door and began feeling her way around the cracks at its edges. Whatever space was beyond the door was dark black as well, but her eyes had adjusted enough to make out a few shadows.

"It's padlocked from the outside," Pete said, with an air of *I've tried everything* behind his words.

But Dally wasn't feeling for the latch. She was feeling for the hinges. "We must be in the jail that's near Welleston Harbor, right? These old cells have a weakness." She had learned about it on her class tour of the Historic Harbor Jail. Few prisoners had escaped the gallows in the harbor's storied history, but the ones who had succeeded did so through cleverness, not force.

The door had two hinges. One was almost too high for Dally to reach. Her fingers brushed the base of it when she stretched up. The other one was down by her shins. She crouched to get a better feel. The hinge was constructed of a pin and a couple of loops. Their roughness suggested a lot of rust. It wasn't going to be easy, but Dally was forming a plan.

She scuttled back across the cell to the empty set of chains. She thought she had felt the key sticking out of the shackles. Was she remembering right?

Dally felt along the wall until the chain jangled under her fingers. The handcuffs were each shaped like a capital D, with the flat side attached on a hinge. The key stuck out the end when the cuffs were unlocked, and then when they were closed around a person's wrists, the key was turned to lock the bar, then removed.

Yes! The key on the loose cuffs was still in place. Whether it was a piece of luck or standard practice, Dally didn't know. All that mattered was that the key was there. She pulled it out and took it over to Pete. Fortunately, the key worked on his cuffs, too.

While Pete rubbed his wrists and shook out his sore arms, Dally took the key to the door. The protruding end of the key was stronger and stiffer than her fingers, so when she positioned it under the hinge and pushed upward (the way you might press the plunger of a syringe), the rusty pin began to move.

It took all her strength, and when her fingertips became angry, she switched to using her palm. Once she'd pressed the key as far into the hole as it would go, the pin was up high enough that Dally could grasp it with her now-very-sore fingers. She tried pulling, but it was too tight.

"Let me try," Pete said. His larger hands, strengthened by years of fieldwork and sailing, rocked and wriggled the hinge pin and pulled it out. Dally freed the key, and Pete went to work on the top hinge, following her strategy. "Brilliant," he muttered.

With a little help from sixth-grade history class, Dally thought. Whoever knew a random school field trip would come in so handy?

Together, Dally and Pete pulled on the door from the hinge side, hoping to lever it open. It worked! Dally was able to squeeze through the gap, but the door wouldn't give quite enough for Pete's larger frame to pass through.

"Well, it seemed like a good idea," Dally said.

"I'm out of the cuffs," Pete said. "That's progress."

Dally hefted the large padlock in her palm. "I could pick this, I think, if I only had something to pick it *with*." The hallway was brighter than the cell, with slivers of light coming from a stairwell, but it was still too dark to see what might be lying around. "What should we do?"

"Just go, Dal," Pete said. "Save yourself."

"I'm not leaving you," Dally answered. She couldn't, not even to try to get help. The mostly black basement was edged in the gray of the fog. The boundary of Pete's secret was relatively close.

Dally leaned her forehead against the bent wood. "I'm not leaving you," she repeated. "And I'm not giving up." She had to be here for a reason, right? "Do you have any secrets you want to get off your chest?" Dally asked. "They say confession is good for the immortal soul."

Pete chuckled lightly. "The only secret I have that's worth anything, you already know."

Dally wondered which secret he meant: the existence and location of the treasure, or his quiet love for Eli. Both seemed worth something, to her. But she refrained from asking. If the secret wasn't in this room with Pete already, then they *had* to be able to escape, didn't they? The secret had to be somewhere beyond this cell, something they'd find together, like the sunken treasure.

"We can do this," Dally insisted. "We have to keep trying—that's all."

"Dal, I don't—" Pete stopped mid-sentence as the stillness around them suddenly shattered.

A voice, a glow of light, and the sound of clattering keys emerged at the edge of Dally's fog, from the place she knew the stairs should be.

"Someone's coming!"

⪦ 32 ⪧

The guard's keys jangled as he thumped down the stairs. "Get back inside," Pete whispered. "We'll catch him by surprise."

Dally and Pete pressed the cell door back into place and stood on either side of it, waiting. The guard moved down the hallway, opening cells one by one and, from the sound of it, dropping off plates of food.

The guard's heavy footsteps approached. Through the cracks around the doorframe, the glow of light grew stronger. Dally could just make out Pete's outline now. A little light went a long way.

The guard fiddled with the key and padlock, then pushed the door, as if to ease it open. Instead, the hingeless block of wood teetered for a moment, then crashed down hard into the center of the cell. The guard rushed in, clomping on the door, holding a cup and bowl. "Here, what's this?" he cried.

Dally jumped forward and threw her whole weight at the guard, aiming her shoulder for his thick waist and shoving him as hard as she could. He staggered to the side.

Pete looped the handcuff chain around the man's neck and pulled tight. The guard dropped the food and water and grasped at his throat, struggling to breathe.

Dally scooted closer and felt around for the cuff end of the chain. She reached up and looped the manacles around the guard's wrists, locked them, then tucked the key into her pocket.

"Okay," she said.

Pete released the guard's throat and let him drop to the ground, panting and retching. Soon enough he'd start yelling for help, Dally was sure. But they were deep in the basement of the jail, and who ever paid attention to screaming from the deep?

The fallen door was beyond repair, so Dally and Pete climbed over it and darted into the hallway. On the way, Dally scooped up the hefty ring with the three huge metal keys that the guard had dropped and took down the lantern that he'd hung on a hook outside the cell. Pete knelt and stuck his face right in the water bucket and took a long drink.

When he rose, Dally handed him the lantern, which was heavier than she'd expected. "Did you see where they were holding Eli?"

"No," Pete answered. "Did you?"

"No, but I have a guess," she said. On the class tour, they had seen several different cellblocks. Black prisoners and white prisoners had not been housed together—not in the pre–Civil War days, when most Black people in the country were enslaved.

Dally led the way up the stairs, with Pete staggering weakly behind her. She didn't know how long he had been in that cell, but he seemed to be making an effort to get some strength back in his legs. The glow from the lantern danced ahead of them and along the walls, creating an effect that was almost eerier than the absolute dark.

As they climbed, Dally could no longer see the edge of the fog. Pete's freedom seemed to have expanded the bounds of his secret, allowing her to breathe a little easier. Metaphorically, anyway—the staircase didn't smell much better than the basement cellblock, though Dally sensed the promise of the sea beyond the walls.

She paused at the top of the stairs and peeked around cautiously. There were likely to be other guards. Whether by luck or by timing, Dally saw no one. Perhaps the guards were overly confident in the strength of the prisoners' chains.

The cells on this floor were separated from the hall by vertical bars rather than proper doors. The only problem was, there were quite a few men chained up within the half dozen cells. Where was Eli? The lantern helped, but not enough to make out faces, especially underneath the fur of unkempt beards and the grime of unwashed skin.

"Up and at 'em," Pete barked, loud enough to sound authoritative, but hopefully not loud enough to rouse any guards.

The prisoners stirred. Chains clanked. Ragged clothing swished softly. Throats cleared and lungs coughed their way out of stillness. Pete scanned their movements and ultimately pointed to a man who hadn't yet stirred. "There," he said.

Another strong wave of bathroom smell hit Dally, and she fought her gag reflex. Only a few minutes more in here, she hoped.

Eli's cell was overall a little drier and cleaner than the one Pete had been in. Dally remembered something Pete had said, when they first met years ago and she was asking him questions about life at sea. *Pirates don't get the best treatment, all around, but people like you and me get the worst of it.*

Dally slid the guard's key ring off her wrist and studied the three metal keys. They looked similar: big, old-fashioned rods with an oval at one end and simple teeth at the other. She chose one and tried it in the padlock. The key turned. Lucky guess!

Eli was curled in the corner, with two other white men chained along the opposite wall. Dally didn't recognize them, but she unlocked their cuffs all the same. They rubbed their wrists and eased upright, moving toward the door.

"Who is that?" Eli said as Dally went to work on his chains.

"Eli, it's me, Dal."

"Dal?" Eli struggled his way to sitting. He was draped in a piece of cloth like a poncho, with a hole cut in the center for his head and the corners flapping down along his sides. He reeked like a pile of the worst-smelling laundry.

"Escape now, explain later," Dally said, scampering toward the door. She listened for the guards.

"May need a hand," Eli said.

Pete thrust the lantern at Dally, then rushed to Eli. He grasped Eli under the arms and helped him to his feet. Eli had put on some weight over the years, and he moved like he was uncomfortable carrying it. The lithe, confident stride that had defined him when they'd met had given way to a strange sort of waddle. His face looked rather gaunt, like Pete's, as if he hadn't eaten properly in ages.

"Are you injured?" Dally asked, struck by the changes in him.

"Not exactly," Eli muttered. "But we can talk about it later." He waddled toward the door.

Eli's face was dirty but still appeared clean shaven, which seemed odd, compared to the other prisoners' inch-thick beards. They must not have been in there as long as some of the others.

Dally led the way. She remembered enough of the tour to know roughly where the nearest door would be. She scooted along the hallways, holding the lantern high. With Pete's help, Eli limped along behind her. The light danced ahead of them, illuminating a crossroads.

From around the corner, a deep voice spoke. "Yer done already, then? Fast rounds."

The three friends froze in place, exchanging alarmed glances. Dally fiddled with the valve on the lamp, turning the flame down low.

"Cliff?" the voice said. "What're ye doing?" A rustling sound, then footsteps.

A tall, thickly built man rounded the corner, carrying a lantern of his own. He had a belt with a keychain and a revolver in a holster. Another guard!

"Cliff is dead," Dally announced in a loud, high, babyish voice. That was not at all true—the other guard was no doubt fine, if a bit angry to be locked up—and Dally didn't know where the impulse came from, but she found herself laughing in a high-pitched child's tone. She let her voice shake, and called, "And you're next!"

Dally swayed her lantern back and forth, up and down, hoping she looked a bit spooky.

"Who's there?" shouted the guard, clearly confused by what he was seeing in the lamplight. He was very large, like a wall made out of boulder, Dally thought. She tilted her head back and back farther to look up at him as he approached. She laughed again, the high-pitched horror-movie laugh.

He stopped a yard or so away and stared at her—a young girl in a place no child should be, carrying a lantern and laughing. She wasn't sure he had even noticed Pete and Eli huddled together in the shadows, so when they started laughing, too, out of the darkness, the guard stepped back a pace and squeaked a not-very-tough-sounding squeak.

His hand fumbled around his belt for the revolver, and then—

Thunk. The guard's face went slack and he stumbled, dropping to his knees. Something moved in the space behind him.

Thunk.

Dally scrambled backward a step as the guard flopped facedown onto the floor, moaning. He rolled to one side, still scrabbling for his revolver. Dally turned her lamplight up and found herself face-to-face with a surprisingly clean-looking Jack. He lowered the long metal pipe he was carrying and grinned at them. "Well met," he said.

Eli lurched forward and snatched the guard's sidearm before his hand could find it. Then Pete supported Eli under the arms again, and they scooted past the flailing guard, who was now struggling back to his feet.

"Being friends with y'all isn't an easy gig," Jack muttered. "Let's blow this pop stand."

⋙ 33 ⋘

I t was nearing sunrise as they darted out of the dark confines of the jailhouse. The predawn streets around Welleston Harbor were nearly still. Signs of stirring came from within a few shops, and lanterns glowed in the windows of a bakery and a fishmonger's. They passed an occasional worker on foot or a cart headed toward the port.

Dally was prepared to sprint as fast as she could to get away from the jailhouse. But Eli's gait apparently did not allow for running. Pete held Eli's arm to steady him as they walked as quickly as possible. Dally's pulse pounded with the thrill and terror of the escape. Even the slow pace didn't calm her racing heartbeat. Being locked in that dark, reeking cell had been horrific—what would happen if they got caught now? Would they be sent back? Or something worse?

"Dal, love, what are you doing here?" Eli wondered, sounding slightly out of breath.

"Just a lucky coincidence?" Dally suggested. "I always hoped we'd see each other again."

"They don't usually put children in a place like that." Eli

paused, thoughtful. "Though you aren't as young as you look anymore, I suppose."

"I ended up here so I could save you," Dally said. "That's really the only explanation."

Eli put his free arm around her shoulder. "You did great."

"You need a wash," Dally told him, plugging her nose. "Bath first, hug later."

Eli laughed, withdrawing his arm. "Don't I know it. But I'd rather eat a bite or two. I'm starving."

"First we need to get out of sight," Pete corrected. As he spoke, a loud clanging bell sounded behind them.

"Oh, barnacles," Eli muttered. "That's the jailbreak alarm."

"Act casual," Jack declared as melodramatically as a character in an old movie. Dally would have giggled if the peril hadn't felt so very real.

Pete cast an urgent glance up and down the street. "We have to hide."

"I know a place." Jack led the others along the cobbled road, heading toward the water.

Walking as swiftly as Eli's strange gait allowed, they made their way to a cove a little down the coast. Dally went behind a boulder for privacy, then stripped and splashed and bathed until she felt clean. The fog lingered well beyond the waterline, but she still dressed quickly. Then she huddled close beside the rock and waited for Pete or Eli to call her out again.

Their voices drifted to her from across the barrier. "We can trust Jack and Dal," Eli was saying. "It's going to be fine."

"It would be easy to leave them behind," Pete answered. "We can find a place on land to disappear for a while. Lie low."

"I'd actually like them to know," Eli said. "But not until we're at sea. It'll be safer for all of us. That's where we belong."

"If you're sure." Pete sounded reluctant.

Eli laughed lightly. "Pretty sure this is going to be an all-hands situation. We might really need their help."

Dally sat very still, trying to hear more, but their voices went quiet. She did not dare go charging around the rocks to join them, lest Pete or Eli decide to share their news now and end the secret early.

Jack's face appeared over the top of the boulder. He waved. "I found some fruit trees nearby. You decent?"

Dally picked up a pebble-sized shell from the sand and threw it at him. "You ought to ask that *before* you poke your head over, doofus."

Jack's unapologetic grin warmed her, as sure as the sun on her salty-sandy skin. "I took a chance."

"The chance I'd take your head off?" Dally quipped.

"Among others," Jack said. "Come on, they're ready."

Dally ventured back around the boulder. Jack jumped down to meet her. She stepped a bit closer and hugged him around the middle. Even though it had been only a matter of weeks for her, for him it would have been four years. Perhaps he had missed her. It was thrilling to be back together with the crew, dodging danger and embracing adventure.

Jack seemed surprised by her affection. He patted her

shoulder awkwardly. "Good to see you, too," he said. Dally pulled away, feeling a little awkward herself. Maybe it wasn't quite proper for girls to randomly hug boys in, um . . . 1854, she recalled, according to the book spine.

Eli was sitting on a rock with his elbows planted on wide-spread knees and his head in his hands, while Pete climbed down from the boulder formation at the other edge of the cove.

"I could see most of the harbor from up there," Pete said. "It's all big ships. Nothing small enough for the four of us to manage."

"We can't sit around and wait," Eli said. "Too risky."

"Then we need a crew," Pete said.

"How?" Dally asked. The port and the city would soon be bustling with people, but how could you randomly ask even a few of them to get on a ship and sail away with you?

"Pirates always find a way," Eli muttered.

"How many people?" Jack wondered, ever practical.

"At least six to begin," Pete said. "We can pick up more along the way if we need to. Or look for a smaller ship." He offered a slight smile. Dally felt that rueful tug of his lips deep in her gut. All Pete and Eli wanted was to be left alone to live their lives somewhere safe, together. Why was that so much to ask? But Dally knew the answer. It was 1854. They were making the best of a tough situation. Like Grandpa always said, *It's up to you to find a way to live your best life, no matter what circumstances the world throws at you.*

"Six whole crew members?" Jack repeated. It seemed like a lot to Dally, too.

"I know how to spot the kind of people we need," Pete said. "Dal, stay with Eli, and Jack, you come with me. We'll find some food and some folks and meet you back here."

"No," Eli said, heaving himself up off the rock. "We're not going to sit idly by. We can help." Pete regarded him with uncertainty.

"At the very least, we should split up," Dally suggested. "They're looking for the two of you, so they're probably expecting you to be together. You two go ahead, and then Eli and I will follow." She tried to send a reassuring glance toward Pete, indicating that she could take care of Eli on her own. That they could go slow.

Pete did seem happier about this plan. "Very well. Let's meet back here at noon with whoever we find."

It was the logical suggestion, but Dally's heart blipped nervously. What if the fog followed Pete? She might need to stay close, although it now seemed the secret might be shared by Pete and Eli. Unless the secret had to do with their jailbreak? But there was no way to know that for sure.

As Pete walked away with Jack, he said, "If we're stopped, you need to do like you've seen Eli do, and pretend you own me."

"Got it," Jack replied, and they strode off.

Dally felt startled by the exchange. She turned to Eli. "Will people who see us think you *own* me?"

"Hopefully," Eli said. "It makes both of us safer if they do."

"Safer." Dally turned that idea over in her mind as they

headed back toward the city streets. She'd read about slavery in history class, but it was an uncomfortable lesson to see come to life before her eyes. In this place and time, most people who looked at her would see her as property? And assume she was *owned*? The thought made her skin crawl.

"People don't pay close attention when you fit their preconceived expectations." Eli waved thanks to a man with a cart who reined in his horse to allow the pair to cross the street. The man tapped his hat brim in response. "Like just now. If they see a man and his slave, it makes more sense to them than seeing two wandering . . . strangers. We become part of the backdrop. Let me lean on your arm now."

"Are you okay?" Dally asked. Eli sure didn't seem okay.

"I'll *be* okay," he said, huffing with every step. "Let's keep on."

The streets that had been empty an hour ago now bustled with early-morning life, as people—some brown-skinned, some white—went about their business. Everywhere Dally looked, she saw servitude: A Black man helping a white man into a carriage. A Black woman in a patchwork dress sweeping the stoop in front of a row house. Two Black women in head wraps lugging sloshing buckets around a corner.

"Pete was enslaved once, wasn't he?" Dally asked. The scars on his back looked like something out of a movie. Dally had the distinct feeling he had escaped from chains before. He must have been so brave, standing up against the law, against society, to make his own way in the world. It made her proud to know that such courage was part of her lineage.

"Yes, he used to be," Eli said. "We are opposites in that way, too."

Opposites. Dally pondered that statement. "Do you mean your family enslaved people?"

"Not in the past tense," Eli said. "We still own them today. About twenty or so, last I knew."

Eli dropped this number so casually, it took Dally aback. "Is that why you left?"

"I wish I was that virtuous," Eli admitted. "I left for other reasons. But I do support the cause of abolition, if that's what you're asking."

Dally felt relieved. It had never once occurred to her that Eli could have come from a plantation family. How odd.

"My ship will never be one of owners and slaves, but a place for all who desire to be free," Eli said. Then he corrected himself. "And by rights, I should say 'our' ship. Pete's and mine. You see, how old habits die hard?"

Dally didn't quite see. Could you love someone, and kiss them, and run away to sea with them, and still view them as not quite equal? The painful layers of racism ran deep.

The slow-walking pair made their way toward the market. There were bound to be a lot of people moving to and fro in that area.

"Are we looking for rough-and-tumble guys? Big muscles?" Dally asked. "Like the last crew?"

"No," Eli said. "We need a crew that we don't have to fight to control. No sleeping with one eye open, right?"

"So how—?"

"Just be with me," Eli said. "I'll know."

They stood at an intersection for a while, watching the morning crowds fill the market square. Then Eli nodded in one direction, and they moved down the block and ducked into an alley. "We can watch from here without being noticed much," he said.

They hung around for maybe an hour. People passed. There were women with shopping baskets. Men with thick wallets. Cooks with aprons. Vendors with wares on carts or in baskets. Small children darting around skirts, giggling and falling in the grass. Some of the marketgoers looked like workers: maids and housekeepers, nannies and grooms, craftsmen and smiths. Some could have been enslaved, buying on behalf of a household that wasn't their own. Some were dressed fancy, delighting in the goods as spectators, and chattering as though it was all a grand lark.

"Her," Eli said finally, nodding toward a dark-skinned woman in a ragged dress, lugging several wrapped parcels. She fretted as she walked, staring at the ground in front of her and speaking to herself as though trying to calm down.

They stepped out of the alley and followed the woman. She turned down the next block. She moved more quickly than Dally and Eli, and Dally wondered if they'd lose her. But when they turned the corner, she was there, standing outside a doorway, speaking with a white man. Or, more accurately, being yelled at by a white man. He now held the parcels she had brought and was thrusting more money into her hand, but he was not happy.

"I already told you to get pineapples, too!"

The woman held her head bowed. "The shops are out of them."

"Well, then go back and find some!" the white man yelled.

He grabbed the wrist that had the money and shook it, causing the woman's whole body to jerk forward by the shoulder. "Didn't you hear me?"

"Yessir, it's just—"

"Do as I say!" The white man shoved the woman hard, and she stumbled away from the door.

Eli nudged Dally. "Her. We want her. Go catch her."

"Pardon, miss?" Dally said, chasing after the woman. She caught up with her around the corner, out of sight of the man who'd issued her the errand.

"Yes?" Her dusty cheeks were marred with wet smudges, and yet she gazed at Dally with clear and patient eyes.

"My, um—" Dally couldn't bring herself to say "master," even for pretend. She motioned to Eli, limping toward them. "He would like to have a word with you."

The woman waited, looking a bit nervous. Eli was not dressed anywhere near as well as the man who'd given the errand, but he was still of a higher station than the woman.

"Is he always like that?" Eli said.

The woman's face flashed with uncertainty. "I—I'm not sure what you mean. Mr. Case is very good to me."

"You don't have to say that," Eli said. "Not to us."

The woman's gaze flicked between Eli and Dally. Perhaps it was noteworthy that he'd included Dally in an "us."

"Begging your leave, sir, but I have to get on with this errand for Mr. Case."

"What happens when you come back empty-handed?" Eli asked.

A shadow crossed her face. "I can't come back empty-handed." She looked at Dally. "Have you seen anyone selling pineapples in town today?"

Dally shook her head.

"We can give you a way out of here," Eli said. "If you come with us."

"We have a ship," Dally added, trying to be helpful.

"Please excuse me," the woman said, scurrying away.

"Barnacles!" Eli took off his cap and smacked it against his thigh in frustration, then carefully repositioned it. He gazed at Dally in despair. "This is never going to work. Not in Welleston."

≷34≸

W hy wouldn't she come with us?" Dally asked. "Life at sea has to be better than that Mr. Case."

"You think it's easy to trust a random stranger and walk away from your entire life? Everything familiar? Maybe she has family. A whole set of roots here that we don't understand."

Eli was right. Dally didn't understand. She considered the hesitation and fear in the woman's eyes. Dally herself was play-acting right now; it was impossible to know how it truly felt to be enslaved. When she read about this time in history, she always figured she'd be one of the people who chose to run away, to resist. But maybe that was thinking too simply. It certainly was more pleasant to believe that she'd have followed a conductor on the Underground Railroad, and maybe even become one herself, leading people to freedom like Harriet Tubman or Zebediah—

Dally's runaway train of thought screeched to a halt.

"Wait, I know a place," she said, squeezing Eli's arm. She looked around for a moment. In her mind she lay the map of modern-day Welleston over the streets where they stood. When she had her bearings, she added, "And it's not too far. Come with me."

She led Eli in the direction of the house she remembered. She'd learned of it, too, on her history class field trip. In her own time, it was a museum, a monument to the Underground Railroad. In the 1840s and '50s, a number of free Black people had occupied the house. There were no secret rooms, no root cellars—just a home from which it was common to see Black folks coming and going.

"What is this place?" Eli asked.

"A house of people of the type we're looking for," Dally said.

"You're certain?" Eli seemed skeptical. The house appeared nondescript. No different from the others in the row, apart from the distinctive mosaic chimney, which had been rebuilt after storm damage using remnant bricks acquired cheaply from various masons. In Dally's present, a drawing of the chimney was the museum's logo, the differing reds, browns, and tans representing the many shades of Black South Carolinians.

"One way to find out." Dally helped Eli settle on a neighboring stoop, then she marched up to the house and knocked.

A woman answered. "Yes?"

"I'm looking for someone named Zebediah," Dally said, digging for his last name in the depths of her memory. "Begging your pardon for the informality. I don't know his full name."

"He's out, I'm afraid," the woman answered.

"It's a matter of some delicacy," Dally said. She tried to make her words sound as formal and appropriate as possible. "I'm hoping for his assistance."

The woman studied Dally for a moment. "We specialize in delicate matters."

"That's what I'm told."

"Please come in," the woman said. "Zebediah—Mr. Douglas—will be home soon, I'm sure."

"I have three . . . friends," Dally said carefully. "We are looking for a quiet place to rest a bit."

The woman paused. "Who sent you?"

"Um," Dally said. She couldn't remember any other names from the tour. "I'd rather not say. I promised discretion, you see. I was told you'd appreciate that as well." *Discretion* was another of her vocabulary words. It meant respecting someone's privacy by not saying too much.

"Very well," the woman said. "Please bring your friends to the garden door." She pointed through the house toward the back. "Around dusk would be best."

The sun was still low in the sky and rising. "I appreciate the thought, but I'm not certain we can wait," Dally said. "Could I go get them now?"

"We welcome travelers at any time," the woman said. "At the garden door."

Dally nodded and thanked her, retreating to the sidewalk.

"It is the correct house," Dally told Eli. "We can get Pete and

Jack and we can all go there. They're part of the Underground Railroad."

"The what?" Eli said.

"They help people escape slavery," Dally said. "We can hide there until we collect a crew. Other runaways."

Eli seemed confused. "A house of runaways?"

Dally didn't know how to explain the Underground Railroad any better than that. And she shouldn't, out here in the open. Zebediah Douglas himself had never been caught, she knew, but not every person who took shelter with him had fared as well.

"You'll see," she promised. "Let's get Jack and Pete."

Eli touched his stomach. "I'd prefer to stay here and wait. You go get them."

That was concerning. "Are you sure? You'd be all alone, out in the open."

"People expect fugitives to be running. I'll barely be noticed if I'm sitting around. Go, Dal. I'll be fine."

Dally glanced around. To her surprise, the edge of the fog was nowhere in sight, so she darted through the streets of old Welleston, back to the rendezvous point. It was well before noon. She expected to have to wait, but there they were.

"Jack!" she called, racing up to them. "Pete!"

"Why are you alone? Where's Eli?" Pete grasped Dally's shoulders with urgency. "Is he all right?"

"He's okay. He wanted to rest. I'll take you to him." It hadn't escaped her notice that Jack and Pete were also alone. "You didn't find anyone either?"

Pete's face drooped with the same dejected expression Eli's had shown earlier. "It's hopeless," he said. "We're used to the pirates' ports, where everyone is looking for a new ride out of town."

Jack added, "We came back early to find you. We need a new plan."

"We have one," Dally reported. "Come on!"

The woman who met them at the garden door regarded Dally with concern. "These are your friends?" She cast suspicious looks at Jack and Eli. Of course. An Underground Railroad house would not be accustomed to welcoming white strangers.

"Conductors," Dally said simply. "Whose work is no longer secret, thanks to their last journey."

The woman hesitated a beat longer. Then she opened the door and allowed them entry. "I'm Eve," she said. "Please come in."

Dally and Pete went first, because Eve motioned to them first. They moved past her into a narrow hallway, wedged between the kitchen and a sitting room. Jack helped Eli in as Dally and Pete moved into the sitting room.

A dark-skinned woman in a simple dress stood near the front window, peering out at the street as though watching for something. Beside her, a lighter-skinned Black girl of about Dally's age sat on a footstool, leaning against the wall.

"Oh, hello," Dally said.

"Hi," said the girl.

The woman turned. Her fingers worried at her lips and chin. Waves of concern and distress radiated from her whole being. "Hello," she said.

Pete and Dally glanced at each other. Nothing was happening in the room, and yet it felt like they'd intruded on something.

Behind them, Eve spoke to Eli and Jack. "We know most of the like-minded in the region. But I don't know you. How far have you come?"

"You wouldn't believe how far," Jack said quietly.

"I grew up not long from here," Eli said. "But not close enough to know Welleston well."

"Men from around the state know Welleston and do business here," Eve countered, in a tone that challenged Eli's claim.

"I suppose," Eli murmured. "Your hospitality is appreciated, and in time, we can repay your generosity severalfold." That meant many times over, Dally knew. Pete and Eli might have lost their treasure once, but when they had a ship again, they could go back to the island for more. Maybe they'd use some of it to help free more enslaved people. Dally hoped so.

Eli edged past Eve into the sitting room. At the sight of him, the woman by the window emitted a small yelp and covered her face with her hands.

"They are our friends," Dally assured her. "Seeking refuge as well." Her words didn't seem to comfort the woman. So Dally tried again. "I'm Dal, and this is Pete, Eli, and Jack."

"I'm Mabel," said the girl Dally's age.

"My name is Amaryllis," the woman said after a pause.

"Pleased to make your acquaintance," Eli said. He moved toward a settee near the fireplace and sat down with a sigh of relief.

Amaryllis fiddled with her dress fabric. A small brown face poked out of her skirts: a child of perhaps two or three. The woman brushed her fingers over the toddler's head and whispered a few reassuring words. A little hand came up and gripped one of her fingers. Then the mother and child stared out the window again.

Mabel, in contrast, regarded the new arrivals with interest. They sat in a loose circle around the room. A fire crackled in the fireplace. Dally watched the smoke rise from the wood and mingle with the fog where it danced at the edge of the room.

"No sign of him?" Eve asked of Amaryllis.

"No," said the woman at the window. "But it's early yet."

"You do understand—you can't stay here much longer," Eve said. "This is a stopping point, not a boardinghouse." She seemed to be speaking to Amaryllis, but her gaze was on Jack and Eli.

Amaryllis nodded, a deep distress in her eyes.

"We won't be staying long," Eli said, answering the question that wasn't asked. "But we could do with some food, if you have any to spare."

Eve nodded. "We'll have ham and bean soup for lunch."

Pete's stomach growled audibly.

Eve's stern face softened into a compassionate smile. "I'll

set it to heat now. And perhaps some biscuits would also be in order."

Mabel got to her feet. "I can help."

The air in the room settled back to a relieved stillness among the four friends, punctuated by Amaryllis's nervous watchfulness.

"Are you waiting for someone?" Eli asked. He leaned back against the settee, studying Amaryllis through barely open eyes.

"My husband," Amaryllis said. "We had to leave the plantation at different times, to avoid suspicion. But something happened. He's been delayed."

"How long have you been here?" Dally asked.

"Nearly three weeks." Amaryllis sighed. "They're growing impatient with me. As is our friend Mabel." Amaryllis shook her head. She stroked her toddler's curls. "Mabel led my daughter and me here. She's been kind enough to wait all this time, but she was expecting us to move on sooner."

"So you don't even know if your husband's coming?" Jack asked.

"He's only delayed," Amaryllis insisted. "We planned to leave on the day Mr. Brunning was departing for a trip. We hoped it meant we wouldn't be missed immediately. I got out first, but then there was a change of plans, and Mr. Brunning ended up taking Buck with him. By the time I found out, it was too late for me to go back. I'm sure he'll still meet us here, once they return."

"You could come with us," Pete suggested. "We can leave word here of a time when we'll circle back to Welleston. Your husband could meet us then."

Amaryllis shook her head. Dally didn't blame her. In a time without technology like telephones or email, it was impossible to guarantee ever finding Buck again if she left their prearranged meeting place.

"Have many others passed through here in the last three weeks?" Eli asked. They were looking for a crew of six, after all.

"No," Amaryllis said.

Dally sighed. Her brilliant plan may not have been so brilliant after all.

After lunch, Jack and Pete ventured out on their own again. In mid-afternoon, they came rushing back into the house. "There's a new ship arriving in the harbor," Jack announced. "Much smaller. We could sail it for sure. The four of us."

"Six would be better," Pete said, looking at Amaryllis. "You truly could come with us. And you have our word—we'll return for Buck as soon as we can."

But Amaryllis was fairly cemented to the windowsill, her child now asleep at her feet.

"What about you?" Dally asked, turning to Mabel. They actually looked somewhat alike, Dally thought, with their light skin and twin braids that had seen smoother days.

Mabel shook her head. "I have to stay with Amaryllis."

"Are you both sure?" Eli struggled to his feet. "In an hour or so, we'll be sailing out of that harbor, bound anywhere we want to go. Do you sail?"

"I've never even been on a boat. I don't expect I would ever want to," Amaryllis said. She looked to Mabel, who raised one shoulder.

"We'll teach you to sail, won't we, Eli?" Dally said.

"Absolutely. You'll be working the rigging in no time, and— whoa." Eli gasped, bending forward a bit and clutching at his belly. He blew out air in a series of little puffs, resting one hand on his knee and the other on his lower back.

Amaryllis looked Eli up and down, then tilted her head and studied him a moment longer. Eli blew out another set of rough breaths, and Amaryllis's expression transformed. "Wait. Are you . . . ?"

"Don't say it out loud," Eli gasped.

"But you're . . ."

"Don't say it." Eli stretched out his fingers. Amaryllis grasped them. "But you could help, couldn't you?" he added.

Amaryllis nodded but pulled her hand away. She cast a nervous glance out the window.

Dally wondered for a moment at the meaning of this exchange. Whatever was wrong with Eli must be very serious. But the urgency of the ship coming in took precedence.

"Those of us who are going need to go right now," Pete said.

Jack rubbed his hands together. "One way or another, the *Celadon* is about to be ours."

"The *Celadon*?" Amaryllis echoed. "That's Mr. Brunning's

boat. He's back?" Her worried preoccupation faded and she leaped to her feet. "I will come," she announced. "Buck will be with him!"

There was a brief moment of hustle and bustle as everyone got ready to leave. No one had much in the way of things to pack. Amaryllis had one small burlap pouch that she slung over her shoulder, but Pete, Jack, and Eli had no bags at all. Neither did Mabel, it seemed.

"In the middle of the afternoon?" Eve fretted. "You'll be in full view."

"They'll be with me," Eli said. "No one will bother us."

"Yes, I suppose that does change things," Eve said. The woman clearly was not used to having a white person be part of the process.

Eli straightened, though his brow remained tinged with beads of sweat. "Come on, then."

≷ **36** ≶

They made their way toward the harbor. Pete, Jack, and Mabel walked ahead, while Dally and Amaryllis helped Eli. They went slowly enough that the toddler walked along beside them, clutching her mother's skirts and sucking her thumb. Dally grew more and more concerned about Eli's condition, but he seemed convinced that getting out to sea would solve everything.

"You're going to love life at sea," Eli told Amaryllis. His voice lit up in spite of the pain. "You'll be free."

"Being a pirate can't be much better than being a fugitive," the woman said nervously. "It sounds about as dangerous."

"I'm the captain of this particular pirate crew," Eli said. "It is what we make it."

Amaryllis nodded.

"It's amazing," Dally agreed. She, too, was thrilled at the prospect of getting back on a ship with Jack, Pete, and Eli.

Eli let out a sharp cry. He slammed his fist into his mouth to muffle it. Dally felt a light splash of water on her ankles, as if Eli's poncho had suddenly begun to drip.

"What . . . ?"

Amaryllis and Eli exchanged a look of alarm.

"It's not going to be much longer now," Amaryllis said. "We should have stayed at the house."

Eli looked squarely at Dally. "I have many secrets," he said. "You are about to learn the biggest of them all."

Dally accepted this with a simple nod. Secrets were par for the course. She refrained from asking any questions, as she hoped a bit more time might pass before she had to go home.

They caught up with the others near the section of the harbor where small and mid-size boats came in. It was much less crowded here than the areas where the larger ships docked. That was a relief.

Pete and Jack stood behind a stack of crates and boxes, staring out at the water. Mabel had climbed up on a barrel in order to get a better view. In front of them, a long, wide wooden pier jutted out into the harbor. Several rowboats and dinghies were docked along the far end of it.

Pete took one glance at Eli's face. "It's happening?"

Eli nodded. "Let's steal that ship."

"Excellent," Mabel whispered. The girl sounded enthused, which was exactly how Dally felt herself. The stakes were incredibly high, and the threat of being caught only heightened the excitement. They *had* to make it to sea. For Pete and Eli, escape meant life or death. Probably for Mabel and Amaryllis, too.

But Amaryllis pushed her child behind her. Her hesitation was painted clearly on her face.

"A few sins in exchange for our freedom," Pete said. He held out his chain-scarred wrists, as if to say, *I've been where you are.*

Eli grasped Amaryllis's arm. "How badly do you want to make your own way in the world? For people like us, this is the cost."

Amaryllis nodded, her eyes shadowed with fear, but she blinked it away. She tossed her head and raised her chest. "All told," she said, "the price they'll pay for what they do is higher."

"Is Buck in the rowboat?" Pete asked.

"Yes." Amaryllis began describing him.

The fog loomed at the edge of the dock. Dally couldn't see the rest of the harbor or the rowboat Pete had referred to. She worried she'd be leaving before she could see her friends safely to their new ship. At least with Mabel and Amaryllis, they'd still have enough people to sail it.

Eli groaned as if the world were ending. Jack blinked at him in alarm. Dally looked at Eli. His crouched posture, the spasms of pain every few minutes . . . it was much like something she'd seen on TV, although . . .

"Dal, you and Jack get that rowboat ready," Pete said, nudging her forward. "We'll get Eli."

"I'll come," Mabel said. "Buck will recognize me."

Jack scampered off down the pier. Dally followed him, and Mabel followed her.

"Let's not go too far from Pete and Eli," Dally said, keeping her eye on the fog.

"They're right behind us." Jack led the way. They moved

among barrels and crates, looking for a good vantage point. As they went, the fog pushed out to sea, expanding its circle such that Dally could breathe a little easier. Now she could see what everyone had been talking about.

The fog receded nearly out of view, all the way to the mouth of Welleston Bay. The water glittered in the afternoon light. Nearly two dozen ships of varying sizes stood anchored out past the shallows of the bay. A beautiful sight.

Dally drew a deep breath of the coastal breeze. The sea felt both like home and as if it could carry her anywhere.

"Third from the end," Jack said, pointing at a vessel anchored about fifty yards offshore. The smallest in the row. "Definitely sailable with our crew."

Between the sailing ship and the dock, a rowboat was headed their way. Dally counted four Black men rowing, a fifth steadying the luggage, and one well-fed and pompous-looking white man along for the ride. He wore sailor's breeches but otherwise seemed out of place, as though he'd never trimmed a sail in all his life.

"We're really stealing his ship?" Dally whispered, her heart in her throat. It was one thing to ride a stolen craft out of necessity while inside Pete or Eli's secret, but it felt odd to actually steal one. Her fingers pulsed with tension. Was this how Marcus had felt at the jewelry counter, waiting for the perfect moment when the clerk turned his back? Had his whole body thrummed with anticipation? Had he felt more alive than ever before?

Dally glanced at Pete, who motioned them forward. She

supposed she and Marcus came by their love of adventure honestly. But it wasn't fun and games this time, Dally reminded herself. This might be Pete and Eli's only chance to escape their fate.

Dally tiptoed ahead, dodging the barrels and crates. "Guess we're really stealing a ship," she mumbled, a smidge of guilt sneaking up on her excitement.

Jack grinned. "It's not like we haven't done it before . . ."

Dally rolled her eyes. "I think you enjoy all this just a little too much." She refrained from reminding him that she hadn't always been part of their crew, and thus had *not* actually done this before.

"You're one to talk," Jack muttered as they scuttled along the pier. "Tell me you're not having the time of your life right now."

Dally smacked his shoulder. She was, in fact, but that was beside the point. Saving Pete and the others was all that mattered. A ship was probably the least of what this Mr. Brunning owed to Amaryllis and Mabel.

"Let's do this thing."

⋙ 37 ⋘

The rowboat arrived at the dock, and one of the enslaved men hopped out to cleat its bow line. Then the portly white man disembarked. He stretched and sighed and looked back at the ship at anchor with pride and a touch of wistfulness. The others clambered out after him, lugging along a valise and a trunk, in addition to their own paltry canvas pouches.

"By God, the sea air is bracing," said the portly man, patting his vest as he walked. He waved at one of his men. "You there. Find me the harbormaster so I can give him a piece of my mind about our anchorage."

"Yessir." The man scurried off ahead of the group. Two others took up the ends of the trunk and followed him. Dally raised her eyebrows at Mabel, silently asking if one of those three men was Buck, but Mabel shook her head.

"Don't they know who I am?" the white man grumbled. "The least they could do is send someone down to greet me when I return."

"Mr. Brunning, we weren't due back until—"

"Did I ask for your opinion?"

"No, sir."

Dally, Jack, and Mabel waited until only two men remained near the rowboat.

"That's Buck," Mabel whispered, nodding at one of the men.

The trio stepped out from behind some barrels and wound around the pilings. Dally tried to imitate Jack's casual saunter.

Buck stretched his arms, rolled his shoulders, and gazed at the horizon for a moment. He was both stockier and taller than Pete, but had similar dark skin and gentle ways of moving.

The other man coiled the end of the last rope and laid it flat on the dock beside the cleat.

"You there," Jack said. "Brunning called for you. Git on and see what he wants."

Buck turned then. His eyes widened as he spied Mabel.

"Yessir." The other man picked up the valise, skirted around them, and started down the pier. Mabel went toward Buck, who greeted her with a hand on her shoulder.

"That can't be all there is to it." Dally surveyed their surroundings. She came from a world of power locks, security systems, and surveillance cameras.

"Don't jinx us," Jack said. "It ain't over till it's over." He knelt down and prepared to untie the rowboat once everyone was on board.

"Beg pardon, master, but that's Mr. Brunning's boat," Buck said, his tone balanced somewhere between sharp and deferential. He was speaking to a white man, after all.

"Well, we're taking it, Buck," Mabel said. She knelt at the

other end of the boat and began untying it. There was no time to waste. She expertly wrapped up the line before Dally could even suggest it. Then she held it tight to keep the rowboat from drifting as the others boarded.

Pete and Amaryllis came huffing down the dock, Eli supported between them.

"Buck!" Amaryllis burst forward and tossed herself into the man's arms. Their embrace was firm, faces buried in each other's necks.

Pete climbed into the rowboat first and reached out to steady Eli. When they were both settled, Mabel picked up the toddler and handed her to Pete, who in turn placed her in Eli's grasp. The little girl whimpered at the separation from her mother.

Buck held Amaryllis tight. "What are you doing here? Why haven't you gone north?"

"We're leaving now," Amaryllis told him. "We were waiting for you."

"Leaving?" Buck echoed.

Mabel eased into the rowboat like a pro. She kept her hand on the dock, holding it steady.

"Mama!" the toddler cried.

"I'm coming, Daisy," Amaryllis cooed, gathering her skirts.

Realization dawned on Buck. "We can't just sail off in Mr. Brunning's ship," he said. "That's not how things work." He cupped Amaryllis's face in his hands, turning her toward him. "It's not right."

"Free is right," she whispered, placing a hand gently on his wrist. "Like we always imagined. Daisy growing up free?"

Buck shook his head.

"There's no time," Eli said. "The others could be back at any moment. Fight us, join us, or let us go." His voice sounded strong and authoritative. "Everyone who's going needs to be in this boat. Right noooooow." The final syllable turned into one of his long, strained cries.

The toddler whimpered.

"Did you change your mind?" Amaryllis whispered. "Because I didn't." She released Buck's hand with a gentle and final "Please." She climbed into the boat and scooped the child up. "Mama's here, Daisy. Mama's here."

"I can't let you do this," Buck said.

"This is our way out," Amaryllis said. "It's different than we planned, but it's a good plan."

"Running on our own, we have a chance," Buck said. "But if we take his ship, there's no way he won't hunt us. We'll be caught."

"We could be caught either way," Amaryllis said. "I've had three weeks to think about the worst that can happen. This is far from the worst."

Pete motioned for Dally and Jack to board the boat. To Buck, he said, "Either send up the alarm or get in."

Dally went first. She grabbed up an oar and showed Amaryllis how to do the same.

"He won't send them after us," Amaryllis whispered. "He'll come along. He has to. Like we wanted."

"Stop," Buck said.

"Want me to punch you?" Jack offered. "I can make it look good. Then you can say we overpowered you."

Buck stood silent. Jack shrugged and hopped into the boat, holding the bow line as he went.

Dally, Mabel, Amaryllis, and Jack rowed as Pete pushed them away from the dock.

"I love you," Amaryllis said, gazing up at Buck. "I'm sorry."

If he said anything in response, Dally didn't hear it, because the secret moved out to sea and Buck was consumed by the fog.

38

Amaryllis wept softly as they rowed. She seemed to be applying her feelings to the oar as well. Rowing to match her took all of Dally's strength. With each pull, her mind echoed a single question: *Why?* Try as she might, Dally couldn't understand why someone would choose not to run from slavery when given the chance. She could no longer see Buck because of the fog, so she tried to imagine his expression. Sad? Angry? Scared? When she glanced over her shoulder toward their destination, she could see Brunning's ship but not much more. Soon she'd be sailing into the fog; she hoped it would shift and dissipate in time. She supposed that to Buck, the life Pete and Eli promised looked like nothing but fog as well, the other side a mystery too scary to contemplate. *The devil you know beats the devil you don't*—wasn't that the saying?

"Dada?" Little Daisy drummed her fists on her mother's legs. Then she waved up at the sky. "Bye, Dada!"

Suddenly, Buck appeared as if from nowhere in Dally's view. His body arced through the air as he dove into the water. He disappeared into the blue for a moment, then surfaced, arms propelling him toward them.

Was Buck coming to stop them or join them?

They had almost reached Brunning's ship. Its hull rocked into Dally's peripheral vision, and she angled her oar to keep from striking the wood.

The rowboat glided alongside the hull until the rope ladder to the deck came into reach. Jack stuck a hand out and caught one of the lower rungs. Bow line in hand, he clambered up to the deck, then cleated the line. Amaryllis slung Daisy across her chest and instructed her to hold tight. She climbed up onto the deck. Dally went next, carrying the rowboat's stern line. Then Mabel.

Eli stifled another cry by biting his knuckles.

"Up!" Pete said, hauling Eli toward the ladder. They climbed with urgency. Amaryllis and Dally helped Eli flop over the rail. He lay on the deck, moaning. His poncho flopped aside and bunched up under his arms, revealing his stomach, which looked like a basketball. The sight of it distracted Dally long enough that Jack suddenly appeared beside her.

"Hoist it up!" he shouted.

Spurred back into action, Mabel and Dally helped Jack raise the rowboat into its place at the side of the ship. Pete bent over the rail and began to pull up the rope ladder just as Buck splashed up.

He treaded water somewhat poorly below. "Please," he begged. "Let me up. Amaryllis . . . that's my family."

Pete dropped the ladder and Buck clambered aboard.

The ship needed three hands, at least, to sail. It went somewhat faster with five. Pete took the helm while Jack, Buck, Mabel, and Dally raised the sails and then the anchor. Mabel seemed to know what to do at sea, responding to their commands without much instruction. Pete shouted directions as he eased the ship through the harbor. Eli was out of commission, lying flat on the deck, with Amaryllis ministering to him.

As Dally ran past to trim the mainsail, Amaryllis had one of her hands on Eli's huge belly and the other out of sight somewhere between Eli's legs. She was saying, "Nearly four fingers. It's almost time. I can feel the head. You're doing great."

The head? Dally gasped in amazement. Could it be?

She adjusted the mainsail, then looked back. Eli was sweating and cursing. He came up on his elbows. His knees were raised, and Amaryllis knelt between them.

"I have to push," Eli grunted. "I can push now?"

"Yes," Amaryllis said. "Couple big breaths and then go."

The ship bounced over the waves that broke along the barrier islands, but Dally had lost all interest in sailing. She moved toward Eli, kneeling beside his shoulder and taking his hand.

"Eli . . ." Dally breathed. "Oh, my goodness."

His words from earlier floated back to her. *I have many secrets. You are about to learn the biggest of them all.*

Eli screamed and threw his head back. Amid the pounding rush of the waves and the wail of gulls, a new sound rose up.

"That's it," Amaryllis cooed. "You did it." Eli's cries were joined by those of the tiny babe now in Amaryllis's arms.

Clouds parted. Late-afternoon sun stroked over them. It was as if the fog had lifted entirely, and the world was bathed in light.

"Eli?" Dally blurted out. "Are you a girl?"

Eli smiled through exhaustion. "Well, I wouldn't go that far," he said. "I've been Eli a long time and I like it better that way. But . . ." Eyes still closed, he offered a two-fingered mock salute. "Eli, formerly Eliza, at your service."

A rush of things suddenly made sense to Dally: Eli's initial tenderness toward her, the knowing ways he'd taught her to hide her girlness.

"Dally, take him so I can attend to Eli," Amaryllis said, lifting the squalling baby toward her.

"Pete should hold him first, don't you think?" Dally said, scooting away. She had never held a newborn, and wasn't sure she wanted to start at sea. She kept on scooting until she was beside Pete at the helm. "I've got this," she said. "Go on."

Pete willingly gave over the wheel. Dally sighed with relief. Being handed a sailboat to steer, even one this big, felt more comfortable than being handed a brand-new, slimy human. Especially given that she was inside a secret that could end at any moment.

Amaryllis set the infant into Pete's arms. The tiny boy was newborn pale at present, but he would likely grow to be a little bit lighter than Pete and quite a bit darker than Eli.

"Look at all those curls," Eli cooed, reaching out to touch the baby's forehead.

Pete laughed. "Maybe we'll have to call him Curly."

As Pete admired his newborn son, Dally marveled at the power of what she was witnessing. Somewhere down the line, perhaps little Curly would have a son of his own. And that son would have a son, who would have Dally's father, Marcus. Or would Curly be one of Marcus's great-great-great-grandparents? Dally didn't know enough about Marcus's side of the family to be certain how many generations back Curly would be found.

Dally looked to the horizon, her hand on the wheel of the stolen vessel. She smiled, because she'd been right. Pete and Eli were in love, and they were *both* her ancestors, and it had to be a secret, if not entirely for the reason she'd thought. She was also pleased that Buck and Amaryllis were reunited, their own little girl tucked between them.

Jack settled beside her, resting his arm across her shoulders. "Would you look at that?" he whispered. "One big happy family."

Dally smiled and leaned into the friendly side hug. She didn't know how much longer she'd be here, but for this moment, at least, it felt like everything was going to be okay.

≋ 39 ≋

The new crew came together quite nicely. Dally had never given much thought to things like destiny or fate, but sailing free with Pete, Eli, Amaryllis, Buck, Mabel, and Jack was a kind of perfection she'd never known to imagine.

The ship was both smaller and nicer than the one they'd sailed with the rougher crew. There was no formal captain's quarters, but there was one small bedroom with a door plus comfortable berths for six in the hold. It still didn't have a bathroom, but everyone was good about using the buckets and emptying them promptly. Amaryllis was neater about the cooking than Doughy had been, so things down below stayed in pretty good condition.

Eli remained in charge, more or less, but there wasn't really a need for a captain when everyone got along and wanted the same things out of the journey—*not* to pirate but to sail for the treasure and build quiet lives somewhere. Perhaps they could settle on the very island they'd discovered, calm, hidden from traffic, tucked away within the safety of the shoals where the roughest of sailors often feared to tread. They'd be starting from nothing, but with access to all the money, they could make supply runs back to any port of their choosing.

They charted a course for a port down the coast, where it would be safe to stock up. That evening, Pete and Buck lay on the deck under the stars, making a list of things they'd need for the first run. Eli held Curly to his breast while Amaryllis steered the ship, each offering advice to the other about how to improve their skills at the task. Daisy sat propped up between Mabel's feet, drumming on her toes.

When Curly was full and milk-sleepy, Eli handed him over to Jack. Dally took Daisy by the hand, and they brought the littles down into the cabin. Jack held and bounced Curly, and Daisy snuggled into Dally's lap. She whispered a simple bedtime story, one that Grandpa had told her a hundred times or more.

When Daisy's eyes drooped shut, Dally lay the toddler down in one of the lower bunks and raised the net Pete had fashioned to keep her from rolling out if the boat rocked.

Curly's tiny round face was slack, dark eyelashes brushing his brown cheeks. "He's asleep, too," she told Jack.

"I know. I didn't want to put him down yet," Jack said. "He feels so nice."

Dally pulled out Curly's blanket-lined crate and tucked the edges of the fabric smooth. She spread out the scrap of cloth designated for his swaddle, and Jack laid him gently on it. Working carefully, they wrapped the newborn up snugly the way Amaryllis had taught them. Then they stood watching him sleep.

"He looks different already," Jack said. "How is that possible? It's only been a few days."

"He's growing," Dally said. "People say babies grow fast. Anyway, everyone changes over time, right?"

Jack winked at her. "Do they?"

Dally looked at him. Pete and Eli had commented on her unchanged appearance, but Jack had said nothing about it up until now. "Yes, of course."

"Sure," he said. "Okay. Nothing unusual going on here at all. Gotcha."

The secretive lilt in his tone made Dally say something she shouldn't. "Why do *you* look the same?" she mused. "It's been four years."

"Four years?" Jack echoed, like it surprised him. "Then I could ask you the same question, I guess."

"It's a secret." Dally spoke slowly. "You?"

"Also secret. I opened a book, or something."

"You . . . you . . . Have you been to the library?"

Jack shrugged. "A secret is a secret."

"When did you come from?" Dally blurted out, unable to stop herself. But she managed to keep her voice to a whisper.

"It's 1960," Jack said. "You?"

No wonder he seemed old-fashioned yet not entirely like he belonged. "Um, 2024," Dally told him.

Jack whistled low. "Dang skippy? You're from the future?"

"So are you, technically." Dally patted the hull. "We're in the same boat."

"Har, har. Twenty-first-century humor leaves something to be desired."

Dally smacked his shoulder. Her mind flooded with questions for Jack, about the library, about the place and time he'd come from, but she knew she couldn't ask. Moments of privacy like this were always fleeting. In the close quarters of the ship, there could easily be someone listening. She fought her excitement at this new revelation, the thrill of the library and the adventures suddenly matched by the thrill of having a fellow traveler.

≋40≋

When Dally landed back in the reading room, she rushed out to tell Jennacake.

"There was some other guy in there from here!"

"Some other guy?" Jennacake echoed.

Dally tried to restrain herself but couldn't. As Jennacake prepared her cup of tea, Dally continued. "Another patron. Someone who read the same secret before me."

"Or after you," Jennacake clarified. "It could go either way."

"No," Dally said. "He told me when he was from."

Jennacake frowned. "You talked about the library?"

"Sort of. It came up."

"You're not supposed to talk about the library. Especially not inside a secret."

"I didn't know that rule," Dally said. "I never even knew that could happen—someone else being there who'd make me even want to."

Jennacake looked troubled. "It's unusual, but not unheard of."

"He lived a long time ago," Dally said. "The library must be pretty old."

"Ancient." Jennacake settled on a stool by the reference desk. She rested her arms on the wood, looking thoughtful. "There have always been secrets, so there has always been a place where secrets go."

"Like a vault?" Dally said, remembering the notes and warnings the library had given on the first day she visited. "Did the library used to be something else?"

Jennacake trailed her fingers through her long brown hair. "I wish I could answer all your questions, my dear. Some things are beyond me. But I do know that the library changes. Things are always changing." She tipped her face toward the atrium ceiling, seeming troubled again.

"Are you okay?" Dally asked. When the librarian didn't answer, Dally said, "Would you like a cup of tea?"

Jennacake smiled. "I have a better idea."

She led Dally behind the curtain that protected the librarian's own secrets. At the back of the nook, there was a door. Jennacake pushed through it, emerging into a small apartment. Everything was neat and beautifully decorated. There was a bedchamber, a bathroom, and a sitting room lined with traditional books. Dally couldn't explain how she knew they were ordinary books, not secret volumes, but she did. Some of them appeared to be for entertainment—novels and comics and all kinds of books with pictures. Others seemed more scholarly, like encyclopedias and atlases and resource tomes. On the coffee table, for example, was a colorful volume titled *Fashion by the Decade*.

"This is where you live?" Dally asked.

"For nearly as long as I can remember," Jennacake said. "But what I really wanted to show you is this."

She pulled a curtain at the far side of the sitting room, revealing a sliding glass door. It led to a small patio. Dally followed Jennacake out into the sunshine. The yard had grass, decorative stones, and a miniature pond with a waterfall. It was a calming space, very pleasant. At the edge of the yard was a copse of trees, though they seemed a bit blurry, with nothing but a gray mist behind.

"Are we still in the library?" Dally asked.

"Yes," Jennacake said. "This is where I come when I need a breath of fresh air." The courtyard was lovely, like everything in the library, but Jennacake's wistful tone sparked questions for Dally.

"Only here? Instead of going outside?"

"The librarian is always on duty, you see. Patrons arrive at all hours."

Dally considered this revelation. "Does that mean you can never leave?"

"I'm afraid not." Jennacake's smile was tinged with emotion. "The library is my home now. I'm quite lucky to have landed in such a beautiful place, don't you think?"

The library was, indeed, stunningly beautiful. Every time Jennacake opened a new door to her, Dally found fresh wonders to behold. It certainly seemed like a place a person could be happy to live.

Dally squinted toward the bright-blue sky. "But the sun isn't real?"

"Do you feel its warmth on your skin?" Jennacake asked.

"Yes," Dally said.

"Then it's real enough, isn't it?"

Dally wasn't sure. But the light clop of hooves distracted her. "Oh, my," she cried as a short, stout goat ambled up to her. "Who is this?"

"I call this one Abe," Jennacake said, scratching the goat between his ears. He bleated happily. "He's one of our last surviving scapegoats."

Abe flapped his ears at Dally. She giggled. "Can I pet him?"

"Of course," Jennacake said.

Abe's fur was soft and warm, yet after one brief touch, Dally yanked her hand back. "Whoa," she said. "When I pet him, I feel . . . I mean, I *know* all these things . . ." Dally shook her head, not sure quite what to say.

"Do you know what a scapegoat is?" Jennacake asked.

"Someone who gets blamed for something they didn't do," Dally said.

"That's how we use the word today. In ancient times, people whispered their sins to a literal goat, like Abe here, then sent the goat into the wilderness. They believed their secrets would be safe and that they would be absolved of guilt."

"And all those secrets came to the library?"

Jennacake's laugh twinkled like the sunlight. "All those goats came here, anyway. There was a flock of hundreds, but that was a very long time ago. Now we have only six."

Dally drew up her courage and petted Abe again. She was suffused with images, emotions. Her mind flashed over the crimes—small and large—and guilt of a long-ago people.

"You once told me that secrets aren't meaningful unless you know the people involved," Dally said. "But these feel meaningful to me. Is that because of Abe?"

Jennacake was silent for a moment. Then she said, "I'm glad you remember the small things I've told you. I'm really quite pleased to be getting to know you, Delilah Peteharrington."

"I'm pleased to be getting to know you, too," Dally said. "Jennacake . . . Hey, you never did tell me what your whole name is."

"I'm afraid that's one of my secrets now, dear," the librarian answered. "Isn't that funny?"

"Quite," Dally said. Jennacake made a clicking sound with her tongue, and Abe trotted off toward the misty trees. Dally smiled after the goat, taking one last look at the courtyard. Was there no end to the library's quirks and surprises?

≫ 41 ≪

Mr. Jerry was on the phone when Dally got back to the car. "Yes, ma'am," he was saying in a deferential tone. "No, ma'am. Of course, ma'am. Will do."

He met Dally's glance in the rearview and raised his eyebrows. That one look, and she sank back into the plush leather seat, closed her eyes, and groaned. Mr. Jerry had a very expressive face.

He finished the call and buzzed the divider farther down. "Uh, Miss Delilah—"

"Busted?" she asked.

"And rightly so, it seems," Mr. Jerry confirmed.

Dally handed him his cupcake through the gap. He took it silently and steered the large car toward Peteharrington Place without another word. This time, he pulled straight on into the driveway.

"Shoulda known something wasn't right," he said as he parked in front of the large double doors.

Breaking his trust was a sad thing, a difficult thing, and Dally felt sure she should be regretting it. But she didn't. She would hate to do anything to hurt Mr. Jerry, of course, but the discovery of the library was very much worth the transgression. She felt rather bad about not feeling bad, though, which was funny. "I hope I haven't caused you too much trouble, Mr. Jerry," Dally said, and she meant it.

"Why did you lie to me?" he asked. "I trusted you, so it never occurred to me to check up on this arrangement."

Since she had lied before, it felt important to give an honest answer now. "Some things are worth breaking all the rules," Dally said. "Don't you think so?"

Mr. Jerry shook his head. "I s'pose. But no cupcake is that good, baby girl."

"Oh, Mr. Jerry. It was never about the cupcakes, I'm afraid."

Dally got out of the car, dragging her backpack and carrying her cupcake wrapper. She tugged open the large front doors. Usually she went in through the kitchen, but today the main entrance was unlocked and ready for her.

Dally entered the cool, airy foyer, a space she rarely used. Her mother stood on the landing, halfway up the wide marble staircase that curved toward the library and sitting rooms. Dally wished she could drop her things, race up the stairs, and disappear into her wing, which was tucked down the corridors beyond the east sitting room.

She settled for dropping her things—her backpack and the crumby ball of her cupcake wrapper—right there on the front hall tile. Grandpa would have looked at her with disappointment if he'd seen her do such a thing. Just because the

Peteharringtons *had* household staff to pick up after them was no excuse for taking advantage of it, he always said. Her mother's eyes merely flicked down to the mess, then back up to Dally's face.

A powerful angry-sad feeling surged through Dally's stomach and chest. She stood with her fists on her hips, staring up at her mother. Between them, in the air, hung the delicate antique-glass chandelier, dangling by its impossibly thin chain.

"Delilah." Her mother turned and walked up the stairs.

Her tone said *Follow me*, so Dally trudged up the twenty-six stairs and trailed behind her mother into the west sitting room. Her mother sat down on one of the uncomfortable-looking armchairs in a half circle of furniture that was normally for grown-ups only.

"Do you care to explain yourself?"

"No," Dally said, tossing herself onto the thin-cushioned, straight-backed sofa and crossing her arms. She barely refrained from kicking her heels up onto the polished wooden coffee table. Rebellious was more than a mood right now—it was everything under her skin.

"Is there anything you'd like to tell me?" Dally's mother said.

Dally raised her eyebrows. "Pretty sure you already found out." She knew better than to confess before hearing the charges. Exactly how much did her mother actually know of what she'd been doing?

"You've been using Mr. Jerry without permission."

"Yes," Dally said. "He's nice to me and a very good driver."

"Do you know how expensive each car service ride is?" her mother asked.

Dally tossed her head, wishing she had the kind of hair that would flow dramatically as she did so. "We can afford it."

"*I* can afford it," her mother corrected. "*You* need permission."

"You wouldn't let me join Adventure Club," Dally blurted out.

Her mother blinked. "What does that have to do with anything?"

"So I found something else to do. Something that fits within my hour. But it's driving distance away."

"That's not a sufficient explanation for this behavior."

Dally pinned her lips together.

"Delilah Peteharrington, do you really think you can get in a *car* and go where you please without asking?"

"Well, we know what happens when I ask, don't we? You say no."

"I'm responsible for your safety, Delilah."

Not *I love you*. Not *I'm worried*. Just *responsible*.

Dally sat up straight. "You don't care about my safety," she snapped. "You care about me spending your money."

Her mother leaned back an inch.

Dally couldn't stop herself. "You haven't asked where I go, or why it's important, or anything!"

Her mother folded her hands, lacing her fingers so tightly her knuckles turned white. "I trust Mr. Jerry," she said. "His account of your activities didn't leave me concerned about your whereabouts, only your impudence." She frowned. "Are you doing something dangerous?"

It was Dally's fault that she'd opened this line of questioning, and now she wasn't sure how to get out of it without a lie.

"How did you even find out?" Dally said, changing the subject entirely.

"Credit cards have bills, you know," her mother said. "Monthly statements of the recent expenses. Surely you've covered this in your finance lessons?"

"Oh." She should have known it was too good to be true. Too good to last. "I didn't think you looked at those."

"Well, I don't. My staff—" Dally's mother rubbed her forehead. "I'm paying your tutor, for what?" she muttered. "Businesses have budgets, Delilah. Unexpected expenses do get noticed, even when there is money to pay them. Which I did."

"Did what?" Dally asked.

"Pay them," her mother said. "I respect Mr. Jerry's business, and he expects to be paid in a timely fashion. Which"—she caught Dally in a piercing stare—"is something you should have thought about before committing yourself to this kind of expense."

Dally gulped. Her mother reached into her blazer pocket and extracted a folded piece of paper.

"What's this?" Dally asked as she opened it. The embossed letterhead said *Peteharrington Enterprises*.

"Surely your lessons are sufficient enough that you can tell."

"An invoice?" Dally's stomach dropped. An invoice was

a document that businesses sent to people who owed them money. This one explained in a nice little chart exactly how much Dally owed her mother. "Yikes," she said. Each ride with Mr. Jerry cost more than her weekly allowance. The amount at the bottom of the page, her "total owed," far exceeded her savings.

"Delilah, we have a lot of privilege, and I know you understand that." Her mother's tone softened enough to surprise Dally into looking over at her. "Dad—your grandfather—worked hard to keep you connected to the real world, not caught up in an ivory tower, so to speak."

It was rare to hear her mother speak about Grandpa. In spite of herself, Dally sat very still and listened.

"You mustn't take these resources for granted, do you hear me? Anyone's world can change in a heartbeat." Her mother paused, and Dally wondered if she was thinking about Grandpa's heart attack. How their lives had changed in a literal heartbeat that day. "You can't assume that there will always be money, always someone there to clean up your mess."

Dally nodded. Grandpa had said so, too. He said the fear of what they could lose was what kept her mother working day and night.

"Do you understand?"

"Yes."

"So now there is the matter of repayment. What do you propose?"

Dally thought about it. "I can pay you back out of my

allowance," she said. "But it will take quite a while." She looked at the invoice to see if there was a due date. There wasn't.

"Then you'll remember this lesson for quite a while, won't you?" her mother said.

"Yes."

"Okay, then." Dally's mother got up and began walking in the direction of her office. Over her shoulder, she said, "Pick up your backpack, please, so Hannah doesn't have to."

Dally grumped and grumbled her way back down the stairs and then to her wing of the mansion, but by the time she got there, her mood was considerably lighter—she had realized something important. Nowhere in the lecture about financial responsibility had her mother said that Dally couldn't go on her adventures anymore. She just couldn't use Mr. Jerry.

≋42≋

That evening, Dally snuck into Grandpa's study again to examine the map. She didn't think she'd be rejoining Pete and Eli on their current run to the island. The last secret had only one volume, she was certain. But she imagined them sailing to freedom, and it felt good to look at the century-old markings that represented their journey.

Dally carefully lifted the framed map from the wall. It was faded with age, but there was no doubt it was the same map they'd created on the ship. She recognized the tea-stained canvas, Pete's rough drawings, and Eli's delicate script. How had Grandpa come to own the map? So much time had passed since it was made—surely it was simply a collector's item now. Had the landscape of the tropical waters changed? Was the island's "toucan beak" eroded? Had it been colonized by condo developers or turned into a luxury resort? Or was there still a shipwreck full of Spanish doubloons and gold and jewels waiting to be dragged into the light?

Dally wondered at the possibilities. It wasn't that she *needed* money—her mother had plenty and provided Dally with more than she required to survive—but what about her adventures? For Pete and Eli, money of their own had meant freedom. Freedom to live, to explore, to step out of the roles society would have forced on them.

At a cost, Eli would say. Freedom always came at a cost, it seemed, no matter how highly it was held in esteem by a person, or a family, or a nation. For Dally, the cost now would be all of her allowance for the foreseeable future.

Worth it, she thought. *Totally worth it.*

Before walking back to her bedroom, Dally studied her printout of the city bus routes and came up with a plan. Now that she knew her time in the library itself didn't count, traveling by public transit could work. If she hurried.

When Dally got back to her wing, her mother was waiting. "It's past bedtime, Delilah. Where were you?"

Ummm. Dally struggled to come up with a cover story. "I forgot I needed to put something in my backpack for show-and-tell." Sixth grade didn't have show-and-tell, but odds were that her mother didn't know that.

Luckily, she'd already folded up the city bus map in her hand. She crossed to her bag and stuffed it inside.

"I see," her mother said.

"Is something wrong?" Dally asked before her mother could inquire further about the item.

"I wanted to talk to you, after how our meeting ended earlier." She motioned toward the bedroom. "Come on, I'll tuck you in."

Dally moved toward her bed. It did not escape her notice that her mother called their conversation a meeting. But it had been a long time since anyone had tucked her in for bed, and it sounded nice.

Dally crawled under the covers and took hold of Raymond, the stuffed koala. Her mother pulled the blankets up to her chin and smoothed them over her.

"Comfortable?"

"Yes." Dally considered closing her eyes, but instead she studied her mother's quiet face.

"You said something earlier, that I only care about money. That I don't worry about you." Her mother stroked Dally's arms through the blankets and swallowed hard. She blinked, then traced Dally's hairline.

"I do worry about you, Delilah," her mother whispered, softening the mood in the room even further. "I worry very much."

"Oh," Dally said. "Well, okay. I'm okay. Really."

"I'm only trying to prepare you for a time when things might not come so easily. We can't act like money grows on trees around here."

"I don't see why we have to worry about money at all," Dally said. "Our family has been rich for a long time. Haven't we?"

"Three generations is not all that long. The business was started by your great-grandfather, and he grew up very poor." Her mother smiled as though touched by a memory. "He liked to say he was a self-made man and a self-made millionaire."

"Founded 1947," Dally recited. The date appeared prominently on the Peteharrington Enterprises logo.

"That's right." Her mother patted her hip. "We can't take what we have for granted, sweetheart. Not ever."

Dally wasn't sure if she took the money for granted, but she was sure she didn't have much of an idea of what life would be like without it. Was that the same thing?

"Your father would be disappointed," her mother said.

Dally couldn't stop the sadness from creeping onto her face.

"In me, not you," her mother hurried to add. "We talked about this problem a lot. We had decided to raise you away from Peteharrington Place so that you could experience a more normal childhood than I did."

"More like how Daddy grew up?" Dally asked.

"Well, not exactly. He grew up without much money, and things were rough for him at times. We hoped for something in between for you. Not the lack that he was used to, but also not the excess that I was used to."

Dally considered her bedroom suite, with its perfect painted walls, shelves upon shelves of wonderful books, and more toys than she could ever thoroughly play with. She pictured Amaryllis's burlap satchel—everything she owned in the world fit in a single pouch. Eli's small trunk of clothing. Belongings and sustenance for eight people jammed into the hold of a ship.

"We do have quite a lot, don't we?"

"Yes, and none of it came easy." Dally's mother continued

to stroke her arm through the blankets. "Grandpa tended to act like money was no object and everything would always be fine. He had a way of making life seem like an endless summer, didn't he?"

Dally quite agreed.

"Marcus had that quality, too, but he was more practical. He knew what it was like to live without, and so he appreciated every penny that ever came into his hands. He was helping me to see it that way, too." Dally's mother shook her head. "Without him, it was harder for me to stick to our more modest way of living. I needed help. From Grandpa. From Hannah. It was all too much on my own. And I was lucky to have that support available."

"We're lucky," Dally said. "I know that. You and Grandpa never let me forget that. This is a wonderful place to grow up."

"I'm glad," her mother said. She bent forward and kissed Dally's forehead. "Get some sleep now, okay?"

"Okay." Dally closed her eyes, but a new question was niggling in the back of her mind.

Marcus grew up poor. But the shipwreck treasure should have been enough to set the family up for generations. What had happened? Had Pete and Eli not made it back to the island? Had the secret of the map been lost to history?

≋43≋

Jennacake seemed to be back in better spirits the following day. She greeted Dally with tea and smiles as usual.

Dally herself was on the moody side of happy. Happy because taking the bus had gone smoothly and she had managed to get to the library. Moody because she kept thinking about the map and everything inside her felt like a stewed mess.

She wandered through Family Secrets, studying dozens of spines. Some days the volumes seemed to be in a certain order, and other times, like now, the dates were all over the place. Even if she found an appropriate year, how could she guess a day and month that would give her the answers she hoped for?

"I wish that I could go to a specific place," Dally told Jennacake. "To find out the exact things I want to know."

"But that's not how secrets work," Jennacake said. "Unfortunately."

Dally sighed. She wanted to know what happened to Pete and Eli and Curly. What happened to Amaryllis and Buck and

Daisy and Mabel. Why Marcus had grown up poor when his ancestors had held the key to incredible wealth.

Library, she thought, *show me what happened.*

Dally emerged from the black in the yard of someone's house. It was a modest house but very well-kept. It appeared quite old-fashioned to Dally's eye, but was probably perfectly in keeping with the architecture of the 1920s. The secret spine had promised a trip to 1924.

"Well, look who the cat dragged in."

Dally spun at the sound of a familiar voice. "Jack!"

"Hey, Dal," he said as though they'd said goodbye only yesterday. She wondered how much time had really passed since he'd seen her. She'd only just left the ship, but for him it could have been much longer.

"Weird to see you looking like a girl again," he said.

"Oh, shut up," Dally muttered. The flapper-style dress and low-heeled shoes Jennacake had picked out for her were not exactly her style. "You're one to talk, with your suspenders and that five-o'clock shadow."

Jack stroked his chin. "Yeah, the beard's looking good, right?"

"Are we calling it a beard?"

"Before, you said I looked dashing." Jack pouted.

Before? Dally didn't remember ever seeing Jack with such serious stubble. Was he remembering a secret she hadn't visited yet? She felt a thrill to know that there were more secrets together to come.

A pickup truck pulled up, loaded down with a large piece of wooden furniture—a desk, perhaps, or a dresser, Dally couldn't quite tell. The man who got out of the cab was brown-skinned, short, and stout. He had a round face and a head full of loose black curls, and he was wearing a clean overcoat and well-worn boots. He lowered the tailgate and began tugging what Dally could now see was a desk toward the back of the truck.

"Need a hand?" Jack offered.

"I could use one, if you have a moment to spare," the man said. He must have assumed they were passing by on their way somewhere.

Jack joined him by the tailgate. When Dally stepped forward to help, too, the man looked at her strangely, so she held back, letting Jack and the man do the heavy lifting. She walked ahead to the house and pushed open the unlocked front door.

"Papa, Papa!" A cluster of three small boys rushed to meet the man.

"Let us through," their father said. "This is heavy." He and Jack placed the desk under a side window in the living room.

New furniture must've been a big deal in the household. The boys buzzed around it as though it were a brand-new toy, all their own.

"We can play island!" the littlest boy cried, sprawling himself across the desk.

Their father glanced at the strangers who'd helped them. "Another time," he said to the boys. "Keep quiet now. We have guests."

"Island?" Dally asked, unable to help herself.

"A game, I suppose," said the man. "Thanks again for your help."

"Anytime," Jack answered, tapping his cap.

Dally and Jack excused themselves. As the door closed behind them, the children started chattering again.

"When are you going to take us to the island for real?" the eldest asked in a solemn tone while Dally was still within earshot.

"When you're older," their father said. "When you're all big enough that we can sail together, just the four of us."

"Hooray!" The boys cheered.

"Now show us the secret compartment Grandpa built," the middle boy said.

Outside, Dally and Jack exchanged a glance. "Do you suppose they're talking about *our* island?" Jack asked.

Dally peeked through the window at the man and his children, squinting at his mop of loose black curls. "Could that be Curly, all grown up?"

Jack joined her at the window and laughed with recognition. "That hair, those cheeks? Sure could. Except wouldn't he be a lot older by now?"

Dally did the math out loud. "He was born in 1854. We're in 1924. That's seventy years."

"That guy's not seventy, I don't think. Maybe it's his son?"

The man pulled open a secret drawer in the base of the desk. He lifted out a familiar scrap of canvas—the treasure map! Jack was right. This had to be Curly's son.

Dally frowned. She had asked the library for answers, but this wasn't one. If Curly's son took his own kids to the island, then the secret of the treasure should have survived.

The fog billowed closer.

"Wait," Dally said.

But Jack disappeared before her eyes . . . and then the darkness rushed in and claimed her, too.

≥44≤

The bus had worked well for Dally once, so when Monday rolled around, she decided to try it again. She greeted Jennacake, chose her secret, and disappeared into the reading room.

The secret spun her into Peteharrington Place. She popped out of the darkness into a room lined with stark white tile. She immediately recognized it as the bathroom in her mother's suite.

From the bedroom she heard Hannah's voice. "Set that over your eyes, honey. We'll get that swelling down in no time. Is it too cold?"

"No, it feels good."

Dally crept to the bathroom door and peeked around the frame. Her mother was lying on the bed. A memory danced up from the recesses of Dally's mind: black dress, white flowers. Her mother had worn that dress the week of her father's funeral. Dally remembered clinging to it as they walked through the grass to the cemetery. She remembered hiding behind it as many large, strange people tried to talk to her. Her mind flashed on a more recent memory—Daisy clutching

Amaryllis's skirt as they stumbled toward their new, mysterious life together. Had Dally herself ever looked so very small?

Hannah clucked her tongue. "Never known anyone to cry so hard their eyes swell shut."

"I've always been an overachiever." Kate laughed, but then quickly broke into sobs.

"Shhh, baby. You let it all out," Hannah cooed. "You earned that broken heart."

"Why did I let him go?" Kate cried. "Why didn't I put my foot down?"

"He was a grown man, honey. He knew his own mind. When he wanted a bit of excitement, there was no stopping him. And you went along a time or two, if I recall."

"He was reckless."

"He wasn't reckless," Hannah chided.

"Then why is he dead?" Kate snapped.

"Accidents happen, love."

"Fewer accidents happen to people who don't go off and—" Kate took a shuddering breath. "Oh, Hannah, never mind. I'm sorry."

"I know, baby. I know."

"I need to check on Delilah," Kate moaned, though she made no move to get up.

"The child's fine," Hannah promised. "Jasper's got her eating six kinds of ice cream."

"I don't want her to see me like this." That was the right instinct, Dally thought. Even now, it was quite alarming.

"Don't you worry." Hannah patted her hand. "We're gonna get her some food and keep her entertained. Then you're both gonna stay the night."

"No, that's not necessary," Kate said. "I'll be fine in a few minutes."

"Nonsense. What's the point of having this big old house if no one's ever gonna use it?" Hannah declared. "I'm gonna send Millie in with some tea for you. You rest now." The housekeeper took a used tray from earlier and bustled out of the room.

Kate lay in silence. Dally shifted her weight in the doorway, causing a creak.

"Millie?" Kate asked. She sat up slightly, raising the ice pack. Her eyes were so red and puffy that she could barely open them.

"Keep the ice pack on," Dally said quickly. "The tea's still brewing."

"Millie," Kate groaned, stretching out her hand. She was expecting the maid, Dally realized, so she assumed that was who had come.

Dally hesitated, but in the end she couldn't resist her mother's call. She perched on the edge of the bed, clutching Kate's hand.

"I can't believe he's gone," Kate cried. "And, oh, our Delilah." She sobbed. "Marcus was the good parent. I can't—"

Dally waited until this bout of tears passed, then she repositioned the ice pack.

"Millie." Kate grasped her hand again. "There's so much to do. The business. His research—he would want me to find a way to carry it forward. And Delilah. I don't know how I can do it all. Alone."

"You're not alone," Dally said. "It's okay to rely on your family right now."

"No. When my eyes clear, I'll be able to drive home."

"You should stay. Delilah's having the time of her life in the kitchen right now."

Dally well remembered this particular afternoon. She remembered her relief and the quiet and calm when the rush of the funeral guests had gone. She remembered eating ice cream with a very big spoon. She remembered the comfort of Grandpa's arms and of Hannah and Jasper bantering about which leftovers to serve for dinner. They'd ended up sampling them all.

It was the day they'd come to Peteharrington Place and never left. The day her mother had disappeared into the large, austere office and never come out again, too.

"Then I think we'll stay," Kate whispered now. "But only for one night."

"Maybe two," Dally suggested. "What's the harm?"

"Maybe two," Kate echoed, rolling onto her side. She tucked herself into a ball. Dally eased away, hearing footsteps in the hall. The real Millie would be along any moment with the tea. She slipped back into the bathroom and waited for the secret to end.

45

Dally stayed away from Family Secrets for a while after that trip. The memory of seeing her mother so overcome with grief was difficult to carry. It tossed Dally right back to that scary time when she was small and her world had turned upside down. Sometimes it felt like it was still turning, tossing her round and round until nothing made sense.

Kate had loved Marcus so deeply that losing him broke a part of her—a part Dally now understood had yet to heal. Even today her mother could barely talk about him. But before that secret, Dally did not remember ever seeing her shed a tear. Had she simply shut it all away? Was she really that good at pretending not to care?

Dally wrestled these thoughts until she could no longer stand it, until the prospect of fighting her feelings for the rest of time became unbearable. She wasn't like her mother. She couldn't let things go, or push them down, or pretend they weren't there. Even the hard things.

The Family Secrets section was always on her left in the stacks, waiting, and after a while, she couldn't resist its call.

Maybe there were more answers to uncover. And she *could* choose a secret that would definitely not bring her face-to-face with her parents. For instance, she still wanted to find out what had happened to the treasure map, if she could. So she focused on the map in her mind as she ran her finger over the shelves, seeking a date that was long before her own lifetime.

Dally endured the familiar rubber-band snap. When the fog cleared, she was standing in a city alley. It smelled of fish and garbage and cooking oil, the odors rolling over her in ever-changing, unpleasant waves. She looked around. Wooden crates. Metal-ringed barrels. No plastic bags. Hard-packed earth and cobblestones. She scooted to the corner of the alley, near the street.

Jennacake had dressed her in a split skirt and dolman top appropriate for the 1940s. The smattering of cars on the street looked exceedingly old—all black and large with humps over the wheels and long snout-like hoods. A wooden sign above the storefront across the way, near the edge of the fog, read CARO-LINA'S FINEST BAIT & TACKLE.

The faces she could see through the windows and those passing by on the street ranged from medium brown to dark. Folks were wearing hats and jackets that befitted early fall. It was a Black community, not poor but not conspicuously prosperous.

Two men approached, caught in such a heated conversation that they didn't even notice Dally lurking in the shadows. "You're not listening," said the taller and lighter of the two.

There was an urgency to his tone, and he punctuated his speech with the waving of arms.

"I don't like what I'm hearing," said the other, hands in his trench coat pockets. "That's not the same as not listening."

"This isn't a game."

"Did I say it was?"

As they walked, the fog shifted to follow them, so Dally moved onto the sidewalk and headed in the same direction, a few paces behind. It was nearing suppertime, perhaps. In the shops they passed, workers appeared to be closing down, locking up. Outside the alley, more pleasant aromas reached Dally's nose. A stew cooking, maybe, and something yeasty plumping in an oven nearby.

"Just hear me out," the light-skinned man said. "When I go downtown, when I'm not with Mom or Pop, or you or Daisy, it's a whole different world."

"Must be nice."

"You gotta understand. How am I supposed to not want that? Even Negroes tip their hats to me, 'less they know me, and downtown most of them don't." He lowered his voice. "I can go into any store. Ain't been questioned yet. Not once, Chuck."

"So what?" Chuck said. "I'm s'posed to be happy for you? Jealous? Well, I'm not. I never wanted any of that. Why do you want so bad to go where we're not wanted?"

The men kept walking. Around them, the city began opening up. The narrow street gave way to a slight clearing, with a path leading across the grass and a wooded area to the side.

Dally crept along the edge of the tree line, hoping to remain out of sight.

"Don't you ever want to be treated like everyone else? Like a white man?"

"This country never treated no Black man equal." Chuck crossed his arms. "And if you don't learn to stay off the sidewalk, you're gonna find that out the rough way."

A pause stretched out between the men as they neared a small white clapboard house. A scattering of fireflies lit up the darkening bushes. Crickets chirped in the gathering dusk. Dally brushed a cluster of mosquitoes off her arm and leaned in to listen.

"What if I didn't have to be a Black man?" the light-skinned brother whispered.

Chuck laughed. "What are you talking about, Jay?"

Jay stepped closer. "Most places I go on my own, no one knows. No one can tell. I didn't know when we were little, because we were always together or with Mom. But remember how people always thought she was my housekeeper? How they'd talk to me in the store instead of her?"

"I guess," Chuck said, laughter still in his throat. "But that don't make you white."

Jay tipped his chin up to the sky. He looked over at the small house, at the sudden lamplight shining in the window.

Chuck's quick side-eye glinted in the darkness. "You know it don't make you white, right?"

"All the things the world tries to tell us about who we can

be—it goes away. All the limits." Jay's face glowed with excitement. "I wish you could feel that."

"I don't want no part of the white world," Chuck said, waving a hand. "You can have it."

"That's what I'm trying to tell you. I—I want it."

"You want what? To be white?" Chuck chortled. "Go on, then."

Jay stood in silence.

Chuck crossed his arms again. "Oh, I see. You come here looking for my blessing? To go off and play whitey?"

"I wanted you to know why—" Jay swallowed hard. "I didn't want to disappear without someone knowing."

"You ain't goin' nowhere, Jay."

Chuck strode away, rounding the side of the house, toward what must be the front door. Jay followed. "Chuck . . ."

Dally crept along the bushes after them, nudged ahead by the fog. Soon enough, she'd lose the cover of the trees, and the sky wasn't dark enough to conceal a whole person standing in the yard. Luckily, the brothers seemed too caught up in the argument to notice.

Chuck strode along a packed dirt walk lined with ragged patches of wildflowers. A few errant chickens pecked the ground next to a raised coop at the far side of the yard. On the wide, grass-flecked, rutted-dirt driveway sat an old-fashioned long black car.

As the men passed the hood of the car, Jay grasped his brother's arm, turning him.

"I—I can't ever see you again. Do you understand?"

"Frankly, no. I *don't* understand. How can you do this to us?"

"I've already enlisted." Jay drew himself up to his full height. "There's nothing to be done. I report to Norfolk the day after tomorrow, just like any other recruit."

"And I'm supposed to walk in there and tell our mother that you've gone off to war without so much as a kiss goodbye?"

"I kissed her goodbye." The tall man's voice snapped defensively. "But I couldn't tell her the whole truth."

"The truth that you're leaving us. Dance on over to the other side of the tracks." His voice took on a funny affect. "Righty-o, massa, you allus know what's best."

"Shut up."

"Your momma Black, your daddy Black, all your siblings and cousins Black, but you wanna walk high and mighty just 'cause you came out a little lighter than the rest of us?"

"This war is bigger than race."

"Hmph. Who's talking about war?" Chuck snapped. "Sounds like you fighting yourself."

"I want opportunities. Things are out there for me, things a Black man could never get. Starting with a chance to serve, and not in no one's kitchen."

"You think enlisting makes this noble somehow, but it doesn't. It's rotten all the way through." Chuck spat into the dirt. "You're willing to go off and die for this country?"

"I'm not going to die."

"Denying who you are is a kind of death. Someday you're

gonna realize that and want to show up at this door, but it'll be too late. You want to disappear? Fine. You're dead to me."

"Chuck—"

"Dead. My brother went off to war, and he died. You happy?"

"That's not—"

But Chuck was done listening. "Take your fancy car and go." He spun around and marched into the house.

Dally inched ahead, certain she'd be spotted at any moment. The fog was at her back, nudging her forward, but forward would mean being seen. It would mean needing an excuse. *Would you like to buy some Girl Scout cookies?* Dally thought. But she lacked, well, cookies.

Jay stood by the car hood, staring after his brother for a long time, though from Dally's viewpoint, Chuck had disappeared beyond the border of the fog. Finally, Jay nodded and moved to the driver's side. The car windows were open, catching the breeze. Maybe it didn't have windows in the first place—Dally wasn't sure. Moment of truth. *Speak now or forever hold your peace,* she thought. But it felt so *wrong* to inject herself into this private moment.

You must stay within the circle created by the fog, Jennacake's voice echoed. *No matter what you have to do.*

The fog tightened around the car. The secret was closing, and Dally *had* to stay inside it. The man was about to get in the car and drive off, and she had best figure out a way to go along with him.

Jay paused beside the driver's door and once again looked

back at the house, after his brother. Dally took this chance and raced forward. She dove through the open rear window, thumped down on the back seat, and rolled to the floor. She hoped against hope that the fog had steered her right, that she wasn't about to be driven out of the secret and lost to time forever.

If he spotted her, how would she explain herself? Homeless child looking for a place to crash? Simply lost and in need of a ride?

Or maybe it didn't matter. The fog loomed over her, around her, even under her, it seemed. The close quarters of the car became the whole world. Dally held her breath and waited for the now-familiar snap as the car lurched forward and lumbered down the washboard of a dirt road.

A sniffling sob came from the front seat. "They will never forgive me," Jay said in a choking whisper meant only for his own ears. "Will I ever forgive myself?"

46

Dally emerged from the stone room, quiet as a church mouse. Jennacake greeted her with a soft smile. "How was it?"

It took Dally a moment to decide how to answer. "Some of the time, the secrets make sense, and some of the time they don't."

"I suppose that's true."

"It's true for me," Dally confirmed.

Jennacake nodded. "Well, yes. I'm sorry. I didn't mean to make it sound like your opinion could be wrong. You're allowed to feel how you feel."

"I don't always know how I feel," Dally explained. "That's kind of the problem."

"Hmm. It's difficult to know one's own heart," Jennacake agreed. "I know you can't tell me about where you went, but if you want to talk . . ."

"No, I probably should be going," Dally said. "I have to catch a bus."

"Well, all right," Jennacake said. "See you soon."

"See you." Dally trudged out of the library, searching her heart for the source of her funk. *Secret traveling is fun,* she reminded herself. But something had felt different today. The ache of the fight between Jay and Chuck was still tangible on her skin and in her gut. She didn't have a sibling, but she'd often wished for one when she was small. Someone to play with when Grandpa was off working or visiting his friends. Someone who never had to exclude her to do grown-up things. Someone who'd still be here to play with. If that person did exist, and then they were ripped from her . . . by their own choice? The heartache pulled her into a swirl of sad thoughts.

Life had been rough in the past for Black people. Many things, even today, could be made easier by the simple fact of whiteness, or even the relative light-skinnedness that Dally herself possessed. But to *choose* to be someone different? That was hard to fathom.

She'd never wanted to be anyone but Dally. Sure, like any kid, she loved to play make-believe, to hold a wide-toothed comb and pretend to accept a Grammy for her spoken-word stylings. But that was different. That was imagining her Dally-ness ramped up to celebrity level. Not imagining to be someone new.

And today's volume had been a family secret, Dally recalled, which meant that somewhere in her lineage was a Black man who'd abandoned his family for the lure of whiteness. How sad. She wondered what had happened to Jay. Had he ever returned? Did he find forgiveness?

Dally checked the time. She'd been waiting at the bus stop for longer than she'd expected, lost in the vortex of her thoughts.

The bus was late.

She was late. *Uh-oh.*

Dally raced into her private classroom at 4:40 p.m. "I'm sorry, I'm sorry! I got a little held up after school and—" She drew up short.

Her mother stood at the front of the classroom, arms crossed over her chest. "Delilah Peteharrington, where have you been?"

Dally glared at her tutor, who was seated at his desk. "You told on me?"

"Of course," he said. "You've never been this late, so I was worried."

His reasonable tone infuriated Dally. How was she supposed to sneak around effectively if she had not one single ally in this entire estate?

"Well?" her mother asked. "We require an explanation."

"I had to go to the library," Dally said. "To do research for a project. And I lost track of time."

"Delilah, you cannot simply run around town without us knowing where you are. Apparently I have not made that clear enough. And punctuality is not negotiable. You have a contract."

"Yes, I know." Dally folded her hands and bowed her head, trying to look apologetic.

"You will report to my office at three fifteen tomorrow, young lady. Is that understood?"

Dally's head snapped up. *What! No free hour?*

"No," she cried. "But—"

"Three fifteen. Is that clear?"

"Three thirty," Dally retorted. "I can't walk home that fast, remember?"

There was no use arguing further. Her mother, when angry, was less like a growling bear or a roaring tiger than a rock-steady, immovable elephant. She pursed her lips and sniffed. "Three thirty," she said. "And not a minute later."

≡ 47 ≡

The next afternoon, Dally did something she had never done before in her life: she snuck out of school two hours early. An hour to get to the Secret Library and an hour to get home should be plenty. She hoped.

Jennacake greeted Dally with her usual calm reverence. If she knew Dally was early today, she didn't let on. Time worked differently in the library, after all.

Dally sipped the blue brew and perused the many stacks, but she knew there was no choice in the end. Family Secrets it was.

Dally emerged from the fog in the middle of the woods. Branches flapped up in her face as though annoyed to be disturbed. *Sorrrry,* Dally thought. *Not my first choice, either.*

She pushed through the leaves in the direction that seemed least thick. Sure enough, there was a dirt road a few yards ahead.

Twigs snapped under someone's footsteps. Dally paused, still hidden by the foliage. A man was approaching along the road: tall, slender, striding with a hurried purpose.

Dally recognized him as the light-skinned man from the car

in the 1940s, except older. Jay. He wore a short-sleeved shirt and denim pants, as if he'd just stepped away from laying brick or something, but he didn't have the overall manner of a guy who worked with his hands. Dally stayed a yard or so behind the tree line and followed him.

Just around the corner, the road met another road. At the intersection stood a second man. Waiting.

"I told you never to call," Jay said, walking up to him.

Dally darted forward, trying to see who he was talking to. It was his dark-skinned brother, Chuck!

"I only need a minute," Chuck said.

"Not here," Jay said, glancing over his shoulder. "We're too close to the house."

Dally looked back, too, but she didn't see anything. No house. No people. Just the barest hint of movement in the trees across the way.

Chuck let out a sigh of disappointment. "After all these years. After all you made of yourself. You can't so much as be seen with a Black man?"

"Come with me," Jay said. "There's a place we can talk." He led his brother into the trees on the opposite side of the road.

It was a warm summer day, but the woods were cool and spacious. Dally used tricks Grandpa had taught her to move as quietly as possible through the underbrush. The men didn't speak as they walked, but she could see them clearly up ahead. They weren't trying to be stealthy. Probably they thought no one was anywhere nearby—that seemed to be the point.

"Who's there?" A soft voice drifted at her from the shadow of a wide oak's trunk. She spun toward the sound. A tall boy emerged from the edge of the fog, and relief flooded Dally.

"Jack! Thank goodness." She launched herself into his arms. She'd survived many secrets without Jack, of course, but the ones with him were the best. The most interesting, anyway.

He received her affection as awkwardly as ever. "Uh—" he said. "Who are you?"

"What?" Dally pulled back, dragging her fingers down his arm and gripping his hand.

Jack jerked away from her touch and gazed at her in confusion. "Have we met? Do we know each other?"

"Jack, it's me, Dally!"

He shook his head. "I don't . . ."

From the ship? she wanted to say. *From the island?* How could he forget? It might have happened a hundred years ago, technically, but—

A realization struck Dally, interrupting her train of indignant thoughts.

She stepped back, studying him. He was still quite tall, taller than Dally, but was he as tall as when she'd last seen him? He'd had stubble then—they'd joked about it—but he didn't have stubble now. Perhaps he was even younger than he had been on the ship? Maybe this was an earlier trip for him.

"I'm sorry," she said. "You look like this guy I know."

Beside her, the fog billowed too close for comfort.

"I'll explain later," she said. "We can't let them get too far ahead of us."

Jack seemed poised to argue, but the pressure of the fog apparently won. As Dally plunged into the woods after the two men, he stayed right on her heels.

Jay and Chuck stopped when the trees stopped. They came upon a field of felled trunks and drying stumps, the whole area littered with fallen leaves and branches. A large tree-clearing effort appeared to be underway, but at the moment, all the trucks and tools were silent.

"Big job," Chuck commented.

"I have plans for the property," Jay said. "A lot of plans."

"You always wanted a big house," Chuck said. "Guess you got it now."

"So what was so urgent you decided to bring me back from the dead?" There was an edge to Jay's tone. Dally wondered if the last time the brothers had seen each other was that day at the car.

Chuck laughed, but not as if anything was actually funny. "You're the one what left. You gonna talk now?"

Jay glanced at the sky and back. "I know. Sorry."

Dally wasn't the greatest judge of age. Grown-ups looked like grown-ups, as far as she was concerned. But the men appeared quite a bit older, she thought. Ten years older? Twenty? She tried to remember the exact date on yesterday's secret. Eighteen years, she calculated.

"I'm sorry, too," Chuck said. "For saying you were dead to

me. At the time—well, anyway, it feels different now. They're both gone, Jay."

Jay sank onto a stump. "Gone?" The word sounded hollow in the vacuum of trees.

"Ma, two years ago now. Pop, just a month and a bit."

Jay's head fell into his hands. He let out a low wail of sorrow.

"What's going on?" Jack whispered to Dally. "Who is that guy?"

"Shhh." Dally didn't want to miss a word.

After a moment, Jay raised his head. "I don't have to ask why you didn't tell me."

Chuck lowered his hefty body onto a stump a few feet away. "You made your bed, that's for sure."

"I thought I'd never see any of you again. It's strange, always wondering, not knowing. I'm glad to know. I'm . . . glad to see you."

Chuck nodded. He reached into his shirt pocket and extracted a folded brown envelope. "Pop wanted you to have this."

Jay opened the envelope and pulled out a scrap of canvas. Dally gasped. The treasure map! Even from this distance, she recognized its jagged shape.

"What *is* it?" Jack leaned forward, trying to get a better glimpse.

Dally smacked his arm. "Would you hush?"

He gave her a look that said, *How dare you?*

Oops. She reminded herself that this version of Jack was not familiar with her.

"This old thing?" Jay's voice turned bitter. "He never let that aimless treasure hunt go?"

Chuck laughed. "Nah, he dug in hard. We been all over the Atlantic coast and the Caribbean. Name an island, we been there."

"But not *the* island," Jay said. "Just like when we were kids."

"Nah, 'course not." Chuck shrugged.

"God," Jay said, fingering the map. "'Just one more run, boys, and all our problems will be solved.' He might as well have been a gambler, for all the money he wasted chasing shadows."

"I did okay for myself," Chuck said. "Climbed outta the hole he put us into in the old days. And you, hell, you done all this." He swept his hand around. "But Pop's last request was that I use this map to bring our family back together. To bring you home."

"So you brought it?"

"I don't know if you or he deserves it. But I do. Can't have it weighing me down no more. I need to be done." Chuck heaved his stocky self off the stump, moving as though he had a couple sore knees at the least.

Jay shook his head. "I'm not coming home." He paused, shaking his head again. "I mean, I am home. This is my home now."

"Suit yourself," Chuck said.

"You could've just thrown it away," Jay said, holding the map to his chest. "That's all I'm gonna do."

Chuck shrugged. "Couldn't do it. If you can, more power to ya." And with that, he ambled off toward the road.

Jay stood up as if dazed. He picked his way through the stumps and felled trunks until he was back in the woods.

Dally started to follow him.

"Where are you going?" Jack asked, falling in step with her.

"Wherever he's going," Dally answered. It wasn't over yet.

"And how did you know my name before? You seem . . . familiar. Have we met?"

"Apparently not."

"Apparently?"

"The library has really done it this time," Dally muttered, unsure how to get out of this particular pickle.

"The library?" Jack echoed.

Dally's mouth may not have moved again, but inside her brain, she frowned. Something wasn't right. First Jack had acted like he didn't know her. Now he was acting like he didn't know the library.

"What year is it?" Dally found herself whispering aloud. The secret spine had said 1958. That was two years before Jack had traveled to the ship.

"Are you serious?" Jack said.

She shook her head. "Never mind. Jack, this is very important. Where is the fog right now?"

He simply stared at her for a moment. "Perhaps it's unkind to ask, but are you all right? When you say things like that, you . . . well, you seem a bit loony."

Dally took Jack's hand. "I'm fine," she said. "There's just . . . there's something happening here that is bigger than both of us."

He tugged his hand free. "Like what?"

Dally felt at a loss to explain. "Look into my eyes," she said. "What's your instinct? Do you trust me?"

"Yeah," Jack said slowly. "I guess I do."

"Then tell me what year it is for you."

He shrugged. "The same year it is for everyone—1958, of course."

48

Dally's eyes popped open wide. As she'd suspected, they hadn't met yet. They wouldn't meet for two more years in Jack's time line, but here they were, in the same secret.

No, only *she* was in a secret. Jack didn't even know about the library, it seemed. They were in his present!

Dally grabbed Jack's arm. There wasn't really time to do math problems in her head. "Come on, we have to stay with him."

"Why?" Jack asked. "It's not like I don't know where he's going."

Dally charged forth. She still had to worry about the fog, after all. "Oh? Where's he going?"

"Home," Jack said. He pulled a small round watch out of his pocket and glanced at it. "It's almost dinnertime."

"I didn't know people still used pocket watches." Dally smiled in spite of herself. Grandpa had had a pocket watch he wore occasionally, and people used to say that to him all the time. Even in this decade, it seemed old-fashioned.

"It was my grandfather's," Jack said. "That's why it's special."

"He gave it to you?"

"No. I never knew him. He gave it to Dad, and Dad gave it to me."

"We have to get into the house, if that's where he's going," Dally said, thinking it over.

Jack was surprised. "You can't just go into someone's house, you know. There are rules about such things and I can't—"

"We stole a sailboat together, for crying out loud," Dally muttered. "Now you're on about rules?"

"We what?"

"Never mind." She had said she'd explain later, but when push came to shove, how was she supposed to tell him, even if she did ignore the rules about secrecy? Would she have believed it if someone had told her? No, the library was the sort of place you had to experience to understand.

Jack frowned. "Who are you, again?"

"I'm Delilah." Dally surprised herself with the use of her full name. Normally she reserved it for very formal occasions, though this was shaping up to be something of an occasion, she supposed.

"And that guy from earlier?" Jack asked. "Was that your dad? How come you didn't leave with him?"

"No, not at all. Neither of them is my dad."

He stopped walking. "Then what are you doing here? I thought you were following them, too."

"I was," Dally said. "Come to think of it, what are *you* doing here? Why are *you* following them?"

"Just curious, I guess. When that fellow called, Dad got all worked up, and he's not exactly the type to have secret meetings in the woods, so—"

Dally stopped short. "Dad? One of those men is your father?"

Jack made a face. "Well, not the Negro, obviously."

"They're both Black," she said.

"Um, no?" He looked at her like she was clueless.

"They're brothers," Dally informed him. "Didn't you hear them talking? About their parents? Jay left his family a long time ago because he could pass as white."

"That can't be." Jack broke into a run. "Dad!" he shouted. "Dad, wait up!"

So much for secrets. Dally groaned. Then she realized that something peculiar had happened. She could no longer see Jay through the fog. Instead, it buoyed along ahead of Jack. The secret she was in wasn't Jay's this time—she already knew his secret. This secret was Jack's.

"Jay's your dad?" Dally repeated as she raced to keep up with Jack's long-legged stride. He certainly got his lanky build from his father.

"Yeah. So?"

Dally didn't know how to answer—her brain was still processing the worldview shift. Jay was Jack's father? Jack's father was Black?

They caught up with Jay at the edge of the woods. He stood in a soft patch of grass beneath an old ash, digging a hole with a stick. When it was a few inches deep, he dropped the brown envelope in and used his shoe to scrape and pat the dirt back over the spot.

"Dad!" Jack shouted, barely winded from the dash. "Who was that man?"

Jay turned, his white-looking skin growing paler. "Jack," he said sharply. "What are you doing out here?"

"I saw you!" Jack blurted out. "With that Negro. Who is he?"

"He's no one. Get back to the house."

Dally looked in the direction Jay had pointed. They were standing in the spacious backyard of a large run-down manor house. Well, father and son were. Dally kept herself out of the way, hovering near the trees.

"But—he was talking about your parents. As if you had the same parents. As if—" Jack tapped his thigh. Even from behind him, Dally could practically see the gears turning in his mind, as if he was replaying what they'd heard the men say.

"Jack—"

The boy shook his head. "It can't be true. He can't be your brother."

"You misunderstood what you heard," Jay said quietly.

Jack glanced back toward Dally. "I thought maybe I did. That's good. Okay." He let out a big breath. "Tell me what it was about, then. Tell me the truth."

Jay's posture slumped. "I never wanted you to find out. Especially not this way." He covered his face with his hands.

Jack was taken aback. "So it's true? You're . . ."

Jay sprang toward his son and took him by the shoulders.

"Jack, you mustn't ever tell. Not ever. Not your mother. Not anyone. Do you understand?"

"Yes," Jack said. "Wait. Mom doesn't know?"

Jay shook his head. "Tell me you understand how serious this is."

"I understand."

"We are not Negroes."

"Of course not," Jack agreed. He glanced at the disturbed dirt by Jay's feet. "What was that?"

"Something best left buried," his father said. Then he turned and walked toward the house, his head hanging low.

Jack and Dally stood silent, watching him go. Then Jack knelt down and began scooping dirt off the envelope his father had buried.

Dally's heart roared and her mind raced. "Jack, what on earth?" she exclaimed. "You're Black? Like me?" Why hadn't he told her?

"You heard my dad. No, we're not." He grabbed a twig to help scrape into the packed spot.

Dally smirked. "Don't worry, I'm not going to out you. But the truth is, you're Black. Negro. Whatever."

"I'm not. I can't be," Jack insisted. "Look at me. I'm no Negro."

Dally crossed her arms. "You're just going to *pretend*? You're going to let him deny his family?"

"What do you mean, let him?" Jack said. "What am I supposed to do about it?"

"Well, I don't know," Dally blustered. "It just seems *wrong*."

"We couldn't buy the new house if people knew," Jack said. "We couldn't even keep the one we have. We'd have to move all the way across town. Why would we do that, when no one can tell?"

Dally took a deep breath to calm herself down. She had forgotten for a second that she was in the past—a time of legal segregation, open prejudice, and structural barriers for people of color. Many of the laws she took for granted that protected against discrimination hadn't been written yet.

Jack pulled the envelope out of its hiding place and flicked the dirt off it. He unfolded the treasure map and began to study it.

"This doesn't look like something that should stay buried," he said.

Dally quite agreed. "What are you going to do?"

"Bring it inside," he said. They started walking toward the house. "And maybe ask Dad about it. Sometime."

"Not today," Dally said. "He's had quite a shock. You should wait."

"Yeah," Jack mused. "For now, I guess it's our little secret." He tucked the envelope into his pocket.

"Sure," Dally said. She glanced at the fog. Jack's secret. She was in on it now.

Jack shook his head thoughtfully. "My dad grew up with Negroes. How is that possible? It's too weird."

She gave him side-eye. "Not that weird. You're talking to a Negro, remember."

He blinked. "Yeah, I guess."

"Anyway, it's all a big lie," Dally said. "There's no difference between you and the people who live on the other side of town. The exact same blood runs in your veins."

Jack was quiet.

"The *exact same* blood," Dally emphasized. "But you get to have all this"—she spread her arms to indicate the expansive lawn—"while half your family can't even own a house in the same neighborhood? Your father is a hypocrite!"

Jack sputtered defensively. "Dad has had his eye on this property for several years. It just came up for sale, and we moved. We're naming it Peteharrington Place, and it'll—"

"What?" Dally exclaimed.

"What?" Jack echoed.

Dally turned a slow circle, studying the landscape. "This is Peteharrington Place?" She scanned the tree line, the lawn. The ramshackle old house was large, but it was built of wood, not stone. The scrubby patch of grass behind it held no trace of the glamorous gardens. There was a weedy, marshy field where the lake should be. "This can't be Peteharrington Place," she said.

"Well, it isn't yet, but it will be. You should see Dad's plans." He brushed his hand through the air in front of him, like an artist presenting a canvas. "Gorgeous gardens, a stable, a pond."

"A lake," Dally corrected. "Dragonfly Lake."

Jack nodded. "Yes, that's what the plans say. How did you know?"

Dally's mind was too hard at work to fully register the

question. "If your dad is building Peteharrington Place, that means you're . . ." Dally's whole being fell utterly still. After a difficult swallow, she managed to speak. "Jack is a nickname? You're . . . John Peteharrington?"

He offered a slight bow. "John Peteharrington Jr., to be precise."

A sound like wind roared in Dally's ears. Blood rushed to her head. Her hands squeezed at the grass that was suddenly close beneath her.

Family secrets, indeed.

49

Dally remained on her hands and knees, in the grass that would one day make up her own backyard. Wind still howled in her ears, and it dawned on her that it wasn't just shock that had knocked her off balance. The secret was ending.

She looked for a place to hide within the boundary of the fog. Jack—the non-time-traveling version of him—could not see her disappear.

"Please excuse me," she managed. The fog was close and growing darker. Dally staggered to her feet and lurched around the corner of the house. Her legs were so unsteady beneath her that it felt like she was back on the ship.

"Wait—" Jack called. But Dally's vision had gone black, and she was flying through time and space.

The cool white stone of the secret reading room came into focus around her. Dally felt sick—not from spinning through time, but from everything she had just learned.

Grandpa, her own beloved grandpa, and Jack, her new adventure companion—they were one and the same person?

Dally burst out of the reading room, startling Jennacake at the reference desk.

"Dally, what's wrong?"

"I have to do another," Dally said.

Jennacake hesitated. "It's really not a good idea."

"No," Dally insisted. "That can't be how it ends today. I found out—" But the librarian gave her a quieting look. So Dally repeated balefully, "This can't be how it ends today."

"I'm sorry, dear," Jennacake said. "You know the rules."

"It's not a real rule," Dally said. "You made it up for me. I know you did."

"That makes it a real rule, I'm afraid. Because I am the librarian." Jennacake maintained her smooth calm in the face of Dally's mounting frustration, which only enhanced it.

"You're the meanest librarian ever!" Dally shouted. Distress overwhelmed her, gathering itself within her body like a coiling snake of steam. Her hands trembled. She balled them into fists and banged them on the reference desk until her pinkies ached.

"Dally," Jennacake said. "Maybe it's time we had that talk."

Dally took two big breaths to try to calm herself. She wasn't the kind of person who pounded her fists and threw tantrums, but suddenly her whole life, all of who she was, had become tied up in the secrets the library held. It had shown her a glimpse, but how much more was there to know?

For most people, being here is about finding out who you really are, in one way or another, Jennacake had said once. The library was changing everything Dally thought she knew.

"I'm going to make us some tea," Jennacake said now. "And we're going to talk."

"I could do another secret while you brew it," Dally said, though she knew what the answer would be.

"You could choose where we sit to talk," Jennacake said. "There are many cozy nooks throughout the library, as you well know."

"Fine." Dally's tone was as grumpy as her feelings. She stomped away from the desk—it felt quite good to stomp, though the rug absorbed the hits with ease.

She chose a pair of brown leather armchairs tucked in a corner, positioned at right angles around an end table. Dally pulled the chain on a small stained-glass lamp with a twisty metal stem to brighten the space, then tossed herself into one of the chairs. She drummed her fingers and bounced her heels against the leather to show her impatience. The arms of the chairs just barely touched at the corners, and when Jennacake sat down, their knees were close enough that Dally had to stop kicking.

Jennacake placed two cups of the grassy-scented blue tea on the table. Dally knew the tea would calm her, and she resented it. She crossed her arms and stared at Jennacake through the steam.

Jennacake lifted one delicate cup and took a sip. "Please," she said. "What I'm about to tell you is very important."

Dally relented—not because she was ready to be done being mad, but because she wanted the information. She took a gulp of the tea, and all the buzzing nerves in her body began to settle.

"What is in this tea, anyway?" Dally asked, taking another sip. It made her feel like she was floating, as though the leather chair had become a cloud and all her worries were somewhere on the ground, far below. Little massaging fingers pulsed through her brain, rubbing away her anger, her anguish, her pain. It wasn't an altered state, like the thick buzz she felt after a dose of cold medicine. She merely felt suddenly clean and pure, and very much like herself.

"A little home remedy," Jennacake said. "The recipe is passed down from librarian to librarian, but each makes it her own. My predecessor's tea was beige and a touch more bitter, like regular tea, but still delicious."

"Is the librarian always a woman?" Dally asked.

"All those I know of happen to be women," Jennacake said. "But the library chooses, and its rationale is not fully known."

"Surprise, surprise," Dally said. "The library keeps secrets."

"The library always chooses someone clever and determined," Jennacake said. "Someone who loves the library at first glance and feels the impulse that they never want to leave. Someone with good instincts and a sense of adventure."

Dally got a funny feeling in her stomach. She took another sip of tea, but the feeling didn't go away. "Good instincts?"

"Yes," Jennacake said. "For example, you're feeling an instinct right now, aren't you?"

Dally did not want to admit it, so she sipped the tea, holding the cup in front of her lips longer than strictly necessary.

"Why did you ask me about the librarians?" Jennacake's voice was even gentler than usual. "You had a feeling?"

"You said you can't leave," Dally said. "You are always in the library. You live here."

"Yes," Jennacake said.

"But you can't read the secrets?" She recalled Jennacake's panic the day they met, when Dally tried to open a secret while the librarian was in the room. *I can't come with you,* Jennacake had said.

Jennacake's face turned wistful. "No, I can't read them. Not the way you do. I know some things about a volume when I pick it up, enough to help the readers prepare, but . . ."

"So, you're stuck here."

"Well, I wouldn't say 'stuck,'" Jennacake's voice was quiet. "There's a great deal to do with my days, and the work is always interesting."

"And eventually you'll retire and the library will choose someone new?"

"Not retire, exactly," Jennacake said. "Being the librarian is a lifetime appointment."

Dally pondered the facts. "So you can never leave the library? Not for the rest of your life?"

"That's right," Jennacake said softly.

Dally's chest felt like it was filled with feathers. She gripped the leather arms of the chair and breathed through the fluttering feeling. "Is the librarian chosen from within the Whisper Society?"

Jennacake sipped her tea. "Most often, she is not."

Inside Dally, the feathers became a bird, trapped and pounding. The *thump thump thump* of her heart shook her chest. "Just tell me," she managed to say. "Tell me what you brought me over here to tell me."

Jennacake's smile was sadness and comfort and darkness and light all at once. "Darling, you already know."

Dally pushed out of the chair and stood. "No," she said. "You have to say it. I won't believe it until you say it."

Jennacake set down her teacup. "The library has chosen you, Dally. It whispered your name to me on the day you were born."

The winged creature in Dally's chest fell still. Perhaps it had grown so large in its small space that it could no longer move.

Dally had been excited about the prospect of joining the Whisper Society when she grew a little bit older. Their work remained rather mysterious to her, but Jennacake had once said the society members' role involved "seeking remedies" when things went awry in the library. That made Dally suspect historical problem-solving might be a part of it. She had looked forward to taking Grandpa's chair at the big table and having a glimpse into the part of his life that he'd kept from her. She'd imagined exploring hundreds or thousands of secrets throughout her lifetime and having a team of friends, like Jack, to do it with. Learning that Jack *was* Grandpa made the idea of those adventures even more enticing, but now . . .

"What about the Whisper Society? Grandpa's seat?"

"Someone else will fill the seat," Jennacake said. "He *did* recommend you, and the society did consider whether they should induct you for the time being. But that is not your destiny."

"So you lied to me?" Dally had thought lies weren't possible in the library. Truth was its foundation; revelations curled in every cobwebbed corner.

"No," Jennacake said. "We temporarily allowed you to believe something simpler than the whole truth."

Lies "for your own good" was such grown-up nonsense. Dally wanted to run and scream and flail, but she was far too used to holding her restless self in stillness. So she just stood there.

"Don't be scared," Jennacake said. "The library will always take good care of you."

But Dally *wanted* to be scared. She wanted uncertainty, and questions and puzzles to solve. She wanted corners to turn that felt unfamiliar.

"I need another secret," Dally whispered.

"Don't you understand, dear? The faster you move through your journey, the faster the transition will happen."

But the secrets felt like adventure, like escape. The only adventures she would ever have, it turned out. She wanted as many as she could get before her time ran out.

"It won't happen until I'm twenty-one, right?" That was the age Grandpa had specified, after all.

Jennacake shook her head. "I'm afraid it'll happen much sooner. The moment you set foot in the library, the moment it met you, our clock started ticking."

Our clock.

"Jennacake . . ." Dally's eyes widened, and the words stalled in her throat.

"I'm afraid so, dear. When you become the librarian, my time will be finished."

Dally's eyes stung, but she refused to cry. It was better, she told herself. All her life she'd been trapped inside the cold stone walls of Peteharrington Place, and soon she'd be living in this warm and magical world. It was better. It was.

⋙ 50 ⋘

Dally trudged her way to the bus stop, clinging to her backpack straps like a lifeline. The bus she needed whistled by as she crossed the street, which meant she'd missed it. She'd probably be late for her lessons again, but she didn't care. What did it matter? What did any of it matter—school, lessons, the very idea of one day taking over the business—if Dally had only days, weeks, or months at best before she'd be pulled into a whole different world? What would her mother think? Would she care when Dally simply didn't come home one day? Would it make her life easier, or would she barely even notice? Would Dally be missed?

She climbed aboard the next bus that arrived, only remembering to check the route number at the last second. She sat by the window, near the back, soaking in the sights of the outdoors. Staring out at all the passing storefronts, Dally suddenly realized—she wasn't late. She was early.

It wasn't even three o'clock when she strode up her driveway. She had more than thirty minutes before she had to meet her mother. She couldn't go inside, for fear of being spotted—not after she'd made such a big deal about the time it took to walk home.

Dally looped around the side of the house. She tucked her backpack under a bush to lighten her load and headed across the grass toward the back of the property. Dragonfly Lake glistened in the afternoon sunlight. Strange, that it hadn't always been there. It must have been quite an expense to install. The water was wide and tinged with deep blues, grays, and black across its rippling surface. Dally longed to strip to her underthings and dive into the freshness—anything to wash herself clean of what she now knew.

To never swim! To never feel the sun on her back or the wind on her face! Dally's chest filled with a weight as if she'd taken on a good swallow of lake water. She broke into a run and let her feet carry her. She burst into the woods, and under the cover of the trees, she felt sure her eyes would explode from the pressure building behind them.

Dally stumbled along, barely seeing the way forward, until she emerged in a small clearing: the family burial plot, with its half dozen sculpted headstones within a wildflower ring. Grandpa's grave. Dally dropped to her knees in front of the double head-stone. Beside Grandpa's name, her grandmother's name was carved into the marble. Grandma's half of the inscription was more than ten years old. Dally traced her finger over the final date beneath Grandpa's name, stark and unweathered by comparison.

"How could you do this to me?" she blurted out. The heat behind her eyes finally broke, and tears streamed forth. "Why didn't you tell me?"

Dally clutched the grass and let herself cry. "I could have waited until I was twenty-one, if you'd only told me."

He knew. The thought struck Dally so hard she felt as if she'd been pushed. He knew she wouldn't wait, because he'd met her when he was a teenager himself. Grandpa had known Dally before Dally was Dally. How strange!

He knew everything. Dally's head spun and her eyes watered, and she gasped for breath. *He knew everything.*

She crawled toward the neighboring stone. Her great-grandfather and great-grandmother. JOHN PETEHARRINGTON SR. Dally touched his name. She had seen him. Jay had lived a decently long life, according to the dates on the stone. Had he ever found a measure of peace with who he really was?

Had Grandpa? Dally moved back to Grandpa's stone. In all the eleven years they'd known each other in real time, he'd never once spoken of the Black heritage they shared. Had her mother known, when she married a Black man, that she was a quarter Black herself?

Dally scooted across to the third stone in line. MARCUS RICHMOND, LOVING HUSBAND AND FATHER, GONE TOO SOON. In smaller type under the pair of dates was a quote: "TAKE LIFE BY THE HORNS AND RIDE IT ALL THE WAY TO THE SUNSET."

"Daddy." Dally spoke aloud, touching the words that bound them. "I'm so glad we got to meet again in this lifetime."

After the tears and the shaking stopped, she lay for a time with her back in the sun-warmed grass and her hand resting loosely on the stone.

The clock on the receptionist's desk said 3:33. Dally resisted the superstitious urge to make a wish and kiss the clock. Her wish could not be granted.

"Hi," Dally said, scooting right past the desk without asking. She opened the tall wooden door and strode inside her mother's office as if everything were fine.

"Delilah, you're late."

"Not very," she said, tossing herself into the tall wingback chair.

"Late is late."

"It's hard to be exactly on time," Dally said. "To the minute and the second? Maybe impossible." She had grown a bit, it seemed. Her feet came nearer to the floor in this chair now, a realization she quite enjoyed. But there was nothing else enjoyable about this moment.

"The way to be on time is to be early," her mother said.

"But then you're early," Dally said. "What a waste."

Dally's mother sighed. "I read this to mean that you did not come straight to my office when you got home from school, as instructed. Where have you been?"

There was no lie that would upset her mother more than the truth, so she told the truth.

"I went to visit Grandpa's grave, and I lost track of time."

Her mother sat silent. When she finally spoke, she said, "How does it look?"

"What?" Dally asked, confused.

"The family plot. Is Hector tending the flowers nicely?"

"Oh. Yes, I think so. It looked fine to me." Dally's mind hadn't exactly been on the landscaping. "The grass is mowed and the flowers are blooming."

"That was your grandfather's doing. The wildflowers. 'Even in death there should be beauty,' he used to say."

"That sounds like him," Dally mumbled. The conversation had taken an unexpected turn. She didn't know quite what to say.

"I know you've been unhappy since he's been gone—" her mother began.

"Unlike you." Dally immediately regretted the thoughtless outburst.

Dally's mother folded her hands. "Delilah, grief is complicated. Don't presume to—" She cut herself off and laid a palm along the side of her face. She sighed. "Your manners leave something to be desired these days, don't they? Perhaps we should be tutoring you in that."

"I'm not the best student."

"So I'm told."

Dally jumped out of the chair. "Why did you bring me here? Just to tell me I'm bad at everything?"

"Delilah, please sit down."

"My name is Dally. Everyone in the world knows that except for you."

"Honey—"

"DALLY," said Dally. Honey was made from nectar, swallowed and spit back out by buzzing, stinging bees. How had it ever become a term of endearment? What business did it have tasting sweet?

Dally's mother stood up, pressing her pale, slender fingertips into the desktop. "Sit *down*, Delilah."

Dally sat.

"What has gotten into you?"

The same thing that has always been in me, only now I'm letting it out. Dally crossed her arms by way of answer.

"You are to come directly home after school each day. You will report here to me by three thirty at the latest, and be on time for your lesson thereafter."

"But—"

Dally's mother silenced her with a look. "Once you've proven that you can be on time, as expected, you may have your free hour back."

"Free *partial* hour, you mean," Dally grumbled.

"Or you can sit here and work on your assignments during that window, indefinitely. Is that what you're angling for?"

"No," she murmured.

"I'd like you to remain indoors until your lesson today. No more losing track of time in the woods."

Dally tried to speak, but the air in the room had grown much too thick. Suffocating. An invisible tightness far worse than the fog.

"Do you understand?"

She pulled hard with her lungs, fighting the sorrow that threatened to engulf her.

"Delilah?"

She rolled her eyes and puffed out the breath. "Fine."

"Answer me properly, please."

Dally folded her hands in her lap like the polite young lady she knew she was supposed to be. It was all an act. She knew it. Her mother knew it. They were performing a skit for an audience only her mother could see.

"Yes. I understand," Dally said. "You want me to turn it off."

Her mother's well-groomed eyebrows twitched. "Turn what off?"

"Everything fun and interesting that I like about myself."

Her mother's lips parted. "What?" she said. "No."

Dally stood up. She felt strangely calm, resigned to the reality before her. But what was a skit without a little drama?

"I'm too much like Grandpa and not enough like you. You didn't like him and you don't like me. But it doesn't matter anyway."

Dally didn't wait for her mother to figure out how to respond. The issue was settled, of course. She turned and put one foot in front of the other, all the way to the door. The last time she'd walked out of her mother's office, she'd been heartbroken, on the verge of tears over being denied permission to join Adventure Club. That day, she'd arrived hopeful. Today, she'd arrived already knowing that her fate was sealed. Her mother could try to lock her away in Peteharrington Place, but it truly didn't matter. All too soon, Dally would be locked away someplace else.

51

I n the morning, Dally did the unthinkable. She went down the driveway as normal and rounded the corner as if to walk to school, but at the end of the street, she turned toward town, got on the city bus, and headed straight to the library. There might be consequences for leaving school yesterday afternoon, and there would definitely be consequences for skipping today entirely, but Dally didn't care. What did it matter anymore?

The logical part of Dally's brain screamed, *Turn around!* If she never went back to the library, she wouldn't become the librarian. She could live her whole life however she wanted. Go anywhere, do anything.

But she couldn't. She couldn't *not* go to the library. It was her only source of adventure these days, yes, but that wasn't all. If she searched her heart (though she tried hard not to), she found that the library had already become a part of her. *The past is pro-logue,* Grandpa had written in his letter. The things that were going to happen had already come to pass, in some sense, in some universe. Dally had already lived the secret she'd explore today, and the one tomorrow, and the one after that, no matter how many remained before the transition.

The instinct that Jennacake had called her attention to was alive and well in Dally, much as she tried to ignore it. There would come a day—and she sensed it was soon—when she would enter the Secret Library and never come back out again.

Dally walked the white entry corridor feeling the weight of her destiny. The ceilings that had once seemed so lofty-high now seemed shockingly restrictive.

Jennacake was quietly reshelving secrets in the stacks when Dally came up to greet her.

"Hello, dear," the librarian said, a hint of resignation lacing her voice. "Welcome, as always."

"Hi, Jennacake."

"Are you feeling all right?" she asked, pressing her palm to Dally's cheek. "You look a mite peaked."

"I don't know," Dally said. "Perhaps it's just the thought of all this . . ." She allowed her voice to trail off and her chin to drop.

Jennacake wrapped a blue-cloaked arm around her. "Nonsense. Nothing to be down about. It's a most enchanted life, dear girl—I can promise you that."

Dally found Jennacake's pronouncement a trifle chipper to be entirely believable. "Mm-hmm."

"Well, let's get you into a fresh volume, posthaste. What'll it be? Perhaps something romantic, for a change?" Jennacake tapped her fingers together.

"Ew, no," Dally said. "Anything else."

"Of course—it's always up to you. Take your time." The librarian swept her finger over the lip of a shelf as if to collect dust. Invisible dust. Obviously, Jennacake didn't need to spend her free time cleaning, as it seemed the library was consistently pristine. That, at least, was a relief.

"Do you want to talk first?" Jennacake offered. "You seem a bit pensive today."

"No," Dally said. "That's okay." She wanted to run, to flee, to fly. Tugged by the now-familiar heartstrings, she wandered toward her perennial favorite: Family Secrets. "I'd like to try something else again at some point," she said out loud to the library, but she was met with a resounding silence.

"There's so much I want to see and do," Dally whispered. "Please." But if the library was listening, or cared, it gave no sign.

Dally looked at Jennacake, who shrugged. Dally nodded, equally resigned to the strangeness in which they found themselves. Her finger tucked into the spine that drew her—1959626—and she tugged it free with a sigh.

With a snap of the fog, Dally was standing inside Peteharrington Place. In the upstairs drawing room, to be precise, though the furniture was not all the same today. But she recognized some of it, and the view of the gardens and lake from the wide bay window could not be mistaken.

"Fine! I'm going!" Jack's voice shouted from somewhere down the hall. A door slammed, like punctuation. A second later, Jack burst into the room, moving at a good clip.

"Oh, it's you," he said, coming up short at the sight of her. "Hi."

"Hi." No matter what, it was always good to see Jack (aka Grandpa). Dally smiled at him. "You okay?"

His hair was mussed, his eyes wild, searching the room as if he'd find some elusive answer tucked away in a familiar corner. "Uh, yeah. No. I don't know. How many times are we going to have this same fight?"

"Who?"

"Me and Dad. Let's get out of here," he said, leading the way toward the stairs. "In fact, how did you even get in here?"

"Well, you can't just walk into other people's houses," Dally said, doing her best to sound matter-of-fact. "So how do you think?" She didn't know how he was going to answer. This Jack knew her. But he had no stubble. Did he know about the library yet?

"I never knew how to find you," Jack said. "Why would you come back after all this time?"

"Hard to say," Dally said. "Guess because you needed me?"

Downstairs, Jack slid open the door that led to the gardens. "Are you my guardian angel or something?"

Dally laughed. "Maybe something like that." She could now see echoes of Grandpa in everything about Jack. It amazed her that she'd ever missed it. *Oops, Dally-bird, too bad my guardian angel isn't on duty yet.* He used to say that all the time, whenever he made a mistake like spilling some juice or knocking over a vase. Dally only now got the joke.

"It's weird that you're here today of all days, when I finally got him to tell me more about that cruddy old map."

"Yeah?" Dally said.

Jack's eyes lit up. "It's a treasure map," he said. "Only, the treasure doesn't exist. According to Dad."

Dally chose her words carefully. "But you think it does?"

"It has to! When I was little, Dad used to tell me bedtime stories about a treasure map. These pirates found a sunken shipwreck full of gold and spent their whole lives trying to make good with it. They got into so many scrapes. It was a gas!"

"It does sound neat." Dally tried to keep her tone neutral.

"The pirates, Pete and Eli, made a map to always be able to find the shipwreck island, but they drew it in code so no one could steal the secret. Later, they passed the map down to their children, from generation to generation, so the family would always know the way."

Dally nodded. "Sure."

Jack pounded his fist on his palm. "I thought it was a made-up story, but now I know it was real. It happened in my family, way back."

"Whoa."

"Today, Dad finally told me the truth. The map got handed down, but the secret of how to read it got lost. His father spent his whole life chasing the dream of the treasure, and nearly drove the family to ruin. So my dad left." Jack's voice shifted deeper, in an imitation of his father. "'I refused to follow a pipe dream of a whisper to the ends of the earth. And turn out penniless? So I carved my own way in the world. I'm a self-made man—that's all that's real.'"

"So, there's still a treasure out there, waiting?" Dally prompted.

"Dad says no, that it was only ever a fantasy to begin with."

"Oh."

"But I," Jack concluded, "I think the treasure could be real."

The treasure is *real,* Dally wanted to say. But she couldn't, of course. It was a secret. A frustrating secret, because she couldn't share it even with the person she'd first discovered the treasure with. But Jack wasn't that person yet.

"It's interesting," Dally told Jack. "Your dad didn't change his last name, even when he tried to run and hide from his family."

"Can you imagine any whiter-sounding name than Peteharrington?"

Dally smiled. "Okay, I will give you that one."

Jack smiled in return. "Dad says we used to be 'Harrington,' once upon a time, actually. But the 'Pete' adds a little something extra."

Dally's lips parted in delight. Pete plus Harrington? Harrington must have been Eli's family name! Dally loved the idea of the two of them taking a new name to represent their union. She wondered what Jack would think if he knew that his last name was an invention that honored everything counter-cultural and biracial about them. That history was tied to Dally and Jack forever.

Grandpa had been the one to suggest—to insist, even—that

Dally be given the last name Peteharrington when she was born. That's why she was Delilah Richmond Peteharrington instead of Delilah Peteharrington Richmond, like most people would expect. The name carried weight, Grandpa had told her. She'd always thought he meant in society, because the Peteharringtons were wealthy and respected. Now she knew the weight he'd spoken of had been something deeper—a nod to the journey they'd shared.

Dally wondered where Jack saw himself now, in the landscape of whiteness versus Blackness. "What I meant is that, deep down, your dad still cares about his family. He couldn't throw away the map. Maybe there's hope that he secretly sees truth in the old treasure stories." Their family was all about secrets, it seemed.

"He ran across town. Not across the country, like he could have." Jack shook his head. "He could have gone so far away that I would never have seen his brother, never known the truth."

"Exactly."

"And we'd still be white, without the knowledge of a few drops hanging over us."

Dally felt uncomfortable with his word choice. She knew she should let it go. It was a different time. A time when a person would be considered Black under the law if they had even one drop of Black blood in their lineage, if even one known ancestor had had brown skin. But Dally couldn't deny the knowledge she brought from her twenty-first-century world.

"Where I come from," she said, "we know that race is a construct."

"What?" Jack laughed. "Like it's made-up?"

"Yeah. People are all different colors—that part is real. But it's society that gives our color a particular meaning."

"Where you come from, being Black or white doesn't matter?" Jack asked. He squinted into the treetops, as if trying to imagine.

"Well, no. It matters." Dally struggled to find the words to explain the ways the world had changed since the days of segregation—and the ways it hadn't changed at the very same time. "I guess what I mean is that your dad looks white, so people treat him one way, and treat his brother another way. They have the same parents, the same family, the same blood, and yet your uncle can't shop in certain stores or have certain jobs because he's darker. That's the construct."

"If we were Black, everything would change," Jack said quietly. "We would lose our house. The business would lose customers. We're already in the red as it is."

"You *are* Black," Dally corrected.

Jack glanced at her sideways. "If people found out where Dad came from, I mean."

"How can it ever be the same, now that you know?"

"I'm not Black," Jack insisted. "Knowing it's in our past doesn't make me suddenly different."

"See?" Dally said. "It's a construct. You feel white because you were raised to feel white."

Jack shook his head. "I don't like it."

"You'll adjust," Dally said, though even as the words came

out, she wasn't sure it was true. The Grandpa she had known, the eighty-year-old man, still moved through the world as white. She didn't know what to make of that, especially because he had helped her be proud of her own Blackness. What did he fear would happen if he told everyone—or even his family— the truth?

Dally self-consciously touched her knots of hair. If she'd been lighter-skinned, or willing to straighten her hair, would Grandpa have raised her differently? She didn't like wondering.

"I have to go in," Jack said. "It's dinnertime. Thanks for the walk."

"Let me come with you," Dally said. The fog was not too terribly close, but she had to stay relatively near him.

"I can't bring you—I can't bring a Negro girl over for dinner," Jack said, lowering his voice to say "Negro." "It's not what people do. Especially with what's going on with my dad and me . . ."

Dally felt like the past was repeatedly slapping her in the face today. She glanced over her shoulder. "Look, can you at least let me come in the house? I'll hide while you eat dinner, and we can talk more afterward."

Jack hesitated.

"We have more to talk about," she said. "We're not done here. Can't you feel that?"

He nodded. "You can wait in my room," he said, leading the way up the palatial staircase and into the wing that would someday be Dally's. He closed her into the sitting room, which was much more sparsely decorated than her own version. There was a small shelf of illustrated books, a variety of wooden toys—a few of which she had inherited—and a very cool model train on an elaborate track.

Dally tooled the train around for a few minutes, feeling bored and far from the action. She wanted to go down and see what was happening at dinner, but she tried hard to be patient.

When the fog moved, Dally had no choice. She crept along the halls toward the dining room. It proved a bit tricky, staying inside the fog. The main staircase fell outside the circle. Luckily, Dally was familiar with the house and its nooks and crannies. She nipped over to the service stairs and slid down the banister (as she was usually forbidden to do).

"We might have to sell," Jay was saying as Dally took up her listening post outside the dining room.

"Sell?" Jack echoed.

"I put too much into building this place," Jay admitted. "And now that the business isn't doing as well, the hubris is coming back to bite me."

"There are ebbs and flows in everything," said his wife. "Maybe we can hang on long enough to see the tide come in again."

"If we do, we risk losing everything. If we don't cut bait or turn things around soon, the house will barely cover the debts."

"What about the treasure?" Jack asked.

"Forget the dang treasure map," Jay snapped. "There is no treasure. It's an old man's fantasy."

"But you said my grandpop swore—"

"What do you think?" Jay said. "We're going to take the boat and sail around the ocean looking for an island shaped like a toucan head?"

Yes, Dally thought. *That's exactly what you should do.*

"Get your head out of the clouds, Jack," his father said. "Money is made in the real world. My father wasted his life hunting that treasure."

"Shhh," said Jack's mother. "No one needs to go treasure hunting. We're not destitute here. There's no shame in selling the property, Jay, if it comes to that. But I believe in you. Let's hold on a little longer and see if things turn around. No one outside the three of us needs to know about this yet, do they?"

"May I be excused?" Jack asked, scraping his chair back.

"Gentle on the floors," his mother said. "If we do have to sell, we want the place in good shape."

"Confidence personified," Jay muttered.

"Oh, darling," said his wife. "I didn't mean it like that. Yes, Jack, go on."

Dally stepped back from the doorway, and a beat later Jack strode through it. He didn't seem all that surprised to see her standing there.

"I wanna go for a walk," he said. "It's so stuffy in here."

Dally followed him out to the yard for the second time. It was still light, signifying one of the longer days of the year. The evening weather was as pleasant as the afternoon's had been, if not more.

"What if *I* went?" Jack mused. "What if I took the map and the boat and went anyway? It's not like I have a business to run.

I could take all summer. What if the map is the key to saving the family?"

"Do you think it might be?" Dally asked.

"The pirate stories feel real," Jack said. "When Dad first told them to me, he said they were passed down from his father." He gnawed his lip. "And today, in his bluster, Dad mentioned that my granddad said *his* father had always meant to show him the way to the island, but then there was an accident. He died before they could get back there together."

"That's sad."

"So all we have now is that map."

"A map with no key," Dally said, treading carefully.

But Jack was lost in his own swirl of thoughts. "I think I'm gonna do it." He turned to her. "Let's do it!"

Dally's heart thumped with the call to adventure. "You should," she said. "It sounds like fun."

"Will you come with me? The boat needs two to sail it right."

With all her heart, Dally wanted to say yes. Her skin stung with thirst for the ocean wind. She could imagine nothing better than to set sail with Jack, pirate-style, once again. To dive into the cool Atlantic and fill the hold with coins. To dance on the deck and drink in the brilliance of the stars.

Yes! screamed Dally's very soul. But behind Jack, the fog billowed closer, as if to remind Dally of her place, her fate, her destiny. She glared at the rippling white wall as if she could intimidate it, but it only undulated nearer.

"No," she said, "I can't."

"Why not? You're always showing up here, with no place else to go, you say. Can't you get away?"

"You don't know anything about me," Dally whispered. "Not really."

Jack was not deterred. He plowed on forward, with the confidence and insistence of a rich white boy who was used to things working out for him in the end. "What I know is that it feels right."

Yes.

"It feels right that I go, and it feels right that you come with me."

Yes.

"You have to, Dally. Please."

Yes.

"We're not done here." He threw her own words back at her. "Don't you feel it?"

Yes.

"You don't understand," Dally told him. "I can't go with you to the island."

"Why not?" Jack slapped his hand against his knee, rocking it from pinkie to thumb, the way Grandpa had always done when he was thinking. Tears sprung to the corners of Dally's eyes.

It was strange to miss someone who was standing right in front of you. But Jack was *not* Grandpa. Not really. Not yet.

Dally thought about the size of the secret she had pulled. It had been thin. "I won't be here long enough. I'll have to go back."

"Back where?" Jack was frustrated, and with perfectly good reason. Dally knew she wasn't making any sense.

"It's hard to explain," she said. "You'll understand someday."

"That's what everyone always says, and I hate it," he retorted.

"Me too," Dally said. "I hate everything."

"This treasure could save my family."

Our family.

"It's now or never, right?"

Grandpa had always said that the old map brought him great adventure, and now Dally knew what he'd meant. She knew what it all meant, and how to find the way. Jack would, too, in a matter of time.

"I—I think so, yes," Dally said. "If you go now, it could save the family." So much for not dipping her fingers in and stirring the past. But the past was *past*, wasn't it?

"Your grandfather was missing the key to the map," she said. "You can find it. I know you can."

"How can you know that?"

Dally shook her head. She didn't know for sure, of course. She was already pushing the boundaries of what she felt she could say. "It's a feeling, okay?"

"This is why I need you to come with me," Jack said. "You're right—I don't know you, but I feel something for you. Maybe it's the whole Black thing? I don't know. But . . ."

Dally's heart pounded. The feelings inside her threatened to burst out of her skin. The fog was but a slender ring now—a little wider than the span of her arms and closing. Closing. Closing.

The secret was ending, and so was something else.

No, Dally thought. *Not yet.*

It wasn't fair, the call to suppress all that was *Dally* about her in order to fit into a preordained box.

But soon the fog would go dark. Dally would be ripped from this place, tossed back to the stone room and trapped in the Secret Library. Never to feel the wind, the sun, never to see the ocean or the stars. The ache in her stretched from her toenails to the roots of her hair. Unbearable.

Closing, closing. Now Dally's world was just her and Jack and a small patch of backyard grass—no more blue sky, just a great swirl of whiteness.

Unbearable.

It was actually unbearable. As in, she couldn't. She couldn't let the fog take her. She couldn't go back.

The realization crystallized in her mind:

She didn't have to go back. She had a choice.

The very thought stunned Dally's racing pulse into near stillness. She breathed in a beautiful calm. She raised her chin and looked into Jack's eyes. Grandpa's eyes. In them, she saw promise, excitement, and tumbling ocean waves. *The past is prologue.*

And then she couldn't see him anymore.

There was but a moment to decide.

In her lifetime, Dally had ranted and raved, kicked and

screamed, argued and logicked, snuck around and omitted the truth . . . but she had never outright disobeyed. Until this week, anyway.

Take life by the horns and ride it all the way to the sunset.

Now or never.

Dally cried out as she dove forward into the fog, a wail of grief, desperation, frustration—everything she had ever felt— exploding in one sound. The fog snapped around her, like a giant rubber band that had been pulled and released. And then . . . everything was normal. Dally stumbled, landing in Jack's arms. He steadied her as her head quieted again.

"You okay?"

Dally stood on the grass of Peteharrington Place. It was all as it had been a moment ago, but there was no trace of the fog— not in front or behind. She could see everything. The house. The woods. The maze of baby shrubs that would one day encase the lush gardens. The trees at the far side of the lake.

"Dally. You okay?" Jack said again.

Dally shook her head. "I did something . . ." She let her voice trail off because she didn't want to frustrate him with the truth: *I did something rash and irrevocable. You can't understand yet, but you will.*

In Jack's view, likely all that had happened was that she'd taken two steps forward and stumbled. He could not imagine how far those two steps had taken her.

What had she done?

Dally shook off the huge wave of fear and uncertainty. This was her reality now.

"Dally?"

"I'm okay." She smiled. "I'm good. We need to get our hands on that old map."

A matching smile took over Jack's confused face. "Yeah?"

"Yeah. We're going to the island."

52

Dally climbed the steps to the Secret Library, perhaps more nervous than she had been the first time. It remembered her, of course.

"*Delilah Peteharrington? As I live and breathe,*" sighed the disembodied voice as she entered. She walked down the white corridor and welcomed in the strange fullness that struck her from ear to ear. How she had missed this place!

She found Jennacake standing expectantly outside the reading room door, waiting for a patron to emerge.

"Jennacake." The softly spoken word went off like a clap of thunder in the quiet-but-not-quiet air.

"I—I didn't hear anyone come in." Jennacake spun around, startled. Of course, on her the whole motion was a graceful twirl.

Jennacake's perfect, youthful features were the same as ever. But the Dally standing before her was in her mid-seventies, slight in build and stature. She had smooth, light-brown skin, wild salt-and-pepper hair, and a twinkle of adventure in her eyes.

Jennacake looked closer, then put her hands on her hips. "Delilah Peteharrington, what on earth have you done?"

≋ 53 ≋

"I wasn't ready when I was eleven," Dally said. "I'm ready now."

"But, your poor mother." Jennacake pressed her hands to her cheeks.

"She'll be relieved, in a way," Dally said. "She loves me, but she also finds me difficult. I've written to her to explain. I logged in to my childhood email account and sent her a message this afternoon."

"Oh, Dally."

"I would have had to leave her anyway, right?" Dally reasoned. "When it was my time to take over here at the library."

"We don't know when that time would have been," Jennacake said, though her eyes drew themselves downward as she spoke.

Dally shook her head. "It's coming soon, isn't it? You can feel it, as I could." She nodded toward the closed stone door. "That day when I left, I knew. It would have been my last adventure. And I couldn't bear that."

"You took a terrible risk." A single tear rolled down Jennacake's cheek. Perfection.

Dally shivered, unexpectedly shy at the thought of her future self. Would she, too, cry perfect single tears? Or would there be no need for tears in this most beautiful place?

"I had to be true to myself," Dally said. "You always said the library would show me who I am, and it did. My mother and I would never have seen eye to eye about my future. Once I was free, I had so many wonderful adventures. And she—well, everything is how it should be. For the two of us, anyway."

"I can't believe she'd have wanted you to be separated like this."

"I've given her directions to the library. She can visit me here, if she likes." Dally pushed down a twinge of sadness, glancing at the reading room door. "When I left here, all those years ago— which is to say, earlier today—I couldn't have imagined my mother visiting this place."

Jennacake took Dally's hand and led her toward the curtain that shielded the librarian's own secrets.

"If she does come," Jennacake said, "and I believe she will, Dally, you should take her here, to your private library." She touched Dally's cheek. "Then she will know you. The true person that you are."

She pulled the curtain back, revealing the square nook lined with bookshelves. The books were spined in various shades of blue, all now luminous with the need to be reshelved. Dally had never seen volumes glowing before, but she instinctively knew what it meant. Jennacake's personal secrets were ready to move on from their place of distinction.

"Yours will arrive soon enough." Jennacake slid a reshelving cart into place alongside the books. "You may need more shelves, of course, and if so, the library will make them."

Dally tingled with anticipation, imagining what her personal library might look like. "My whole life has been a secret," she said. "From you, from the people I met, from the mother I left behind."

"I shall put every good thought into believing that she will come," Jennacake said.

"Oh," Dally said, "but she will come. When eleven-year-old me disappeared into the library, my mother came after me. She read many of my secrets over the years, which means she traveled to visit me time and time again. She read so many of my secrets that I've had her all my life, just not in the normal way."

Jennacake smiled, though something about her presence had begun to seem faint. "I'm glad."

Dally ran her finger over the edge of the librarian's shelf, as if checking for invisible dust. "Kate will have many, many volumes to choose from. She'll get my email, and then she'll be here soon, I expect. You can meet her."

Jennacake shook her head. "Probably not," she said. "It's happening."

"Yes, I feel it, too," Dally said. A softening. A lightening. Her body growing closer to some kind of peace.

Jennacake gripped her hand. "Good luck, then, my darling girl."

Dally squeezed back. "Are you scared?"

"No," said Jennacake. "I feel at peace. It's . . . been a long time." Her silky arms enclosed Dally.

"What happens now?" Dally asked.

"I don't know." Jennacake's voice was reduced to a whisper, quite fitting for this moment in this place. "But I know I must go alone." She reached within her gown and withdrew the slender secret-opening key and lifted its chain from around her neck. She looped the necklace over Dally's head. "Steward it well."

Dally gave Jennacake's fingers one last squeeze. "Good luck, dear friend."

Jennacake was out of words. She pressed her fingers to her lips and blew a kiss.

Dally stepped back, as she knew she had to. From within her nook of secrets, Jennacake drew the curtain one final time.

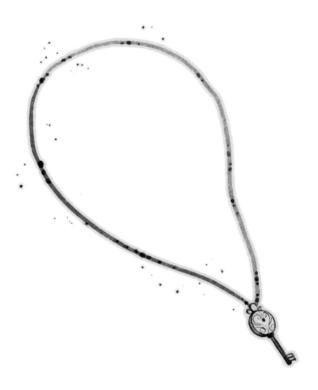

≋ 54 ≋

Dally sat behind the reference desk, alone and uncertain in this new place. She did not know how long she had to wait before she could open the curtain, but she had a feeling that it wasn't time yet. Things within her and around her were still changing. She hoped her nervousness would soon give way to a settled calm, the sort of quiet confidence that Jennacake exuded. How long had it taken the former librarian to feel comfortable in this role? Suddenly, Dally knew she hadn't asked nearly enough questions of her predecessor.

"I will miss you, Jennacake," Dally said into the whisper-quiet room. With that, she realized that the very air had changed. She no longer felt the familiar pressure in her ears, the sound of a million voices about to speak. It was finally quiet.

Dally closed her eyes, and when she opened them, she found that yet another thing had changed. Her arms were draped in soft gray fabric, long fitted sleeves with a slight swoop at the wrists. She wore a royal purple vest with smart gray buttons and matching pants, smooth around her hips and thighs with a slight bell out over a pair of low-heeled boots that felt more like sneakers. It was the most comfortable, most Dally outfit she had ever had the privilege to wear. "Thank you," she said to the library. "It's lovely."

She went to the curtain, now purple as well, and drew it back. Sure enough, the nook was several times larger, and the shelves were lined with new secrets, bound in every imaginable shade of purple.

The reshelving cart Jennacake had prepared was loaded down with her volumes, their once-vibrant blues now faded to near-gray. Dally rolled the cart out and entered the stacks. No time like the present to get to work, she supposed. As she picked up each volume, she could feel where it belonged. A handful for Family Secrets, a couple for Childhood Mischief, surprisingly few Transgressions. Quite a number of volumes went to Unrequited Love. Now that Jennacake was gone, it felt strange, almost like a violation, to know these private things.

Dally returned to the reference desk and consulted the calendar and clock that were calibrated to the outside world. The Whisper Society would arrive within the hour, according to the calendar, but it was unclear to Dally how long that time would feel to her. She pulled the list of members and looked it over. Grandpa's name was still there, with an asterisk. Perhaps his replacement had yet to be appointed.

Aloud to the library, Dally said, "Jack took care of me all my life. Both of my lives. It shall be painful, living without him." The first time she had lost her grandfather, she had gotten him back. This time, he was gone from her forever.

But what a life they'd lived! Together, Jack and Dally had

returned to the island and cemented their family fortune. Free of the need to earn a living, they'd sailed the seven seas. They'd rafted through rain forests, explored ancient ruins, gone spelunking in the greatest caves, luxuriated in waterfall pools, and climbed mountains. When it came time to take over the family business, Jack had come home, but Dally's adventures continued. She had marched for civil rights, protested for LGBTQ+ equality, and monitored elections all over the world. She'd visited landmarks in every state, set foot on every continent, stood up at Jack's wedding, and so much more. A miraculous life, all told.

When Katherine was born, Dally had begun to distance herself from Jack to protect their shared secret. Instinctively, she knew she and Kate mustn't ever meet. Jack started to call Dally "Dee" to avoid any confusion around his daughter. It had been the end of an era, and the start of fresh adventures for them both.

Dally pushed open the door to her new living quarters. They looked much as they had when Jennacake occupied them. Dally supposed it was her own task to adjust the space to her liking. She would enjoy decorating a home, she imagined, after living a life on the move.

As she turned to reenter the library, she noticed one very significant change to the decor. A large framed drawing hung on the wall beside the door. From this distance, it appeared to be a lightly colored pencil sketch of a leafy tree. Dally approached it, looking closer.

It was a family tree, full of names she recognized.

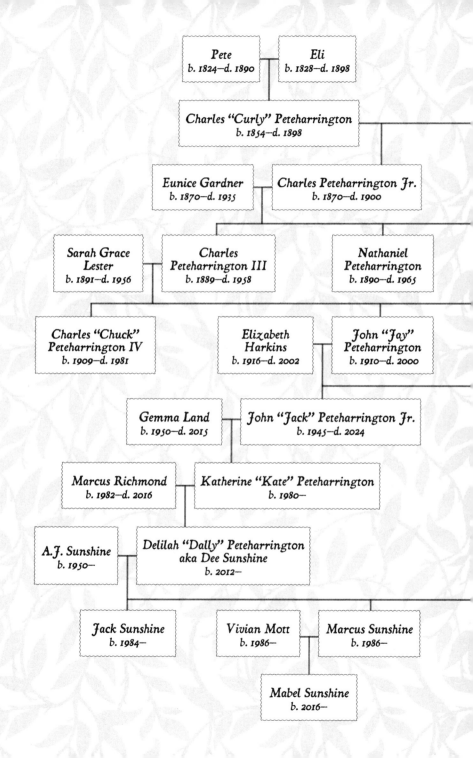

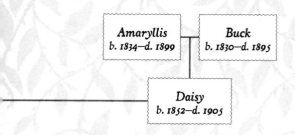

Amaryllis	Buck
b. 1834–d. 1899	b. 1830–d. 1895

Daisy
b. 1852–d. 1905

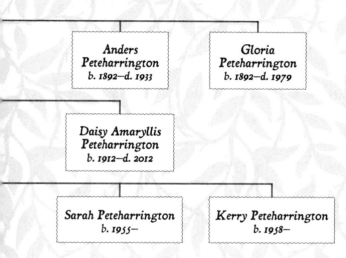

Anders
Peteharrington
b. 1892–d. 1933

Gloria
Peteharrington
b. 1892–d. 1979

Daisy Amaryllis
Peteharrington
b. 1912–d. 2012

Sarah Peteharrington
b. 1955–

Kerry Peteharrington
b. 1958–

Kate Sunshine
b. 1988–

The
Peteharrington
Family

Dally touched the names of her loved ones. It had been a miraculous life, indeed. She would miss adventuring with her three children, of course, but they were grown now. She'd explained her destiny as best she could, seeking their acceptance. And one day soon, she'd see young Mabel embark on her own adventures. Dally smiled. She'd left her granddaughter a letter and a map in an envelope just as Jack had done for her so many years ago.

The library was not through with her family quite yet.

As if to prove her point, at that very moment a light wind stirred up around her. Above Dally's head, a tinkling sound echoed, like door chimes—which, in fact, they were. Someone had entered the library. Dally could hear the announcements and warnings read out softly in the background. A newcomer. Dally smoothed her vest—not that it needed smoothing—and walked down the hallway to greet the arriving patron.

She did feel calm. She did feel confident. The library's power was alive within her. As she moved down the hall, the intricate lines on the wall no longer seemed random. They spoke of connections across time and space.

She waited in the dim corridor as the library finished its introduction. A brief glow flared as the mystical parchment went up in peachy flames.

"Yes, you've come to the right place," Dally began, pressing a bit more light into the foyer as she spoke. She could do that now. "Only those who are meant to find the—" Her voice caught in her throat when she saw who it was.

Dally's mother rushed in. "I'm looking for my daughter," she said, urgency and panic in her voice. Her suit blouse was untucked, and a few strands of hair had come loose from her bun. "She's sent me a message. She's been very upset—we're grieving, you see—and the email, well, I don't quite understand what it means, so I'm concerned. Is she here? Is she all right?"

Dally smiled upon the woman, this young, frenzied version of her mother that she hadn't seen in many years. It was odd, knowing that, for her mother, the best of their relationship was still in the future.

"I'm looking for my daughter," she said again.

Dally placed a gentle hand on her mother's back. "Delilah's here, and she's perfectly fine, Katherine. Come on inside. Everything is going to be all right."

⇗Acknowledgments⇖

My family is ever supportive of my work, particularly my parents, who let me write in their living room and on their porch for many years. My brother, sister-in-law, and nephew sent a glorious LEGO pirate ship to celebrate the completion of my final revision on this novel. My cousins remain the best cheering section, from near and far.

My cats, Jed and Leo, offered enthusiastic editorial advice on a daily basis—they will gleefully take credit for any typos found within, especially if it involves errant use of the Caps Lock button—their favorite.

My friends always have my back, *especially* when I'm being artistic and weird, which continuously surprises me. Thanks to Kerry for coming along to all the shipwreck museums, and to the Dodge-Alexander family for providing constant affection and support and welcoming me to their dinner table when deadlines loomed.

Thanks to the early readers, content experts, and supportive fellow writers who offered advice, wisdom, and a listening ear, including Will Alexander, Meg Frazer Blakemore, Amy King,

Emily Kokie, Cynthia Smith, Parrish Turner, Linda Urban, and Nicole Valentine.

Special thanks to Mike, the sailing instructor from Newport, Rhode Island, who taught me to sail so that I could earnestly write about rigging, knots, and coming about. I still made most of it up, but at least I got to feel the wind in the sails and the salt air on my skin, like Dally.

My agent, Ginger Knowlton, graciously puts up with me wanting to try every genre and explore every new idea, and I'm grateful that she didn't blink when I said, "So what about a time travel fantasy . . . ?"

None of this would be possible without my wise and wonderful editor, Andrea Tompa, and the entire team at Candlewick that helped bring this book to fruition, including Juan Botero, Anna Dobbs, Martha Dwyer, Hannah Mahoney, Larsson McSwain, Sarah Chaffee Paris, Maya Tatsukawa, and my fabulous publicity and marketing support team of Anne Irza-Leggat, Stephanie Pando, Sawako Shirota, and Jamie Tan.

Finally, I'm grateful to all the enthusiastic young readers out there who inspire me to keep telling stories, asking questions, and creating imagined worlds. Thank you!